Lieutenant B'Elanna Torres stopped and pounded her fist . . .

. . . against the cold stone barrier in front of her. She couldn't expect any help from the ship. For all intents and purposes, she was on her own.

Gritting her teeth, B'Elanna pushed away from the cave wall and fired in the direction of her adversaries. As her ruby-red beam lanced out, she heard a grunt and saw one soldier slump to the ground.

A lucky shot. At least it seemed so at first.

Then a whole bunch of them came roaring into the cave, scalding the air with a wild barrage of seething blue energy. Suddenly the shot didn't seem so lucky anymore.

For orders other than by individual consumers, Pocket Books grants a discount on the purchase of **10 or more** copies of single titles for special markets or premium use. For further details, please write to the Vice-President of Special Markets, Pocket Books, 1633 Broadway, New York, NY 10019-6785, 8th Floor.

For information on how individual consumers can place orders, please write to Mail Order Department, Simon & Schuster Inc., 200 Old Tappan Road, Old Tappan, NJ 07675.

STAR TREK®
VOYAGER™
HER KLINGON SOUL

DAY OF HONOR
BOOK THREE OF FOUR

3

MICHAEL JAN FRIEDMAN

POCKET BOOKS
New York London Toronto Sydney Tokyo Singapore

An *Original* Publication of POCKET BOOKS

POCKET BOOKS, a division of Simon & Schuster Inc.
1230 Avenue of the Americas, New York, NY 10020

ISBN: 0-671-00240-6

First Pocket Books printing October 1997

10 9 8 7 6 5 4 3 2 1

Printed in the U.S.A.

To Estelle Mass, for her wit and generosity

Author's Notes

It was September 8, 1966. Thirty years ago, though it's pretty hard to believe.

This is how I remember it. I was eleven years old, sort of a bean pole with a Beatle haircut. I was also about as big a science fiction fan as you could find, which was why I'd been so intrigued by the promos I'd seen all week.

Something about a new show. A science fiction show. Like *Lost in Space,* but different. More serious. More adventurous. More like the novels and the comic books I'd always enjoyed.

Anyway, that was the promise. Even at that age, I knew the chances of it being fulfilled were pretty negligible. Still, at a couple of minutes before the hour, I turned the television to Channel Four, leaned back into my pillows, and waited for the commercials to end.

And then I saw it. "The Man Trap," it was called. A story about love and illusion and loyalty and courage. Looking back, I can't say it was the best episode of the original series. But at the time, it was the *only* episode, and it was much better than anything I'd seen on television before.

My god, I thought. This is so cool. It's so amazingly *cool.*

I didn't know that, thirty years later, I'd be toiling in the vineyards Gene Roddenberry planted with such care and vision. And after eighteen novels and more than a hundred comic books and a *Voyager* story credit, I'm still eager to toil some more.

If you ask me why *Star Trek* has been around so long, you won't get any special wisdom. I'll mention the same things everyone else does—the spirit of optimism, the sense of inclusion. But it's more than that. It's something I can't express, some resonance with my psyche I can't put into words. Except to say . . .

This is so cool. It's so amazingly *cool.*

Michael Jan Friedman
Long Island, New York
October, 1996

HER KLINGON SOUL

CHAPTER 1

HER SHIFT OVER BY A GOOD TWENTY MINUTES, CHIEF Engineer B'Elanna Torres exited engineering and headed for the ship's mess hall. As she had hoped, the predictable change-of-shift traffic was over. There was no one in the corridor but her.

So far, so good. If she kept to herself, she imagined, she would get through the day with a minimum amount of agony.

"Lieutenant?" said a voice from behind her.

Oh, no, she thought. Reluctantly, she turned to look back over her shoulder.

It was Paisner from stellar cartography. He was smiling in his beard at her, smiling as warmly as she'd ever seen him smile.

"Happy—"

"Yeah," she said, "thanks."

And before he could finish his greeting, B'Elanna ducked down an intersecting corridor. Nor did she turn around until she was sure she'd left Paisner behind.

Unfortunately, as she approached a turbolift on her left, its doors opened and a couple of her fellow officers came out. One was Trexis, a stocky Bajoran who'd been with her in the Maquis. The other was Morganstern, an attractive redhead who ran the bio lab.

"Lieutenant," said Trexis. "A brave—"

"Right," B'Elanna interjected. "Uh-huh. See you later."

And she accelerated her pace, passing the two of them before they could say anything else. Again, the engineer found another corridor and took it.

She cursed inwardly. This was harder than she'd believed it would be.

Coming to another turbolift, B'Elanna ducked inside it. "Mess hall," she said, slumping against the side panel. But just as the doors were about to close, someone slipped inside with her.

It was Wu, who worked with her in engineering. He was obviously pleased to see her.

"Lieutenant," he said as the doors closed.

"Mister Wu," she responded, looking at the ceiling and not her colleague. She could feel the slight vibration that meant the lift compartment was moving.

"I didn't think I was going to see you today," he told her. "But since I have, allow me to wish you—"

"Hang on," she interrupted. Turning to him, she asked, "Why aren't you in engineering?"

Wu looked at her, surprised. "It's my day off."

B'Elanna eyed him. "Are you sure about that? I could've sworn I saw your name on the duty roster."

He thought about it for a moment. "I don't see how that could be. I distinctly recall—"

Suddenly, the doors opened. "Now that you mention it," the lieutenant remarked, "it *is* your day off. My mistake." And she exited the lift before Wu could say another word.

Turning left, she set her sights on the double doors of the mess hall. She was almost home free, she told herself. If she sat by herself and grimaced enough, she could eat and get out without meeting any more well-wishers.

Then, just as she was about to enter, the doors opened and a half-dozen of her crewmates spilled out. She sought a way around them, but there wasn't any—not unless she wanted to bowl them over.

"Lieutenant Torres," said onc of them.

"Just the woman I wanted to see," said another.

"After all," said a third one, "it *is* your day, isn't it?"

B'Elanna wanted to crawl into an EPS conduit and die.

As First Officer Chakotay entered *Voyager*'s brightly lit mess hall, he wasn't looking for B'Elanna Torres.

Chakotay had no reason to be looking for her at that particular moment. After all, everything was running smoothly in the ship's engineering section, and there weren't any emergencies elsewhere on *Voyager* that required B'Elanna's special expertise.

Still, it was difficult not to pick out the lieutenant in the midst of all the other uniformed personnel in the room. After all, she was half-human, half-Klingon. That made her rather noticeable—the only one of her kind on the entire starship. Indeed, the only one of her kind in the entire Delta Quadrant.

But what made her even more noticeable was the fact she was sitting all by herself. The ship's engineer had sequestered herself in a corner of the mess hall, facing one of the observation ports, her back to the entrance and therefore to him as well.

Alone.

Though the first officer couldn't see her face, he couldn't imagine she was very happy right now. People usually didn't seclude themselves when their hearts were bursting with joy.

As her commanding officer in their days with the Maquis, Chakotay had known B'Elanna to be moody on occasion, even volatile. She had never resented his company, however, not even when she was at her worst. In fact, she had always welcomed it.

He hoped she would welcome it now. And beyond that, that she would let him help her with whatever was on her mind. It was tough enough to be a lifetime's journey away from home, but to make that journey by oneself was too great a burden for anyone.

Crossing the lounge, he headed for B'Elanna's table. But before he could get halfway there, someone else beat him to it.

It was Neelix, the ship's Talaxian chef and semi-official "morale officer," carrying a large metal pot with a flat bottom. No doubt it held another of his strange and exotic concoctions, thrown together from whatever planetary flora *Voyager*'s foraging parties could supply him with.

But something was different here, Chakotay told himself. Usually, Neelix served up his creations with undiluted eagerness. Right now, that eagerness was tempered with a certain . . .

Revulsion.

"Here you go," said the Talaxian, forcing a smile.

B'Elanna looked up at him, then at his pot. Clearly, she had no idea what Neelix was talking about.

"Here I go with *what?*" she asked.

"A mélange of traditional Klingon dishes," said the Talaxian, failing to suppress a shudder as he placed the pot on the table. "Serpent worms, heart of targ, and rokeg blood pie. All fresh from the replicator, no less. I'll just leave it here on the table, and you can . . ." He grimaced. ". . . pick it over at your leisure."

The lieutenant seemed surprised as she surveyed the contents of the pot. As he approached, Chakotay could see them as well.

Not being a connoisseur of Klingon cuisine, he had only a vague idea of what Neelix had come up with. One part of the pot held what looked like a mess of snakes, another some kind of internal organ.

None of it was cooked. Even Chakotay knew that Klingon delicacies were generally served raw—and whenever possible, still alive. Not up my alley, he thought. Even sushi made him a little queasy.

B'Elanna gazed at Neelix, perplexed. "You used your replicator rations to make these?" she asked.

He nodded proudly. "I sure did. But I felt it was something I had to do. After all, I've made plomeek soup for Mister Tuvok and pineapple pizza for the Devlin twins, but I've never attempted anything Klingon before. Then I got wind of this wonderful holiday of yours and . . ." He shrugged. "I couldn't resist. Bon appetit, Lieutenant." He leaned a little closer to her. "That means knock your socks off in French."

B'Elanna shook her head. "I can't eat this," she said. She pushed the pot away from her.

The Talaxian was mortified. "I . . . I don't understand," he replied after a moment. "I did extensive research on your cultural background. I could have *sworn* this was the way I was supposed to present these dishes."

The engineer got to her feet. "It's not the presentation," she said, her tone cold and blunt. "I don't eat Klingon food. In case you haven't noticed, I'm not your run-of-the-mill Klingon."

And with that, she stalked off, leaving Neelix and the pot behind. The Talaxian looked to Chakotay, who was the nearest person around.

"I didn't mean to offend her," Neelix explained, clearly at a loss. He watched B'Elanna's departure with genuine disappointment. "I knew she hadn't eaten these things before, but I thought it was because they weren't available. I didn't have any idea she would—"

The first officer put a hand on the Talaxian's shoulder. "It's all right," he said. "Your heart was in the right place."

Neelix glanced at the writhing, pulsating contents of the pot and sighed. "So was the targ's. But it didn't seem to make a difference."

Chakotay frowned. He didn't approve of B'Elanna's behavior. No matter what was bothering her, she had no right to take it out on the cook.

As the engineer exited the mess hall, Chakotay made his decision. "Excuse me," he said, and went after her.

Ensign Harry Kim glanced at his shuttle's instrument panel. On the monitor to his right, he could see the asteroid belt as his sensors saw it—a series of green blips, each a different size and configuration.

There was a path through the blip field, but not an easy one. In fact, it was kind of torturous. And at warp seven, it looked virtually impossible to maneuver through.

"You can do it," said his copilot.

Kim glanced at Tom Paris, who was sitting beside him. As always, Paris was the picture of casual confidence. "What makes you think this time is going to be different from the others?" the ensign asked.

"I've got a feeling," said Paris as he consulted his own monitors. "Pay attention now, Harry. Those asteroids are coming up fast."

They were, too. In a few moments, they'd be right on top of them. The ensign took a breath and let it out. At this speed, their shields would be of no use to them. One collision and they'd be space debris—if there was anything left of them at all.

"Ten seconds," Paris told him. "Nine. Eight. Seven . . ."

"I get the idea," Harry said.

Then he was operating on pure instinct. The first asteroid loomed on his port side; he cut it as closely as he could. That put him in position to cut even more sharply to port when the second asteroid appeared.

The third one required a quick dip, the fourth a sharp rise. The fifth and sixth required only minor adjustments. And the ensign handled them all without an error.

Then again, it wasn't that first sequence that had scared the daylights out of him. It was the next one. Harry gritted his teeth.

Hard to starboard to avoid a large asteroid, the largest he'd seen yet. Hard again, this time to port, to miss another one. To starboard; starboard again. And then a backbreaking ascent.

The shuttle shivered mightily with the force of each turn, but it managed to hold together. More importantly, there were no collisions, not even a particularly close call.

And there were only two asteroids ahead of him, virtually side by side, only a few meters apart. Two asteroids to beat and he was home free. The ensign bore down, concentrating harder than ever, rotating his craft ninety degrees in an attempt to slip between them.

You can do it, he told himself.

"You can do it," Paris echoed. "You can—"

Before the lieutenant could finish his sentence,

Harry's shuttle wavered ever so slightly from the vertical—and clipped one of the asteroids. The impact sent it bouncing into the other one.

The ensign heard his copilot utter a curse. Then, before he could take another breath, his craft exploded in a cataclysm of light and sound.

Harry closed his eyes and scowled as he embraced oblivion. Then he felt Paris tapping his shoulder, and he opened his eyes again. The holodeck grid was all around them, a mocking reminder of the ensign's failure. Or at least, that's how it seemed to him.

"You did it again," said his friend. "Too much starboard thruster."

Normally, Harry didn't like to let his frustration show. He made an exception this time.

"I tried to keep her from heeling," he said. "I *thought* I had it."

Paris grunted. "If you'd had it, you and I would still be safely ensconced in the shuttlecraft, popping open some champagne—not standing here in the middle of the holodeck doing a postmortem."

The ensign pressed his lips together and turned away from his friend. If he'd cracked up just once or twice, it wouldn't have been such a big thing. But this was the *seventh* time he'd tried the very same maneuver—and each time, he'd run into the same crushing results.

"You know what?" he said at last.

"What?" Paris responded.

"I think I've had it with this program," Harry told him, shrugging. "I mean, what's the big deal? I'll probably never run into a situation like that one anyway. How many asteroid belts have we seen since we got ourselves stuck here in the Delta Quadrant? Two or three altogether?"

The lieutenant eyed him soberly. "I see. When in doubt, retreat. Or better yet, just run away."

Something in the ensign stiffened. "I'm *not* running away," he answered. "I'm just conceding my limitations. It's not as if everyone can be the kind of pilot *you* are."

Paris smiled. "Harry, I'm not asking you to be the kind of pilot I am. I'm just trying to prepare you as best I can. Don't forget, we're in terra incognita. We don't know what to expect here. And that's all the more reason to be prepared."

Truthfully, the ensign *wanted* to be able to execute the maneuver, and not just to get his friend off his back. It irked him that any move—no matter how difficult—could make such a monkey out of him.

"Tell you what," said Paris after a moment or two. "I'm going to let you in on a little secret. No, scratch that. It's actually a pretty big secret."

Harry regarded him. "I'm listening."

"The starboard thrusters aren't the problem," said the lieutenant. "Not really. The problem is you're afraid to go for broke."

"Go for broke?" the ensign repeated. "What does that mean? I'm not completing the maneuver because I haven't got the guts?"

Paris winced. "I didn't want to put it quite that way, but—"

"That's what you're saying?" Harry pressed. "I'm

screwing up because I don't have the backbone for it? The nerve?"

"What I'm saying," his friend explained, "is you care too much about the outcome. The secret of piloting, whether it's in a holodeck or out in the real world, is to loosen up, to not give a damn—to not even entertain the *possibility* of failure. And then, if you lose—hey, it happens to the best of us. At least you gave it your best shot."

The ensign was beginning to get angry now. "I *am* giving it my best shot—for what it's worth."

Paris shook his head. "You only think that's your best shot. Stop worrying, stop thinking altogether—and maybe *then* we'll see Harry Kim's best shot." He clapped his friend on the shoulder. "Be a risk-taker, Harry."

The ensign threw his hands up in exasperation. "All right, all right. We'll try it again. And this time, I'll try not to think." He sighed deeply. "Whatever that means."

Paris winked at him. "That's the spirit." He looked up at the ceiling. "Computer, program Paris beta—"

Abruptly, the empty holodeck rang out with the voice of authority. "This is Captain Janeway. All senior staff officers are to meet me in the observation lounge immediately. Janeway out."

Kim felt relief more than anything else. What's more, his friend seemed to sense that.

"I'm not done with you," Paris assured him. "Not by a long shot."

"Hey," said the ensign, "I'm just as disappointed as you are. I really wanted to tackle that program again."

"Yeah, right," his friend muttered, rolling his eyes. "Just like Tuvok wants to learn how to dance."

As the corridor curved, obscuring his view of the lieutenant, Chakotay lengthened his strides. He called after her.

"B'Elanna!"

After a moment or two, he caught up to her. She had stopped at the sound of her name. Or was it the fact that it was *he* who had called her?

"What is it?" she asked.

Chakotay could tell by her attitude that she didn't want to have this conversation. Tough. She would have it anyway.

"What is it, *sir,"* he corrected.

The engineer scowled. "What is it, sir," she echoed.

The first officer looked around to make sure no one else was present in the corridor. What he had to say wasn't necessarily for public consumption.

"You were rude to Neelix back there," he told her. "All he wanted to do was please you, and you shot him down. I want to know why."

"Isn't that between me and Neelix?" she asked. "Or am I under orders to eat whatever he puts in front of me?"

Chakotay sighed. "All right, forget I'm your superior. I'll speak to you as your friend—who was embarrassed by what he saw."

B'Elanna's lips pulled back, as if she were about to lash out at him. But in the end, she seemed to think better of it.

"Fine," she said, looking away from him as her anger ebbed. "Maybe my reaction was inappropriate. But you know how I feel about Klingons. And that includes the things they eat."

Chakotay knew, all right. He had served with B'Elanna long enough to hear the whole story. How her Klingon mother and her human father had separated when she was very young, so she had never really known her father.

How she and her mother had lived in a mostly human colony, where she was self-conscious about her Klingon characteristics. And how she had always emphasized her human characteristics, in an attempt to belong.

That desire for acceptance had gotten her all the way to Starfleet Academy, where she had excelled in the sciences. However, her Klingon side had surfaced there as well—manifesting itself in the way she argued with her teachers. Finally, it had forced her to quit the place.

But several months ago, B'Elanna had obtained a new perspective on her Klingon heritage. Abducted by the Vidiians, she had been split into separate Klingon and human personas, each with its own positive and negative attributes—and each incomplete without the other.

In order to escape her captors, B'Elanna's two halves had been forced to work together—to, in effect, form a whole. In the process, her human self had come to appreciate how much of her courage and determination came from the Klingon within her.

The first officer considered his protégé. "I don't buy

it," he replied. "When you were sitting in sick bay, after the doctor had announced he would have to merge you again with your Klingon DNA—"

"I said I was incomplete without it," the lieutenant recalled. "I said I had come to admire my Klingon self. For her strength, her bravery."

"Exactly," said Chakotay. "And even though you'd never be at peace with her savagery, it seemed you'd at least come to terms with it."

B'Elanna shrugged. "So?"

"So, why did you abuse Neelix that way in the mess hall? His intentions were good—as always. And you treated him as if he'd insulted you."

The lieutenant sighed. "All right. Maybe there's more to it." She paused. "Maybe it's this damned holiday."

At first he didn't know what she meant. Then he recalled the Talaxian's reference a few moments earlier. "Holiday?" he prodded.

She frowned. "Yes. The Day of Honor. It grew out of an incident a hundred years ago. A Starfleet captain named Kirk risked his life to save some Klingons, and now the day is celebrated throughout the Klingon Empire."

Chakotay grunted. He had heard of Kirk, of course. The man's exploits were required reading at the Academy. And now that he thought about it, he remembered something about Kirk rescuing some Klingons early in his career.

"But why does that bother you?" he asked.

B'Elanna looked at him. "It would bother you, too, if you'd spent your life denying a part of yourself. The

Day of Honor has always been a reminder that I'm different from everyone else. That no matter what I say or do, people will always look at me as an outsider."

Chakotay regarded her. He was starting to understand.

"To make matters worse," she went on, "my mother always wanted me to spend the day contemplating its meaning. And of course, I would run away when she wasn't looking and have some kind of bad luck. No—make that *horrible* luck. When I was six, I went exploring outside the colony and fell into a big hole. They had to send a search party out for me. And I didn't get found until well after dark, when the temperature had dropped below freezing."

Chakotay grimaced at the thought of it. "Not one of your fonder childhood memories, I imagine."

"It got worse," she told him. "When I was eight, I was fiddling with the controls to a sensor array when no one was looking. All I did was change the angle on a single data collector—no big deal, right? How was I to know a damaged ship was sending out a distress call, and that we would miss it because the collector was off?"

The first officer winced. "Was the crew rescued?"

B'Elanna nodded. "Eventually—after someone noticed that the collector was off and corrected it. But I caught hell for my fiddling—from my mother, especially."

He got the point. However, the engineer wasn't finished yet.

"When I was nine," she said, "I accidentally locked

myself in a storage room. When I was eleven, I nearly lost my leg to a falling cargo container. When I was thirteen, the boy I liked—"

Suddenly she stopped. Her face was a bright shade of crimson.

"What?" he asked.

"Nothing," she muttered. "But you see what I mean? This holiday has been nothing but trouble for me. And yet, people always seem to want to thrust the Day of Honor on me, as if it were a badge of pride. If I—"

Suddenly, an intercom voice interrupted the conversation. Chakotay recognized it instantly, even before it identified itself.

"This is Captain Janeway. All senior staff officers are to meet me in the observation lounge immediately. Janeway out."

He looked at B'Elanna. She seemed relieved to have been provided with a distraction.

"I guess we'll have to continue this another time," Chakotay told her.

"Another time," she echoed as they headed for the turbolift.

B'Elanna and Chakotay were the last to arrive at the ship's observation lounge. As they took their seats around the table, the engineer saw the others look up at them.

Tuvok, the security officer, was as stone-faced as ever. But then, he was a Vulcan, and Vulcans had mastered their emotions hundreds of years earlier. Whatever he was feeling at the moment, he kept it well-hidden—even from himself, the engineer suspected.

Tom Paris, the helmsman, smiled a perfunctory smile at B'Elanna. In some ways he was the opposite of Tuvok, reveling in his human foibles and faults. But right now, he seemed pretty businesslike.

Harry Kim, the young ensign who'd been making his maiden voyage when *Voyager* was whisked into the Delta Quadrant, had taken a chair to one side of Paris. As always, he seemed eager to apply his intellect to the problem at hand—no matter what it might be.

Neelix was in attendance as well—not just cook and morale officer, but also their resident authority on people and places in the sector. As a being who had scavenged and traded his way from star to star, he was an invaluable guide in what often proved to be hostile territory.

The Talaxian didn't mention B'Elanna's behavior in the mess hall. But then, he didn't look at her either, so it was hard to tell if he harbored any resentment over it.

Finally, there was Janeway, their captain. She sat at the head of the table, her usual place. As always, she seemed calm and unruffled, hopeful without being demanding.

But then, she was the commanding officer of this vessel, the only real Starfleet presence in the entire Delta Quadrant. If she didn't maintain an even keel, who *would?*

B'Elanna was glad Janeway had summoned her staff when she did. More than likely, the engineer would soon have something to occupy her mind. If she was *really* lucky, this damned Day of Honor would be over before she had a chance to think about it again.

Janeway looked around the table, from one to the other of them. "Thank you for being prompt," she said. "This shouldn't take long." The captain leaned back in her chair. "Long-range sensors have identified a Class M planet not far from here. There's a good chance it'll have the kind of plant life we've discovered elsewhere—and put to good use."

"Excellent," said Neelix. "We're running low. As always." He had muttered the last part under his breath, but there wasn't anyone at the table who failed to hear it—or to understand what he meant.

As a ship on its own, with limited energy and raw material, *Voyager* couldn't produce large quantities of food through its replicators. The crew had to depend on natural flora for much of its diet. Some of it could be produced in the aeroponics bay, but the majority had to be foraged from the surfaces of alien planets.

"We'll send down three teams of two people apiece," Janeway announced. "Each team will take a different area, examine the local plant life firsthand—and coordinate its transport, if it fills our needs."

Janeway leaned forward in her chair. "Any questions?"

B'Elanna tried to think of one that wouldn't be a complete waste of time. But she couldn't. And no one else had a question either, apparently.

The captain nodded. "Dismissed." Then she

turned to the engineer. "And, by the way, B'Elanna—I want to wish you a brave Day of Honor."

The lieutenant could feel herself blanch. Somehow, she managed to say, "Thank you, ma'am."

Then, with a glance at Chakotay, she made a quick exit—before someone decided to echo the sentiment.

CHAPTER 2

JANEWAY EMERGED ONTO THE BRIDGE WITH CHAKOTAY alongside her. "She doesn't *like* people saying that?" the captain asked.

"Apparently not," said the first officer.

Janeway frowned. "I'll have to remember that in the future." She thought for a moment. "You think I ought to—?"

"Apologize?" Chakotay ventured. He shook his head. "No, I think that would only make it worse."

The captain sighed and headed for her center seat, her thoughts reverting to a more immediate concern.

Neelix's remark at the briefing earlier had been an absolute understatement. Their provisions weren't just low—they were lower than they'd been at any time she could remember.

That made their foraging mission more than just necessary. It was nothing short of essential. And where was that planet anyway? By now, she estimated, it should have been well within—

"Visual range," said Tuvok. He was standing at his customary post, as poker-faced as ever.

The captain chuckled softly to herself. Vulcans were supposed to be able to read one's thoughts only during a mind-meld. However, Tuvok often seemed to read hers without one.

"Let's see it," Janeway replied.

In accordance with her orders, the flowing star field on the forward viewscreen gave way to the image of a Class M planet. She could tell by the degree of magnification that it was somewhat smaller than Earth, but not by much—though its continents were considerably larger.

The captain turned to Paris, who was manning the helm. "Estimated time to orbit?" she asked.

"One hour and forty minutes," he told her.

Janeway nodded. "Thank you, Lieutenant."

It was an hour and forty minutes longer than she cared to wait, but even warp drive could propel them only so fast. Taking her seat, she settled in and prepared herself for the vigil.

Fortunately for her, as well as everyone else, Janeway didn't enforce a rigid silence on her bridge the way some captains did. She felt comfortable with a certain amount of chatter, as long as it didn't distract anyone's attention from his or her duties.

Tuvok never took part in these conversations. But then, no one expected him to. By contrast, Paris liked to needle everyone a bit, the Vulcan included—though the helmsman's favorite target was Ensign Kim.

After all, they'd become close friends over the last several months. Whenever Paris made a remark, Kim would always frown good-naturedly and let it roll off his back.

But today seemed to be an exception. Paris didn't send a single barb in the ensign's direction. And that made the captain wonder. Had the helmsman jabbed his friend once too often?

No doubt, she told herself, she would find out in due time. Very little went on between the bulkheads of this ship that Kathryn Janeway didn't get a whiff of eventually.

B'Elanna had purposely waited until mealtime was over and the mess hall was likely to be deserted. As it turned out, there wasn't a soul around—except for the one who was cleaning up behind the serving counter.

Not wishing to take him by surprise, the lieutenant cleared her throat. A moment later, Neelix poked his head up. When he saw who it was, he paused a moment—then went back to his cleaning.

B'Elanna folded her arms across her chest and sighed. Apparently, the Talaxian wasn't going to make this easy for her.

"Listen," she said, "I'm ashamed of the way I acted earlier. It was uncalled-for. And I hope you'll accept my apology."

There. She'd said it. But there wasn't any reaction.

Somewhere below the level of the counter, Neelix continued his chores rather noisily. But he didn't give her a response.

The lieutenant bit her lip. She'd tried, hadn't she? She'd done the right thing. If the Talaxian didn't think it was enough, there wasn't much she could do about that.

Except apologize one more time. "All right. Maybe I deserve the silent treatment. I just wanted you to know I'm sorry. Really."

Still no answer. Just more of Neelix's puttering. If anything, it was even louder than before.

B'Elanna looked at the floor and steeled herself. Then she forged ahead, despite the difficulty she had in saying such things.

"Look," she told the Talaxian, "I know you went to a lot of trouble for me. I know I acted like a spoiled child. And I know you're under no obligation whatsoever to speak to me, now or ever again. But I really wish you would. Not only because I would miss your company, but because every time you gave me the cold shoulder I'd be reminded of what an absolute jerk I was."

The puttering continued unabated. But no reply. Not even a hint of one. Obviously, she thought, she wasn't going to get anywhere with Neelix, no matter what she did or said.

The lieutenant was just about to leave the mess hall, her mission unfulfilled, when Neelix appeared above the level of the counter again. And this time, he had a plate in his hands.

"You turn *this* down," he said, "and I'll really be upset."

B'Elanna looked at it. "Cheese quesadillas? With salsa verde?"

The Talaxian nodded, obviously pleased with himself. "A traditional meal from the *human* side of your family tree. It's my way of saying I understand your being mad at me. Now come on. Dig in before it gets cold and the cheese starts to congeal."

The engineer couldn't help smiling at him as she accepted the plate. "Well . . . what can I say? Thanks, Neelix. Um . . . care to join me?"

"I've already eaten," he told her, "but I'll be glad to keep you company. I get a kick out of watching people enjoy their food."

As B'Elanna led the way to the nearest table, she took another look at the quesadillas and suppressed a grimace. Truth be told, she didn't like Mexican food either. But under the circumstances, she knew she'd better eat it—or lose Neelix's friendship forever.

Brave Day of Honor, she remarked inwardly. This holiday was nothing but torture for her.

Thanks in part to her curiosity about Paris and Kim, time passed quickly on the bridge for Janeway. Almost before the captain knew it, *Voyager* had reached the system that housed their target world.

"Reduce to impulse speed," she told her helmsman.

"Taking her down to impulse," Paris confirmed.

Janeway stood, as if to get a better look at the Class M planet, and glanced at Tuvok. At this range, the sensors could pick up a good deal more data than before.

"Sentient life forms?" she asked.

The Vulcan examined his instruments for a moment, then shook his head. "None, apparently. The little fauna that exists shows only rudimentary signs of intelligence."

The captain nodded. "I see. In your estimation, will any of it present a significant danger to us?"

Again, Tuvok consulted his instruments. "There are predators, of course, but nothing out of the ordinary."

"What about surface conditions?" she inquired. "Radiation? Unusual gases? Geothermal activity?"

"Nothing significant," the Vulcan told her. "At least not from the point of view of safety."

Janeway absorbed the information as she joined the Vulcan at his console. "And what would you say are the most promising beam-down sites?"

Tuvok didn't answer right away. But then, the security chief was a Vulcan through and through. He seldom made recommendations without carefully considering all his options.

"Here," he said finally. His monitor showed the two hemispheres that made up the planet. Tuvok pointed to a spot that displayed a concentration of foliage—or, to be more accurate, a particular sort of foliage.

It wasn't the kind of plant they needed to supplement their food supplies; that stuff often grew in amounts too sparse to identify with ship's sensors. Still, as the captain had learned from experience, the plant Tuvok had found was an indication that what they needed was probably nearby.

The Vulcan pointed again. "And here." He pointed to a second spot on his monitor, this time in the other hemisphere. "And lastly, here." He showed the captain a third location.

Janeway nodded. "I agree—although it appears there are some sensor blind spots in the vicinity of the third site." She took a closer look. "Probably mineral deposits. That could hamper communications."

Communications were important, considering how little they knew about most of the worlds they visited. But on the whole, she was willing to take the chance, given the lack of other hazards.

On other planets, the captain had been forced to overlook a promising source of supplies in the interest of keeping her people from harm. Fortunately, she mused, that wouldn't be the case here.

"Put together some landing parties," she told Tuvok. "I'll want them to beam down as soon as we establish orbit."

The Vulcan nodded. "Aye, Captain."

As he left the bridge, another officer moved over to take his place. Smooth and efficient, thought Janeway. She liked that. With a little luck, this entire mission would go that way.

* * *

As B'Elanna ascended the transporter platform, Kim was right beside her. Adjusting his shoulder strap and the tricorder that dangled from it, he winked in her direction.

"Ready, Maquis?" he asked.

She nodded, smiling a little. "Ready, Starfleet."

It was a private joke born of their experiences on the Caretaker's planet, shortly after their arrival in the Delta Quadrant. They had woken side by side in a stark, colorless laboratory, having never met each other before—but cognizant of the fact that they were the only two familiar elements in an otherwise alien picture.

At the time, she was hostile—mistrusting him. Since then, they had learned not only to get along, but to depend on each other—to watch each other's back. These days, B'Elanna wouldn't have thought twice about entrusting Harry Kim with her life.

Of course, this was slated to be a routine mission. And since the other survey teams had all beamed down already without incident, there was no reason to believe she would have to entrust Kim with anything—except maybe collecting his share of the data.

Best of all, he hadn't mentioned the Day of Honor to her. Not once.

The transporter operator, a petite, blonde-haired woman named Burleson, smiled at their banter as she made some small adjustments in her controls. "Stand by," she told them.

"Standing by," Kim assured her.

Finished with her ministrations, Burleson looked up at them. "Energizing."

When she was younger, B'Elanna had always wondered what it would be like to be transported. What it would *feel* like. Now, as an adult who had transported to and from space-going vessels hundreds of times, she knew the answer.

Nothing. It felt like *nothing.*

One moment, one was in a transporter room, with its muted lighting and hard echoes. The next moment, one was somewhere else.

In this case, it was a gently rolling hillside under a big, yellow-orange sun. As the sensors had indicated, there was plenty of vegetation around. The dominant form of flora was a plant with wispy blue tendrils, each the thickness of her pinky finger.

Kim took out his tricorder and started analyzing the stuff. After a moment, he grunted. "Poisonous. And even if it weren't, it's all but devoid of nutrients. At least, the kind *we* need."

B'Elanna tried another kind of plant. It wasn't poisonous to them, but it also didn't suit their needs. Nor did the next specimen she tried. Or the one after that.

She was beginning to get frustrated. So was the ensign, if his tight-lipped expression was any indication. "Let's expand the scan," she suggested.

Kim nodded. As B'Elanna adjusted her tricorder to analyze everything within one kilometer, he did the same.

"Still nothing," he told her. "Wait—maybe I spoke too soon."

She saw it, too. "In that direction." She pointed west. "Some kind of vegetation. And it seems to be more the kind of thing we're looking for. Of course, it's hard to tell for certain from this distance."

Kim shrugged. "So let's close the gap."

Putting away their tricorders, they headed in the direction B'Elanna had indicated. It wasn't an unpleasant walk, with the sun on their faces and a gentle breeze stirring the blue tendrils all about them.

And as she had predicted, her friend didn't mention the Day of Honor. They talked about the soil, the atmosphere, the temperature, and the ways in which they missed the Alpha Quadrant.

But they didn't refer to the Day of Honor.

There was something else they didn't talk about—something that was bothering Kim, though he tried not to let on. Out of respect for his wishes, B'Elanna didn't press the issue.

Before long, they arrived at the spot where they had detected the patch of edible vegetation. It turned out to be the mouth of a cave set into a particularly steep hillside.

The vegetation itself—something that looked like cabbage, except it was orange with white streaks running through it—was in sparse supply. But a glance deeper inside the cave revealed more of it, as well as evidence of some other useful-looking plants.

Unfortunately, neither B'Elanna nor Kim could tell just how deep the caves went. According to their tricorders, the signal-blocking minerals Tuvok had warned them about seemed to be in vast abundance here.

"We should take a look inside," B'Elanna said.

Her companion nodded. "But first, we'll let the captain know what we're up to." He tapped his comm badge. "Kim to Janeway."

The communication was plagued with static, but the captain's voice was recognizable nonetheless. "Janeway here. What can I do for you, Ensign?"

"We've located what appears to be edible vegetation," he said. "But it seems to prefer the dark. More specifically, a cave we've discovered."

"And you'd like to explore it," the captain deduced. "Taking all possible precautions, of course."

"Of course," B'Elanna chimed in.

There was a chuckle on Janeway's end of the communication. "Very well," she told them. "But don't stay down there long. I want a report in, say, fifteen minutes—no later."

"Acknowledged," said the ensign. "Kim out."

He turned to B'Elanna and indicated the cave mouth with a gesture. "Shall we?" he asked.

Snapping the palmlight off her uniform, B'Elanna shone it into the darkness. Then she hunkered down and took the lead. As it turned out, the cave was bigger than it looked—not just taller and wider once they got inside, but deeper as well. And if anything, it was more profuse with usable flora than they had imagined.

"This place is one big larder," Kim laughed. "Neelix is going to have a field day with this stuff."

"No doubt," she agreed. "I'll take the wall on the left, you take the one on the right."

"Sounds good to me," he told her.

Little by little, they worked their way deeper and deeper into the cavern, following its twists and turns. The orange-and-white stuff gave way to something big and fluffy and scarlet, then something that looked like a bunch of tiny purple tubers.

And all of it was edible, with a good variety of vitamins and minerals. The way it tasted was another matter—but, as always, B'Elanna would leave that to Neelix. Maybe her discovery would make up for the way she'd growled at him that morning.

The lieutenant was so busy cataloguing the cave vegetation, she didn't see her friend turn his head to look at her. That is, until he cleared his throat and drew her attention.

"Something on your mind, Starfleet?"

"Well," Kim said, "now that you mention it . . ."

Oh no, she thought. I can't escape it even *here.*

". . . I understand you were a pretty fair pilot," the ensign finished. "You know, when you were with the Maquis."

B'Elanna smiled with relief. "I suppose. But then, we were all good pilots. We *had* to be." She tilted her head. "Why do you ask?"

Kim sighed. "There's a holodeck program Tom keeps running me through. We're in a shuttlecraft, and there's this asteroid belt . . ."

He went on to describe it for her—and how it was that one last obstacle that gave him the most trouble. "I can't seem to get the hang of it," he confessed. "I was wondering if you might have any . . ." He shrugged. "I don't know, any hints."

She went back to cataloguing the vegetation.

"Well," she said, "you might want to try applying your thrusters sooner, then reversing them when you rotate too far. That's worked for me."

Kim shook his head ruefully. "I tried that. It didn't—"

Suddenly, they heard a *crunch.* It seemed to have come from the direction of the cave mouth.

Stopping in mid-remark, the ensign looked at her. B'Elanna swallowed and deactivated her palmlight, throwing her half of the cave into darkness. Then, as Kim extinguished his own light, she put her tricorder away and took out her phaser.

Of course, she was probably being overly cautious. There were animals on this world, after all. One of them had probably disturbed a rock. But it could also have been something more. And as she had heard often enough growing up, it was better to be safe than sorry.

Kim pulled his phaser out as well. But try as they might, they couldn't hear anything more. B'Elanna began to relax a little.

Then a bright blue beam sliced the air mere inches from her face, blinding her for a moment. She heard a shuffling, as of many pairs of feet. Pressing her back against the hard, sloping wall of the cavern, she blinked away her blindness and fired back.

The Kazon used directed-energy beams of that color. She cursed silently.

Kim looked at her from across the cave, little more than a shadow. He had likely come to the same conclusion she had. And if it *was* the Kazon, they could expect no mercy—only hostility and savagery and death.

Another directed-energy beam pierced the darkness, throwing the cavern into stark relief. Then a third beam, and a fourth. All of them missed—but by their light B'Elanna could see several large, poorly clad forms poking their bizarrely coifed heads around the bend.

Kazon, all right. She tapped her communicator. "Torres to Janeway. We've got a problem down here, Captain."

A moment passed. Then another.

"Torres to Janeway," she repeated.

Again, nothing. Was it the fault of the signal-blocking minerals in the ground? Or were the Kazon interfering with their communications?

At this point, it hardly mattered. Either way, they couldn't expect any help from the ship. For all intents and purposes, they were on their own.

Gritting her teeth, B'Elanna pushed away from the cave wall and fired in the direction of their adversaries. As her ruby red beam lanced out, she heard a grunt and saw one of the Kazon slump to the ground.

A lucky shot. At least, it seemed so at first.

Then a whole bunch of Kazon came roaring into the cave, scalding the air with a wild barrage of seething blue energy. Suddenly, the shot didn't seem so lucky anymore.

B'Elanna felt something hit her in the midsection—so hard it knocked the breath out of her. She staggered, fell. And as she lay gasping, she felt a second hammer-blow—this time, to her shoulder. And a third.

She fought hard to stay conscious, to hold on to the phaser in her hand. But it was no use. Against her will, darkness claimed her.

CHAPTER 3

"CAPTAIN?"

Janeway turned to look at DuChamps, the dark, stocky former Maquis who had replaced Tuvok at the tactical console.

"What is it?" she asked.

DuChamps frowned and shook his head as he consulted his instruments. "Some kind of unidentified vessel," he reported. "Heading our way at full impulse—three million kilometers and closing."

The captain sighed. Tuvok would have detected an approaching ship at twice that distance, maybe more. And by now, he almost certainly would have found a way to identify it.

But Tuvok wasn't here right now, was he? He was with Tom Paris at one of the beam-down sites.

"I've identified it," DuChamps said at last.

Janeway grunted. "Is it in visual range?"

"Aye, ma'am," the lieutenant responded.

A moment later, the main viewscreen filled with an all-too-familiar sight—that of a Kazon battleship under impulse power. The captain didn't have to know any more than that to realize there was trouble in the offing.

"Transporter room," she intoned, keeping her eyes on the screen. "Bring back the away teams—and I mean *immediately.*"

Janeway then turned back to DuChamps. "Lower shields." Otherwise, the transporter wouldn't work worth a damn. Of course, in the case of Torres and Kim, it might not work anyway.

The lieutenant nodded. "Lowering shields, Captain."

The captain gritted her teeth, watching the Kazon vessel on the viewscreen. At any second it could fire a devastating barrage, and *Voyager* was—at least for now—completely unprotected.

"Raise shields again," Janeway ordered, unable to wait any longer.

DuChamps did as he was told. "Shields up," he informed her.

As the captain watched, the Kazon ship slowed and assumed a parking orbit. It gave no outward sign of hostile intentions, but one never knew when it came to these people.

"What's the status of the Kazon vessel?" she asked DuChamps.

"Quiet," the lieutenant told her. "For the time being, anyway. Their shields are up, too, but they're not charging any weapons."

And the Kazon couldn't beam down to threaten the away teams, if there was anyone left on the surface. Thanks to Janeway's caution, *Voyager* still had the only transporter technology in the Delta Quadrant—and as far as she was concerned, it was going to stay that way.

"Hail them," she told DuChamps. Then she returned her attention to the away team personnel. "Janeway to transporter room. What's going on?"

"We retrieved two of the three teams," came Burleson's reply. "But I couldn't seem to get a lock on Torres and Kim."

Of course you can't, the captain remarked silently. They're in that damned cavern.

"Janeway to Torres," she said out loud.

No answer. Apparently, the mineral deposits were keeping Torres and Kim from hearing the summons.

Then again, there was another possibility—that something more intrusive was keeping Torres and Kim from responding. A cave-in, perhaps? Or—

"The Kazon aren't answering our hails," DuChamps informed her.

The captain bit her lip. "Keep trying."

On the viewscreen, the Kazon vessel was maintaining its position. But surely it was here for a reason. It hadn't made the trip just to admire *Voyager*'s lines.

She didn't like this. She didn't like it at *all.*

As she was pondering what to do, she heard the soft swoosh of the turbolift doors. A moment later, Tuvok and Paris emerged onto the bridge. Smoothly and efficiently, their replacements gave way to them.

The captain nodded to both her senior officers, glad to see them safe and sound—and pleased to have them at her side again. She hated the idea of facing the Kazon with anything less than her best people on hand.

Encouraged, she returned her attention to the viewscreen. The Kazon vessel showed no signs of changing its position.

"What is our situation?" asked the Vulcan, taking in the information on his tactical monitors at a glance.

"Torres and Kim are still down there," Janeway told him. "We can't seem to raise them. And while the Kazon aren't making any threatening moves, they're not speaking to us either."

Paris looked at her. "If you're thinking about a search party, I volunteer to go back down."

The captain frowned. "Don't anticipate me, Lieutenant."

Still, a search party might be their only option. The question was whether or not Torres and Kim had stumbled into a trap—and if so, whether she'd accomplish anything by throwing additional lives at the problem.

She was still considering the option when Tuvok

called out her name. Janeway whirled, energized by the urgency in his voice.

"What is it?" she asked.

"There's a vehicle rising from the planet's surface," he told her. "It is Kazon in design, but smaller than any Kazon ship we have seen to date."

"On screen," she commanded.

As the Vulcan complied, the image on the viewscreen changed. Instead of a full-blown Kazon cruiser, the captain found herself looking at a shuttle-sized vessel. And it was indeed rising from the planet's surface, where it had been hidden until just a few seconds ago.

But why hide there—unless it was part of a trap to snare a *Voyager* away team? And why leave its hiding place now, unless it was trying to rejoin its Kazon mothership?

"Get a tractor beam on the smaller vehicle," Janeway snapped. "I want it intercepted immediately."

But before Tuvok could carry out her order, the larger Kazon vessel left its position. And it was all too clear what its commander had in mind.

"They're maneuvering to shield their shuttle from us," she observed out loud. "Compensate, Mr. Paris."

"Aye, Captain," said the helmsman, sending *Voyager* in the direction of the ascending shuttle.

But it was too late. Janeway saw that even before Paris made his move. And even if it weren't, the Kazon ship had begun firing at them for all it was worth, lighting up the heavens with its deadly barrage.

The bridge shivered with the impact. "Shields

down twenty-two percent," Tuvok barked in the wake of it.

"What about that tractor beam?" the captain barked in return.

"I am finding it exceedingly difficult to establish a lock," the Vulcan reported as he wrestled with his controls.

And then it became downright impossible, as the smaller vehicle slipped behind the larger one. There was no way the tractors could snare the shuttle with the mothership blocking their line of sight.

"Come around her," the captain instructed. "Quickly, before we lose the shuttle."

Paris did his best. But by the time they reached the far side of the Kazon ship, the smaller vessel was already inside its cargo bay.

Janeway cursed beneath her breath. She wasn't going to give up Torres and Kim without a fight.

"Target phasers and torpedoes," she cried out. "Fire!"

Phaser beams sliced through the void, finding their objectives. Photon torpedoes exploded on impact. But the Kazon's shields held up.

And a moment later, it took off at warp speed, leaving a momentary trail of photon spill. The captain was just as quick.

"Stay with her," she told Paris.

"Aye, ma'am," came his response.

Before she knew it, they were proceeding at top speed. Unfortunately, that was only good enough to keep pace with the Kazon, not overtake them.

Janeway moved to her helmsman's side. "Can we wring any more speed out of the engines?" she asked.

Paris shook his head. "Not without risking a shutdown."

For a moment, the captain was tempted to try it anyway. Then she backed off from the idea. For now, she would go with the conservative approach. At least this way, they could stay in the game.

"Steady as she goes," she told Paris. "Steady as she goes."

Teeg'l, third Maj of the reknowned and feared Kazon-Ogla sect, stood over his helmsman and inspected his craft's monitors. Unfortunately, surrounded as they were with sensor-foiling energy fields, the monitors were all but useless.

Of course, it was those same energy fields that had allowed Teeg'l's vessel to go undetected until this time—without question, a great convenience. But now they were keeping the third Maj from ascertaining when it was safe to leave.

His helmsman, whose name was Shan'ak, looked up at him. "I await your orders, third Maj."

Teeg'l frowned and remembered his instructions. This was an important mission with which he had been entrusted—the first one since his promotion to third Maj. He didn't want to make any mistakes.

"How long has it been since we left the cave?" he asked.

The helmsman consulted his chronometer. "Twenty-seven small cycles."

Teeg'l's frown deepened. "Not enough. Our ship may still be in orbit, awaiting the other shuttlecraft—the one that will serve as a decoy. And if that is so, *Voyager* will be in orbit as well."

The third Maj glanced at the door behind him. Beyond it, the rest of his men were maintaining an armed guard over their *Voyager* captives. All had gone according to plan so far—at least from *his* point of view. It wouldn't hurt to remain here a little longer.

"We continue to wait," Teeg'l decided at last.

Shan'ak nodded. "As you wish, third Maj."

As soon as B'Elanna woke, she sat bolt upright and scanned her surroundings. She was in some kind of cargo hold, small and dark and pentagon-shaped, one of its five walls a yellow energy barrier that prevented her from seeing anything beyond it.

And she had the feeling the place was moving. She imagined she could hear wind on the outside of the walls.

Kim was lying a meter or so away, moaning as he began to regain his senses. There was a large purple bruise on his chin.

Neither one of them had their comm badges. More than likely, they'd been destroyed.

"Harry," she said, crawling over to him and gripping his shoulder. "Wake up."

His eyes opened instantly at the sound of her voice. Then they looked past her, trying to match a location to what they saw.

The ensign sat up. "Where are we?" he asked.

B'Elanna shook her head. "I don't know. But I'm guessing we're in the hands of the Kazon. The last thing I remember is the cavern flooding with them."

He nodded. "I saw them hit you with a couple of those energy beams." His face took on a more serious expression. "I thought they'd killed you—and that I wasn't too far behind. That's when I rushed them, figuring they wouldn't fire at close quarters. You know, for fear of hitting each other?"

"And?" she asked.

Kim winced and touched his black-and-blue mark. "I was right about them not firing. But one of them found another use for his weapon."

"He belted you with it," B'Elanna concluded.

"Knocked me right on my back," the ensign admitted. *"Then* he fired at me, for good measure."

The lieutenant sighed heavily. "And here we are. Neither one of us dead." She looked around again. "I shudder to think why."

"Very simple," said a voice. It seemed to have come from the other side of the energy barrier.

A moment later, the barrier crackled and disappeared—revealing three tall, burly Kazon warriors in the corridor beyond. B'Elanna stood to get a better look at them.

It had been hard to tell in the cavern, but now she recognized the garb of the Kazon-Ogla sect—the first one *Voyager* had encountered in the Delta Quadrant. Not that it mattered much. Janeway and her crew were despised by every Kazon they had run into.

Two of their captors were armed with handweapons. The third, by far the stockiest of the three, entered the cargo hold and smiled savagely.

"Very simple indeed," he said. "You see, you have something and we want it. Give it to us, and we will let you go."

"Just like that," Kim commented.

"Just like that," the Kazon echoed. "As entertaining as it might be to torture and kill you, we will forgo the pleasure if you cooperate. You have the word of Teeg'l, third Maj of the Ogla."

"And how do we know you'll keep your word?" asked B'Elanna.

The Kazon shrugged. "I don't see you have much of a choice."

The lieutenant scowled. "What is it you want?"

"I think you know the answer to that," their captor told them. "After all, we have asked for your transporter technology before. And you have declined to share it with us—though it would benefit our sect immensely."

"Enabling you to dominate the other sects," Kim suggested.

The Kazon nodded. "And others of our enemies as well."

B'Elanna looked the warrior in the eye. "You must know we can't give you what you're after."

"On the contrary," he growled, his smile fading suddenly. "I know you *can*. That is, you have the expertise. But for now, you have decided against it. We are not fools, you know. We have anticipated such a reaction."

"You have to understand," she explained, "we're sworn not to give such technology to anyone, friend or otherwise. It's our most sacred rule."

The Kazon's eyes narrowed. "Do not play games with me, Lieutenant. You are alone in this part of space. You are afraid to share your technology because it would take away your military edge—and therefore impair your chances of survival." He smiled again, but it was a thin-lipped smile. "You may have other reasons—but this is the most important one."

Not true, thought B'Elanna. But there was nothing to be gained by arguing the point.

"Maybe you think your friends will find you," Teeg'l went on. "Maybe you think all you have to do is hold out for a while, and they will free you. But I am here to tell you it is not so. In kidnapping you, we did not merely see an opportunity and take advantage of it. You are the result of a trap we have been planning for some time."

"A trap?" the lieutenant echoed.

She wanted to keep the Kazon talking. The more she knew, the better equipped she would be to find an escape route.

"Indeed," said Teeg'l. "The Ogla tracked your progress through the quadrant for months, seeing what kinds of planets attracted your attention and why. Once we realized what you were after and where you were headed, we determined the location of the next attractive planet in your path."

"And that's where you caught us," Kim deduced.

The Kazon frowned. "No, not right away. Twice

before we set a trap and you went off in some other direction. It was only this third time that everything went according to plan."

"Which was?" B'Elanna prodded, perhaps a little too hard.

"A matter of misdirection," Teeg'l explained, unperturbed by her aggressiveness. "While you and your comrades were still foraging on the planet's surface, a Kazon cruiser appeared. No doubt wondering what this might mean, your captain retrieved your fellow crewmen. But, to her regret, she could not retrieve you."

"Because of the minerals in the crust," the ensign noted.

The Kazon laughed. "That's how it must have seemed. The truth is, we projected a field around the cave—one which simulated the effects of certain sensor-foiling minerals. The field also served to conceal this vessel—which was located on the surface all the time. And not just this vessel, but another as well."

B'Elanna was beginning to get the picture. But she let Teeg'l finish, still hoping he'd reveal something she could use to good advantage.

"Shortly after our cruiser arrived," the Kazon boasted, "that other vessel rose from its concealment—and eventually found safety in the cruiser's cargo bay. But not before it gave your captain the idea she had been duped. As far as she could tell, you had been captured by the Kazon and were being spirited away. It was then that our cruiser took off.

"Predictably, your captain chose to give pursuit. As far as we know, she is pursuing still—and will continue to do so until she realizes the *true* extent of our deceit." Teeg'l chuckled. "By that time, *this* vessel will have rendezvoused with a *second* Ogla cruiser, in an entirely different sector of space. And before long, we will have obtained the secret of your transporters—one way or another."

B'Elanna had no illusions as to how far the Kazon would go to get what they wanted. After all, they had two captives. If one died in the course of their tortures, it would only serve to loosen the lips of the other one.

Or so they believed. But it wouldn't work. Certainly not with B'Elanna herself, and probably not with Kim either. Starfleet officers took their vows pretty seriously—and the promise to observe the Prime Directive was the biggest vow of all.

"So, you see," said Teeg'l, "you have no choice but to cooperate. And as long as you must do that anyway, why wait until the rendezvous? Why not cooperate with *me?*"

Kim smiled humorlessly. "So you can get credit for it?"

"Credit I *deserve,*" the third Maj insisted. "Believe me, it will go better for you if you speak to me. I am, let us say, a good deal more generous than the other Kazon-Ogla you will encounter."

"Is that so?" asked the ensign. "Well, you and the other Kazon-Ogla can go straight to—"

"That's enough," B'Elanna snapped.

Kim was clearly surprised by the interruption. But, recognizing it as an order, he kept his mouth shut.

The lieutenant turned to Teeg'l. "Thanks for the advice," she told him. "We'll consider it."

The third Maj's eyes narrowed as he looked from one captive to the other. "See that you do," he replied.

Then he turned and led the other Kazon out of the room. As they departed, one of them reactivated the yellow energy barrier.

Only when she was sure their captors were out of earshot did B'Elanna turn to her companion. "Listen," she said, "I don't have any intention of giving them our secrets either. But if Teeg'l's not the one ultimately in charge here, why not keep him on the line? He'll be more inclined to treat us better for a while."

"But not forever," Kim reminded her. "Ultimately, we'll be turned over to someone who won't take maybe for an answer."

"With any luck," the lieutenant rejoined, "we'll have escaped by then."

The ensign smiled despite the bruise on his face. "The way you say it, I'm almost tempted to believe it."

"Believe it," she said defiantly.

Had he been a member of a species other than Vulcan, Tuvok would have been expressing considerable frustration. As it was, he was only mildly perturbed.

Since *Voyager* took off in pursuit of the Kazon vessel nearly fifteen minutes earlier, Tuvok had been probing for information they could use to their advantage. He had looked for anything and everything.

Weaknesses in the Kazon's shields, for instance. Blind spots in their sensor array. Gaps in their weapon spread, their structural integrity field—anything that might prove valuable in the recovery of Lieutenant Torres and Ensign Kim.

He hadn't found a thing. The vessel was remarkably sound, considering the Kazons' apparent lack of discipline.

The Vulcan didn't like to admit defeat. However, in this case, it seemed unavoidable.

Then another possibility occurred to him. If he could pinpoint the locations of their missing crewmates on the Kazon vessel, they might be able to beam them off—even with the Kazon's shields up.

It would mean finding the necessary frequency—no easy task in itself. And it would be a difficult maneuver, full of danger for those being transported. But it was less obtrusive and less likely to provoke retaliation than any attack they could mount.

At the very least, it was an option. And right now, the captain needed all the options she could get.

Cocking an eyebrow, Tuvok set to work. He couldn't detect any comm badge signals; no doubt the Kazons had destroyed the badges. Undaunted, he programmed the sensors to look for human and Klingon life signs and began a search—a time-consuming procedure, since Kazon biology didn't differ greatly from that of those other species.

But it wasn't the amount of time involved that took the Vulcan by surprise. It was the result.

"Captain Janeway," he said, looking up.

Janeway turned in response. "Yes, Lieutenant?"

Tuvok frowned. "Captain, I detect neither human nor Klingon life signs aboard the Kazon vessel."

Janeway's eyes opened wide as she started toward tactical. "Are you certain about that, Mister Tuvok?"

The Vulcan nodded. "As certain as I can be," he told her.

Joining him at his console, the captain inspected Tuvok's monitors for herself. What's more, he took no offense at this. It was, as he had learned years ago, simply human behavior.

"Damn," Janeway grated, looking up at him. Her face was ruddy with anger and embarrassment. "They conned us, didn't they?"

A rhetorical question, he thought. Once, he would have supplied an answer. But over the course of his Starfleet career, he had become conversant with human foibles—the captain's in particular.

Janeway set her jaw and glared at the viewscreen. "Mister Paris," she said, her voice low and determined, "bring us about. Set a course for the world where we lost Torres and Kim."

The helmsman didn't say anything. He just followed orders. No doubt he shared in the captain's embarrassment.

As they all did, Tuvok mused. He wished he had thought earlier to confirm their crewmates' presence on the Kazon vessel. However, as humans were fond of saying, that was water under the bridge. The important thing now was to find out what had really happened to the ensign and the chief engineer, so they could devise a new rescue strategy.

And hope they were not too late.

CHAPTER 4

JANEWAY PACED THE BRIDGE OF *VOYAGER* AS IT ORBITED the Class M planet where they'd lost Torres and Kim. Not for the first time, she wondered how she could possibly have been so gullible. How she could have jumped to a conclusion so eagerly, without giving thought to the possible alternatives.

Dumb, she told herself. *Very* dumb.

In her own defense, she'd had to respond to the Kazon's departure in a heartbeat. If she'd let even a minute go by, the cruiser would have left them in the dust.

At the same time, she could have been more skeptical. She could have concentrated more of their resources on achieving a positive identification of her officers. She could have made *sure* they were aboard before she traversed half the sector trying to recover them.

Now she had lost precious time. Worse, she was compelled to start from the beginning, checking and rechecking her facts, before she decided on a course of action. Nor would she cut any corners this time around. She would sacrifice speed for accuracy, because—unfortunately—there was no other way.

An intercom voice cut through her internal dialogue. "Captain?" called her first officer.

"What have you got for me?" she asked Chakotay.

"Lots," he told her. "Evidence of a firefight, for starters. The walls of this cave have been scarred with directed-energy beams. And the ground's full of footprints that aren't B'Elanna's or Kim's."

Janeway nodded to herself. "So they were abducted—just not by the Kazon we took off after."

"That's the way it looks," Chakotay agreed.

"What else?"

"We found a field projector. One set to baffle our sensors, apparently. But get this—the field reads like a mineral deposit to our tricorders."

Janeway bit back her anger.

"Acknowledged," she said. "Bring your team back up, Commander. I think we've learned enough."

"Aye, Captain," came the reply.

Janeway felt her hands clench into fists at her sides. With a conscious effort, she unclenched them. Bad enough she'd let herself be fooled once. Letting her emotions distract her would only invite other mistakes.

"Captain?" said Tuvok, who was standing at his customary place on the bridge.

She turned to him. "Something?" she suggested hopefully.

The Vulcan nodded. "I have discerned an ion-trail."

"Good work," she told him, joining him at his post.

She could feel her hopes rising. This could be the breakthrough they needed to find their comrades.

"Judging by its density and spatial parameters," Tuvok went on, "I believe the trail was produced by a Kazon vessel—though one considerably smaller than the cruiser we were pursuing. Also, the trail leads in the opposite direction from our previous heading."

"Which would make sense," said the captain, "if they were trying to throw us off."

"Indeed," the Vulcan agreed.

Janeway regarded him for a moment. "Make this information available to the conn, Mister Tuvok."

He nodded. "Aye, Captain."

"Transporter room," called Janeway. "Has the away team returned yet?"

"They're back," Burleson reported. "All present and accounted for."

Unlike the last time, the captain thought. She turned to her helmsman.

"Mister Paris, you'll be receiving data on a Kazon ion-trail. Plot a course and follow at best speed."

"Understood," Paris confirmed, already making the necessary adjustments on his control panel.

Janeway was glad to be taking action finally. It was only a beginning, she realized, and there were no guarantees they'd be successful—but at least they were *doing* something.

On the viewscreen, the planet waned as Paris brought the ship about and applied thrust from the impulse engines. It would be a little while before *Voyager* escaped the system's gravity well and the helmsman was able to engage the more powerful warp drive.

At this point, the captain was all but superfluous. She could have left the bridge and found something to do in her ready room. But she didn't want to give the impression she was hiding from what she'd done. She wanted—needed—to be out in the open with her crew.

Taking her seat, she leaned back and closed her eyes for a moment. Just for a moment. But as soon as she did, there it was. The embarrassment. The pain of loss . . . the litany came to mind again. Unasked for, it echoed in her brain.

Dumb, she told herself. *Very* dumb.

Teeg'l was disappointed as he hovered over his helmsman, awaiting the rendezvous with the *Bar-ach'ma.* At first, he had believed he'd made a dent in the *Voyager* officers' resolve. Apparently, he'd been wrong about that.

They had no intention of telling him about their transporter technology. He saw that now. When the female had said she would consider his offer of leniency, she'd obviously been lying.

Under normal circumstances, he would have killed her for such audacity—or come close enough to it to make her *wish* she was dead. Unfortunately, that wasn't an option in this case.

Maj B'naia would want to see the prisoners in good condition when Teeg'l delivered them to the *Barach'ma.* If they were damaged unnecessarily, B'naia would know Teeg'l had risked the success of their mission to further his own ambitions—and that would go hard on him.

So the third Maj had swallowed his pride and left the *Voyager* officers alone. As it was, he told himself, he would see more than his share of honors for his part in their capture. He tried to picture the possessions that would be bestowed on him—the glory that would be his.

And he would deserve it, would he not? After all, the *Voyager* scum held the key to preeminence in the quadrant. The plan to obtain them, of course, had been Maj B'naia's from the beginning. But Teeg'l was the one who had executed it to perfection.

"Third Maj," said the helmsman. Shan'ak was leaning a little closer to his monitors, as if to see better.

Roused from his inner dialogue, Teeg'l grunted. "What is it, Shan'ak? Have you found the *Barach'ma* yet?"

The helmsman turned to look at him. Something in his eyes made the third Maj's stomach muscles tighten.

"The *Barach'ma* is not here," Shan'ak told him. His voice was tight with anxiety, his brow creased with concern.

"Then it is not here," Teeg'l allowed. "We will wait for it to appear."

The helmsman shook his head. "You do not understand," he said. "It is not going to meet us. Not *ever.*"

Is'rag, the Kazon at tactical, turned around to look at them. Obviously concerned, he searched his own monitors for an answer.

The third Maj grew angry. Grabbing the front of Shan'ak's leather tunic, he twisted the helmsman around in his seat and brought Shan'ak's face close to his own.

"What do you mean, it is not going to meet us?" he demanded. "Aren't these the coordinates we agreed on? Don't we have the prisoners second Maj B'naia coveted so much?" He rapped Shan'ak sharply on the nose with his forehead. "Speak, damn you!"

The helmsman recoiled in pain, blood spilling from his nostrils. "Look!" he cried, clutching his damaged nose. "See for yourself!" And he pointed to one of his monitors.

Teeg'l glowered at it. "What?" he spat. "I don't see anything."

"Look closer!" Shan'ak told him.

The third Maj looked closer. And at last he saw what his helmsman was talking about.

"Debris," he muttered.

For that's what it was. Tiny fragments of metal, scattered throughout the void. And, according to their sensors, it was the same metal used in the manufacture of the Kazon-Ogla's vessels.

"No," he whispered. "It can't be."

"It *is,"* the helmsman insisted. "Those are the remains of the *Barach'ma.* Someone got here before us and destroyed it. *Voyager,* perhaps."

Teeg'l reeled as he considered where that left him and his little ship. He would have to seek out the Ogla's main fleet. But they were far away, and there were hostile races in between.

A vessel like the *Barach'ma* could have eluded them with its speed or intimidated them with its armaments. But a craft like Teeg'l's could do neither of those things. For all intents, it would be defenseless.

Swallowing hard, the third Maj grabbed Shan'ak again. But this time, he was too scared to be angry. "We've got to get out of here," he said. "Whoever did this might still be in the sector."

His words proved prophetic. They were barely out of his mouth when a proximity alarm went off on the helm console. Peering at the monitors, Teeg'l saw the cause of it.

It was a ship, even bigger than the *Barach'ma,* and more heavily armed. A Nograkh ship. And though it was nearly a million kilometers away, it was closing fast.

The third Maj cursed at the top of his lungs. It had been a Nograkh ambush all along. And he had fallen for it—just as the *Voyager* captain had fallen for the Kazon trap.

Still, Teeg'l told himself, he was Ogla. He would likely die this day, but he would die bravely.

"Is'rag," he said, still intent on Shan'ak's controls, "activate the cursed weapons banks."

There was no answer. Turning to the tactical station, Teeg'l saw that Is'rag had frozen, his eyes fixed on the monitor that showed him the approaching ship. Snarling, the third Maj lumbered across the bridge and shoved Is'rag aside. Then he took charge of the station himself.

As Is'rag looked on sullenly, Teeg'l activated the intercom system and called for N'taron and Skeg'g, whom he'd sent to check on the prisoners in the cargo hold.

"What is it, third Maj?" asked N'taron.

Teeg'l told him. "Forget the prisoners. I want you up on the bridge. *Now.*"

"As you wish," came the response.

The third Maj didn't really believe the presence of N'taron and Skeg'g would make any difference in the long run. But if Shan'ak was killed, at least one of them could fly the ship.

Teeg'l himself needed his hands free to work the weapons controls. Powering up the appropriate energy sources, he consulted his monitors.

And waited for the enemy to appear.

At first, when B'Elanna saw Teeg'l's henchmen enter the cargo hold, she imagined the worst—that the third Maj had lost his patience and was going to execute them, against all reason. After all, he was a Kazon. One never knew what passions ruled them from moment to moment. In that respect, they were a lot like some Klingons of her acquaintance.

Then she realized the pair was just checking to make sure their prisoners were secure. B'Elanna breathed a sigh of relief. So did Kim.

That's when Teeg'l contacted his men over the intercom, to tell them about the mysterious ship that was bearing down on them. As soon as he was done, they started out the door.

"Wait!" cried B'Elanna. "We can help!"

But the Kazon ignored them. Suddenly, the lieutenant's mouth went dry. In a matter of seconds, they had gone from the proverbial frying pan into an all-too-real fire.

Happy Day of Honor, she told herself.

Kim looked at her, the muscles working in his temples. "We've got to get out of here," he told her.

Her instincts agreed with him. In the event they were boarded, this cell would put them at a distinct disadvantage. Of course, if the Kazon vessel was blown out of space, it wouldn't matter if they were free or not—but B'Elanna tried not to think about that.

Teeg'l's jaw clenched as the enemy ship loomed. He rolled to starboard just as it fired, its weapons ports illuminating the void with a yellow-white directed-energy display.

Obviously, he thought, his adversary had underestimated the Kazon's maneuverability—and the skill of its pilot. The third Maj brought his vessel about and targeted the larger ship's weapons banks. Then he unleashed some directed energy of his own.

What's more, he hit his targets dead-on. But the enemy's shields held as they wheeled for a second pass. Teeg'l watched intently, trying to decide which way he'd move to avoid the next barrage.

Unfortunately for him, he never got a chance. Too late, he realized his adversary had been playing with him—testing him. And now that the test was over, the next stage had begun.

The larger ship spat stream after stream of yellow-white fire, each of them with unerring accuracy, battering Teeg'l's shields until there was nothing left of them. But the barrage didn't stop there. It went on, jolting the Kazon with hit after devastating hit.

The section of bulkhead beside Is'rag exploded, killing him instantly and showering the rest of the crew with flaming fragments. The deck shifted and bucked beneath their feet, throwing them this way and that.

Shan'ak struggled to regain mastery of their vessel, tapping his controls desperately in the lurid light of the emergency back-up system—until his helm console erupted in a geyser of sparks. Burned badly, he toppled from his seat to the deck below him.

"Skeg'g!" cried the third Maj, jerking his head in the direction of the empty helm station.

Immediately, Skeg'g lurched across the bridge to take Shan'ak's place. But no sooner had he taken a position behind the sparking helm console than the forward viewscreen went white with fury.

As Teeg'l flinched, blinded by the spectacle, he braced himself for the impact that would certainly follow. And follow it did.

B'Elanna could hear the pounding of enemy fire on the hull and feel the pitching of the deck beneath them. It only spurred her to greater efforts as she and

Kim tried to pry away a plate from the bulkhead behind them.

"Damn," said Kim. "If we had a tool of some kind—"

"But we don't," she rasped, clawing at the plate for all she was worth. Her fingers were already scraped and bloodied, but she ignored the pain and focused on her objective.

If she could get to the circuitry that was almost certainly in the bulkhead, she could disable the barrier and give them a fighting chance. And really, that's all she'd ever asked for—a *chance.*

Suddenly, the deck rose up on one end of the cargo bay and made an impossible incline of the floor beneath her feet. With nothing to hold on to, she felt herself sliding toward the barrier.

The impact would stun her, make her woozy. She couldn't afford that right now. And neither could Kim, who was sliding along beside her, pressing his cheek and hands against the deck in an attempt to slow himself down.

It wasn't working—not for either of them. B'Elanna closed her eyes, dreading the jolt that was sure to follow. Somehow, it never came. The next thing she felt was the smooth, hard surface of the bulkhead next to the exit.

She looked at Harry, who pointed to the emitter grid that had produced the barrier. There were thin plumes of white smoke coming from some of the emitters, but no energy field.

The barrier was gone.

"Some kind of short circuit," he noted.

"From all the pounding," she agreed.

Just then, the ship staggered again, leveling the deck. B'Elanna and Kim got to their feet and tapped the padd by the side of the door at virtually the same time. A moment later, the metal surface slid aside, giving them a vision of the freedom they'd earned.

It wasn't pretty. The corridor was filled with white smoke and a sharp, sickening stench. Every few feet ahead of them there was a crackle and a pulse of naked energy.

"Let's go," she told Kim.

"Right behind you," he assured her.

It wasn't difficult to find their way. The corridor was short and it led to only one set of doors. Again, she placed her hand on the padd beside them, ready to fight if necessary.

It wasn't necessary at all. Control consoles were burning everywhere she looked. And the five Kazon who'd been their captors were strewn across the bridge, at least one of them dead of a broken neck.

Clearly, the priority was to try to save the ship. If they succeeded in that, they could take care of the surviving Kazons later.

But before either B'Elanna or Kim could move toward the controls, the ship jerked and sent them hurtling across the open space. Though she tried to protect herself with her arms, the lieutenant took a nasty blow to the head on one of the consoles.

She felt herself losing consciousness, but fought it off. Come on, she told herself. You've got to get up, dammit. You've got to get this Kazon bucket moving again.

Rolling over onto her side, she opened her eyes—and found herself staring into the eyes of a dead Kazon, half of his face a bloody ruin. Biting back her revulsion, B'Elanna took hold of the lip of the console above her and dragged herself to her feet.

Then she heard something—the creak of metal on metal. The turning of a hatch, she thought, somewhere in the rear of the ship. Whoever had attacked them was doing their best to force their way aboard.

Beside the door they'd used to come out onto the bridge, there were two others. One of them must have led to a hatchway. That's where the attack would come from.

"B'Elanna . . ." moaned a familiar voice.

She saw Kim roll out from under another section of console. There was a bloody gash just above his brow to go with the purple spot on his chin. He was grimacing in pain.

"Are you all right?" she asked, negotiating the body of the staring Kazon to get to him.

He nodded as he grabbed her for support. "I think so."

"Can you use a weapon?" she asked, helping him get to his feet.

He nodded a second time. "Are they here yet?"

Clearly, he'd heard the creak of the hatch just as she had. "Just about," she told him.

Leaving him to stand on his own—by no means a certain proposition—she turned to the corpse behind her and hunkered down beside it. As she'd hoped, there was a handweapon stuck in the Kazon's belt. Slipping it free, she stood and handed it to Kim. He leaned back against a control panel and peered at it, as if he'd never seen anything like it.

"Can't tell which one is the stun setting," he muttered.

"That's the least of our problems," she hissed at him, as another bulkhead plate blew out with a crackle of rampant blue energy.

True, they ran the risk of punching a hole in one of the bulkheads. But there was no time to study their hosts' weapons technology. Not with a boarding party knocking on the door.

Crossing to the next-nearest Kazon, she rolled him onto his back and wrested his weapon from him. In the process, he murmured something and even moved his hand to try to stop her—but he was too badly stunned.

Suddenly, B'Elanna heard the tramping of heavy boots. She turned to face the door to the left of the one she'd come through. Then there was more tramping—this time, from beyond the door to her right.

"Damn," said Kim. "They're coming at us from both sides."

He was right, of course. Raising her weapon, the lieutenant trained it on one door, then the other, uncertain as to where to use it first.

Then the choice was taken out of her hands. Both doors slid aside at once, revealing huge, hulking figures in stiff, dark bodyarmor. She caught a glimpse of angry red skin, heavy brow ridges, and wide, cruel mouths. Seeing her, one of them barked a guttural command.

She didn't try to figure out what he'd said. She simply began firing at the invaders on her left. As if by silent agreement, Kim sent a beam at the aliens on her right.

The first of B'Elanna's targets went down. Then another. But before she could lay into a third, the invaders erected some kind of invisible shield. Her beam just bounced off it.

Glancing at the other door to the bridge, the one Kim was firing at, she saw the same thing happen. The ensign's barrage splashed off the deflective surface, wreaking havoc on a bulkhead instead.

That's when the invaders started retaliating. A series of yellow-white bursts stabbed at the lieutenant. The first one punched her hard in the left shoulder, numbing her arm as it spun her halfway around and sent her stumbling into a console. The second one blasted the weapon out of her hand.

A moment later, Kim was disarmed as well. He looked to her across the width of the Kazon bridge, blood streaming down the side of his face. After all, she was the ranking officer here. It was up to her what they would do next.

What they would do, she decided bitterly, was surrender. As much as it went against her grain, she couldn't ignore the fact they were outnumbered and outgunned. And even if they somehow regained control of the ship, it wasn't going anywhere as long as the enemy was standing guard over it.

Slowly, so there would be no mistake, she raised her hands above her head. Seeing her move, Kim did the same.

The invaders looked about to make sure there was no one else worth worrying about. Then they came out onto the bridge, weapons at the ready. One of them inspected the fallen Kazon, while another walked up to B'Elanna.

He didn't say anything. He just stood there, peering at her from beneath his protuberant brow. His eyes, which seemed small compared to the rest of him, were silver grey with a vertical slash of black pupil.

"My name is B'Elanna Torres," she began, though she had her doubts the brute in front of her would care. "I serve as a lieutenant on the starship *Voyager,* a vessel from another quadrant. The Kazon took me and my companion captive against our will. If you could arrange to see us back to our ship, we would be—"

Suddenly, before she could defend herself, the invader backhanded her across the face. The next thing B'Elanna knew she was lying flat on her back, her mouth tasting of blood. It took her a moment to gather her senses and look up at her assailant.

"You will not speak," he told her, his voice as harsh as two stones grinding together. His mouth twisted. "Get up."

Kim started toward her, either to defend her or to help her up. Either way, she wanted no part of it—not when it meant he'd get the same kind of treatment she'd gotten. Or *worse.*

"No," she snapped.

Kim stopped in his tracks. But he still looked as if he didn't like the idea of leaving her to her own devices.

B'Elanna leveled a glare at him for emphasis. Then, though her head was swimming with the force of the blow she'd endured, she managed to stand herself up.

The invader's eyes narrowed. He seemed to approve of her obedience. Still looking at her, he jerked his head toward the door he'd come through and barked an order to his comrades.

Three of the other invaders bent and picked up the Kazon who weren't obviously dead already. Then they stood them up against the bulkhead and struck them smartly across the face.

After a while, the Kazon woke. Two of them, anyway, Teeg'l included. The third must have had a concussion or something worse.

He wouldn't live long enough for anyone to find out. Seeing that he was incapable of moving on his own, the invader who'd lifted him held his hands to the Kazon's temples.

By the time B'Elanna realized what was about to happen, it was too late. There was a cracking sound, and the Kazon crumpled to the deck, limp and lifeless. If his fellow Kazon cared at all, they didn't show it. And as far as the heavy-browed invaders were concerned, the corpse might have been an insect they'd squashed underfoot.

Without ceremony, the other two Kazon were rousted from the bridge. Then the invader in front of B'Elanna jerked his head again—this time for her benefit. It was clear he meant for her to leave the bridge as well.

Which she did. A moment later, Kim followed.

True, she thought, the two of them were still prisoners. Their fates were still in the hands of others, and those others didn't seem particularly inclined toward benevolence.

But if one wanted to look on the bright side, one might say they were no worse off than before. And more important, unlike some of the Kazon who'd abducted them, they were still alive.

CHAPTER 5

JANEWAY WAS SITTING IN HER CENTER SEAT, ONCE AGAIN going over the events that had led to her officers' abduction.

She couldn't stop thinking about it, couldn't stop turning it over in her mind. Couldn't stop wondering if she might have prevented it.

She was so intent on her mental playback, she didn't notice when Tuvok came to stand beside her. Then he said, "Captain?"

She turned to look up at him. "Yes, Lieutenant?"

"I would like a word with you," the Vulcan told her. "In private."

Janeway nodded. "Very well. Let's go."

She led the way to her ready room. The door slid aside automatically, admitting them, then closed when they were both inside. In silence, they took seats on either side of her desk.

"All right," she said, "I'm listening. What did you want to talk about?"

Tuvok frowned. "You seem distracted. If I may be allowed to speculate, it has something to do with Lieutenant Torres and Ensign Kim."

The captain had to smile. "And the way we were duped by the Kazons."

The Vulcan tilted his head slightly. "Yes. It occurs to me you may be engaged in a process of self-recrimination. Of course, under the circumstances, that would be illogical."

Janeway sat back in her chair. "Oh? And why is that?"

"Because any experienced officer would have done the same thing—myself included. You made a rational choice based on the facts and probabilities at hand. Nor did you have a great deal of time to make that choice, considering the Kazon were attempting to escape."

"Or appearing to," the captain remarked.

"As it turns out," Tuvok conceded. "Though you had no way of knowing that at the time."

Janeway shrugged. "The bottom line is I took a guess. In this case, I guessed wrong."

"One cannot control the outcomes of one's decisions," Tuvok reminded her. "One can only make the best decisions possible."

"In other words," she said, "I shouldn't beat myself up over it."

The Vulcan cocked an eyebrow. "Not the precise words I would have chosen, but I agree with the sentiment."

Janeway was touched by his concern. She said so. "And don't worry," she added. "I'm not going to whip myself over what happened. But by the same token, I'm not going to forget about it. I want to make absolutely sure it never happens again."

Tuvok seemed satisfied. He stood. "That is all I wished to say."

The captain smiled, this time a little more freely. "I'm glad you did, Lieutenant. It seems I never fail to benefit from your logic." She paused. "You may resume your duties."

With a slight inclination of his head, he turned and left the room. Janeway watched him go.

He was right, of course. She couldn't allow herself to get distracted by what had happened. Otherwise, she might miss a chance to get her people back.

And one thing was for certain: she *was* going to get them back.

Up ahead of B'Elanna and the other prisoners, there was a hatchway that seemed to provide egress from the Kazon vessel. It seemed that was how the invaders had gotten aboard.

Apparently, she mused, they didn't have any more access to transporter technology than the Kazon did. More than likely, they hadn't even *heard* of such a technology. And unless Teeg'l and the others opened their mouths, they might *never* hear of it.

At the moment, neither of the surviving Kazon-

Ogla was in much of a position to talk. Only now starting to regain consciousness, they were being herded along on legs that could barely support them, both of them nursing a host of cuts and bruises. Still, all in all, they'd been lucky—none of their injuries looked permanently debilitating.

One by one, the Starfleet officers and the Kazon were thrust through the open hatchway. One by one, they were grabbed on the other side and shoved down another corridor.

At one point, B'Elanna stumbled into Teeg'l. The third Maj turned and snarled at her with his bruised and swollen mouth, but didn't go so far as to retaliate. Obviously, he had no more desire to incur their captors' wrath than she did.

Finally, they reached their destination—a heavy door set into an inner bulkhead. One of the heavy-brows opened it, hefted his weapon meaningfully, then gestured for the prisoners to go inside.

B'Elanna was the last in line. Apparently, she didn't move fast enough, because she felt a meaty hand on her back. The next thing she knew, she was sprawling on the far side of the entrance. Then the door swung closed and shut with a resounding clang.

The lieutenant got to her feet and looked around. Clearly, she and Kim and their Kazon friends weren't the only ones that had been taken captive. The circular hold was full of prisoners—perhaps twenty in all.

Surprisingly, more than a few were of the same brutish race as their captors. But the majority were aliens whose ilk the lieutenant had never seen before.

As if with one mind, they turned to get a gander at the new prisoners on the block.

B'Elanna had no reason to expect a hearty welcome from these people. Hell, they'd probably never even heard of *Voyager* or the Federation, so a certain wariness was probably the best she could have hoped for.

But the other prisoners were acting more than wary. The way they were glaring at the newcomers, one would have thought they were already guilty of some serious offense.

Kim looked at her. "What's going on? We haven't been here more than a couple of seconds and already we're not very popular."

"I wish I knew," she replied.

Their fellow captives were murmuring among themselves and looking angrier by the minute—angry enough to jump them, perhaps. If that was so, the lieutenant told herself, they wouldn't find her an easy adversary—though she already felt as if she'd been rolled through Neelix's pasta-maker.

"They don't hate *you,*" Teeg'l remarked unexpectedly. He sneered, despite the pain it must have cost him. "They hate *us.*"

Only then did B'Elanna realize what was going on. Apparently, the Kazon-Ogla had made a few enemies in this part of space—not a difficult thing to imagine, given the coarseness of their personalities and the itchiness of their trigger fingers.

She and Kim had only been thrown into the hold with Teeg'l and the other Kazon. They weren't allies by any stretch of the imagination; only moments ago, they'd been bitter enemies. But in the eyes of the other prisoners, the two of them were already guilty by association.

She eyed the third Maj of the Ogla. "What's going on, Teeg'l? What are we doing in this place?"

The Kazon grunted. "We're prisoners of the Nograkh, one of the races that dominates this part of space. They're miners for the most part, traders when it suits them."

"What do they want with *us?*" asked Kim.

"There's a Nograkh station not far from here," said Teeg'l. "It was built by the race that ruled this sector before them. The Nograkh use it to mine precious minerals from an asteroid belt."

"And?" B'Elanna prodded.

The Kazon's eyes narrowed as he regarded her. Clearly, he didn't like to be rushed. "The minerals in question are radioactive. As a result, the workers don't survive very long—which is why the Nograkh need to replace them so often."

The lieutenant understood now. "We're here to supplement the work force on their station?"

Teeg'l nodded. "That's my guess."

"Slave labor," Kim remarked.

Judging by his expression, the prospect didn't sit well with him. But then, it didn't sit very well with B'Elanna either.

"Lovely," she said. But then, it *was* the Day of Honor. She jerked her head in the direction of the heavy-browed prisoners on the other side of their cell. "And these Nograkh down here with us?"

The Kazon's mouth twisted with disdain. "Who

knows? Maybe they're criminals—the dregs of Nograkh society." He laughed. "But knowing the way the Nograkh treat each other, it's hard to imagine what sort of behavior would qualify as a crime."

B'Elanna looked at their fellow prisoners in a new light. Quite a character reference, she thought—to be called uncivilized by someone as low and vicious as a Kazon-Ogla.

"Thanks for the warning," she said.

Teeg'l shot a glance at her. "For all the good it'll do. To my knowledge, no one has ever escaped from the Nograkh."

"There's always a first time," Kim noted.

The Kazon eyed him. "Surely you're joking. Look around you at your fellow prisoners, human. Many of them are powerful warriors—the Nograkh even more so than the others. If they cannot escape, how will you?"

The ensign smiled mysteriously, despite the gash above his eye. It was more to taunt the third Maj than anything else.

Clearly, thought B'Elanna, if this conversation progressed much further, Teeg'l would go for Kim's throat. And she didn't want to draw any attention from their captors.

"Come on," she told her comrade. "Let's take a load off our feet."

Kim hesitated for just a second. Then he allowed her to guide him to a curved bulkhead, where they sat down side by side and placed their backs against the unyielding metal.

"All this for a bunch of vegetables," the ensign

sighed. "There's got to be an easier way to put food on the table."

B'Elanna couldn't help but smile. "When we get back, you can come up with one, all right?"

"It's a deal," he told her.

But privately, she knew, he was wondering the same thing she was. Asking the same questions.

Where in blazes was *Voyager?* And how were they ever going to get out of this without her?

Leaning back in her center seat, Janeway used her thumb and forefinger to massage the bridge of her nose, where stress and weariness had conspired to form a growing ache.

A small price to pay, she remarked inwardly, if their efforts produced the desired effect and their friends were returned to them. Not that she knew for certain they would be, but she had to nurture the hope.

After all, she was the ranking officer around here. If she didn't maintain an air of confidence, who would?

"Captain?" said Tuvok.

She turned to look back at him. "Yes, Lieutenant?"

The Vulcan was intent on his instruments. "Sensors have detected a small object point nine million miles off the starboard bow. It appears to be a ship—of unknown origin."

Janeway looked surprised. "On screen," she ordered.

A moment later, the viewscreen showed her what Tuvok was talking about. It was a small vessel, little bigger than one of *Voyager*'s shuttlecraft. But that was where the resemblance ended.

This ship was slender and dark and elegant, with two bubblelike features—one near its bow and a second at its midpoint. Three slender, almost flat nacelles protruded from it, like the fins of a Terran fish.

She turned to the Vulcan. "Hail them, Mister Tuvok."

The Vulcan complied. But a moment later, he shook his head. "No response. In fact, I believe they may be incapable of responding. There seems to have been a plasma leak in their engine compartment."

He paused, his brow wrinkling. "The radiation appears to have killed everyone on board—except one individual in the aft compartment. And she will likely die as well if left to her own devices."

Janeway frowned. "Mister Paris, fix on the craft's coordinates and bring us within ten thousand kilometers."

"Aye, Captain," came the accommodating response.

It would only be a matter of seconds before that was accomplished. Knowing that, Janeway turned back to Tuvok. "Have the survivor beamed directly to sick bay," she told the Vulcan. "Then establish a link with her ship's computer and download its data base."

Tuvok nodded and went about his task. At the same time, the captain looked up at the intercom grid and summoned the ship's holodoctor into existence.

"Computer, initiate emergency medical holographic program."

In a heartbeat, the Doctor's balding, sardonic image appeared on her personal monitor. "Please state the nature of the medical emergency," he said, in a voice just this side of annoyance.

Of course, the Doctor would be far from annoyed to learn he had work to do. He had been created to heal the sick and infirm. However, his programmers had created him with several—unfortunately—disingenuous qualities, his tone of voice being only one of them.

"We're beaming over a patient from a derelict ship," Janeway advised him. "She'll be suffering from radiation exposure and perhaps other problems as well, but we'll probably have some medical data for you to go on."

"I see," the Doctor said simply.

"Is Kes down there?" the captain asked.

"She is," the Doctor confirmed. "I've had her working on a research project the last several hours."

Janeway nodded. "Then you'll have help if you need it."

The Doctor scowled. "I doubt I will require assistance if we're only talking about a single patient, no matter how alien she may be. But it'll be good for Kes to lend a hand. A learning experience, if you will."

"Whatever you say," the captain replied. "Janeway out."

She glanced at Tuvok. He seemed troubled. Rising from her seat, she joined him at his console.

"Problem?" she asked.

He nodded. "The radiation spilling from the vessel's power source is making it difficult to effect transport. However, I believe I can overcome the difficulty by boosting the annular confinement beam."

Leaving the Vulcan to his work, the captain turned again to the viewscreen, where the alien craft gave no indication of the turmoil and death inside it. It simply hung in the void, silent as the tomb it had become.

But not for its last surviving passenger, Janeway thought, lifting her chin as if facing down an adversary. With any luck, the data they would take from the vessel's computer files would give the Doctor a head start in treating her—and sometimes that made all the difference.

Of course, she wished they hadn't had to deviate from their course. Every moment they spent here was another setback in their pursuit of Torres and Kim, another nail in their proverbial coffins. But when Janeway had signed on as captain of *Voyager,* she had sworn to lend assistance to those in trouble—even when it meant jeopardizing her own crew in the process.

Suddenly, the vessel on the viewscreen exploded in a flare of blazing white light. The energy output was immediately dampened by the sensor mechanisms that fed the screen, but it made the sight no less horrifying.

The captain whirled to face Tuvok, fearing the worst. "The survivor . . . ?" she asked.

The Vulcan's countenance was as unreadable as ever. As the seconds passed, he checked his instruments carefully, so there would be no mistake. Then he looked up again.

"She is in sick bay," Tuvok reported at last. "Much

of the vessel's computer data was salvaged as well—though, regrettably, not all of it."

Janeway breathed a sigh of relief. "Don't give it a second thought," she said. "You did your best." And after all, the survivor had been the priority. "Resume course," she instructed.

"Aye, Captain," said Paris. He looked relieved as well as he made the necessary adjustments on his control console.

"I'll be in sick bay if you need me," Janeway announced, naturally curious about the being they'd taken on.

Without another word, she made her way to the turbolift.

CHAPTER 6

VOYAGER'S DOCTOR WAS AS WELL-EQUIPPED TO HANDLE an emergency as any physician in the history of the Federation. After all, his program encompassed not only all the Federation's medical research and clinical experience, but a great deal of its distilled genius.

He could apply the diagnostic approaches of hundreds of doctors on dozens of worlds, and he could do it all in the blink of an eye. It was a good thing he could. With all *Voyager* and her crew had encountered here in the Delta Quadrant, it was unlikely any single physician could have pulled them through as effectively as he had.

So when he saw the alien female materialize on a biobed, writhing in agony, her scaly, purplish flesh ravaged with third-degree burns, the Doctor didn't even raise an eyebrow. He made a quick and necessarily superficial scan of the medical data downloaded from her vessel's computer and went to work.

Of course, Kes was by his side the whole time. For her sake, he described his strategy step by step.

"According to our instruments, the patient's biochemistry is similar to that of several Alpha Quadrant races. That means we can rely on familiar medications."

First, he checked her status on the bed's readout. She appeared to be in stable condition, at least for the time being. It would make treating her a lot easier.

However, that wasn't all he saw in the readout. There were indications of something else in her system as well—something that had nothing at all to do with radiation exposure.

"What is it?" Kes asked, obviously picking up on his surprise.

The Doctor shook his head. "We can talk about it later," he told her.

Concentrating on the task at hand, he introduced a drug to reinforce her vital signs and another to deaden the pain. In a matter of seconds, the woman seemed to relax.

"So far, so good," he remarked offhandedly. But he was still bothered by what he'd seen in the readout.

Next, the Doctor gave the woman a dose of hyronalyn to mitigate the effects of the radiation on her system. That, too, produced a favorable reaction. Encouraged, he went on to give her a healing agent for her burns and yet another agent to prevent infection.

Finally, he erected an electromagnetic field around her to keep her safe from germs in her new environment. Of course, there was no indication that she would have a particular vulnerability to them, but it was always better to err on the side of caution.

All in all, a smooth operation. Especially when one considered what he had found in the woman's bloodstream.

"Doctor?" said Kes.

He turned to her. "I know," he replied. "You're wondering what it was I saw in her readout."

"And what *did* you see?"

The Doctor sighed and considered his patient anew. She was sleeping soundly now, all her vital signs deceptively normal.

"This woman has a disease I've never seen before," he announced. "A disease that is communicable only by intimate contact, fortunately. But if left untreated, it will kill her in less than a week."

Kes swallowed. "But surely there's something you can do for her."

Just then, the door to sick bay slid aside and the captain entered. "How is she doing?"

The Doctor frowned and brought Janeway up to speed. "But before I can give you a prognosis," he explained, "I need to take a look at the data we salvaged from her ship. There may be something there that will help."

The captain eyed him. "Doctor, if there was a course of treatment contained in the data bank, wouldn't her own physicians have applied it already?"

He shrugged. "Certainly, that's a possibility. But I

prefer not to jump to conclusions. Now, if you'll excuse me, I've got work to do."

Janeway smiled understandingly. "Of course. Just keep me posted on her condition, will you?"

"As you wish," he assured her.

Then, without waiting for the captain to leave, he deposited himself in his office and accessed the requisite data from the ship's computer. As he was himself little more than a computer program, it wouldn't take long to assimilate everything they'd downloaded.

Then he would put the Federation's best medical minds to work. With luck, they would do the trick.

One hour, maybe even a little less. That's all it took for bedlam to break out in the hold where Harry and his companion were being held.

The ensign had been resting his head against the bulkhead and looking up at the ceiling, trying to guess from the shape and size of the crisscrossing energy conduits what kind of power supply the Nograkh ship ran on. He'd have said it was microwave-based, along the lines of a Cardassian system, except there was no evidence of the rhodinium sheeting that usually went with the microwave approach.

Suddenly, there was a flurry of activity on the other side of the cargo hold. And a string of angry, guttural shouts. And before Kim knew it, a fight had started.

It was between two of the most powerful-looking Nograkh. None of the other Nograkh tried to break it up, either. In fact, they grew more excited by the moment, cheering the combatants on.

The ensign's first reaction was to look for B'Elanna,

to make sure she was safe. As it turned out, she was standing by a stretch of bulkhead nowhere near the melee. But as it progressed, she joined Kim anyway.

He watched, fascinated despite himself, as hammerlike fists pounded at flesh and bone, each blow eliciting a resounding thud. But no matter how many times they were hit, neither of the Nograkh seemed daunted in the least. If anything, the punishment spurred them on to inflict some of their own.

B'Elanna sat down beside him. "Nice roommates," she said.

The ensign winced as one of the Nograkh drove his fist into the other's face, snapping his adversary's head back. "You think they might get tired of pummeling each other and come after us next?"

"A distinct possibility," said a voice to one side of them.

Following it to its source, they saw Teeg'l standing there, his fellow Kazon at his side. The third Maj smiled savagely at them.

"Didn't I tell you they were animals?" he asked. "A barbed remark, a misplaced elbow, and before you know it they're bludgeoning each other."

Still smiling, he turned to observe the Nograkh. There was no letup in the intensity of their combat, no abatement in the ferocity with which they went at one another.

"And no one makes a move to stop it," Teeg'l pointed out. "Not even the guards. And why should they? They're Nograkh, too."

Kim was so wrapped up in the violence of the

spectacle, he had forgotten about the guards. But now that the Kazon mentioned it, he cast a glance in their direction.

Sure enough, the watchmen had taken note of what was going on. They would have to have been blind not to. And deaf as well. But the brawl didn't seem to faze them in the least. Hell, thought the ensign, they looked like they were enjoying it.

"Their only regret," Teeg'l remarked, "is that they can't jump in themselves. That they can't get in there and pound each other to pulp, the way their brethren are doing it."

Kim took a closer look at the guards and decided the third Maj was right. What had he called them?

"Animals," the ensign said out loud, answering his own question.

B'Elanna looked at him. "What did you say?"

The ensign shook his head. "Nothing."

The jabbing and the smashing and the clubbing went on for another minute or so. Then one of the combatants fell to his knees, unable to continue.

It was over, Kim thought.

He thought wrong. Hauling back, the other Nograkh—a strapping specimen with a scar along his jaw—drove his fist into the center of his opponent's face. There was a loud crack, audible to everyone in the hold.

Then, as a horrified Kim bore witness, the loser's head lolled back and his body fell sideways to the deck. A trickle of blood ran from the corner of the victim's mouth.

He was dead. Just like that.

What's more, it was no accident. It was murder, plain and simple.

But none of the Nograkh seemed to care. Oh, the guards intervened finally, but they didn't pay any special attention to the murderer. They just took hold of the dead man by his ankles and pulled him out of the hold.

"My god," Kim heard himself saying.

Beside him, B'Elanna grunted. "Quite a show." Her voice was hollow with dismay.

That's when the lights dimmed. It didn't take a genius to figure out their captors wanted them to sleep. And more than likely, there would be punishment for those who opposed that wish.

What's more, the Nograkh seemed to accept the situation. If they grumbled, they did so quietly. A couple of moments later, the other prisoners settled down as well.

It was almost peaceful in the cargo hold. But that didn't mean it would stay that way.

"Tell you what," B'Elanna suggested. "We'll sleep in shifts. I don't want to wake up in the middle of their next disagreement."

"Amen," said Kim.

It was bad enough he'd become a slave. He didn't want to become a *dead* slave into the bargain.

It was Kes's job to stand watch over the scaly-skinned female on the biobed and make sure her vital signs followed the expected course. As always, she took her job very seriously.

At the moment, their patient was sleeping soundly, still feeling the effects of the sedation the Doctor had prescribed for her. More important, she was healing. Nearly half her burns were already gone and the rest would likely disappear over the next couple of hours.

From all outward signs, she was well on her way to recovery. But then, those signs didn't take into account the disease that was festering in her, threatening her life.

Kes turned to look at the Doctor. He was hunkered over his computer terminal on the other side of his transparent office wall, brow furrowed, mulling over the data downloaded from the patient's vessel in significantly greater depth than before.

At first glance, one might have thought he was scanning the monitor screen, like a flesh-and-blood organism. But a closer look would have shown there was nothing on the screen. He was just standing there, his eyes intent on a point no one else could see.

That was because the data had been dumped directly into his program. It was faster that way, or so the Doctor said. Of course, he still had to sift through the information. He still had to test hypotheses and establish connections, and that could take a considerable amount of time.

In the meantime, their patient inched closer to death. The Doctor didn't seem to notice; he was too engrossed in his work. But his assistant noticed. She noticed all too well.

Kes regarded the woman and sighed. Not much longer now, she assured herself. Just a matter of time.

Funny, she thought. Growing up, she had always thought of herself as the patient sort. She had never pestered her elders as often as the other children, always willing to wait a while if it meant getting what she wanted in the end.

Then circumstances had landed her a berth on *Voyager,* where she was the only one of her kind. It didn't take long before she realized how short her life span was—at least, in comparison with the other races on board.

Tuvok could expect to live for a couple of centuries—perhaps more. The captain might live more than half that length of years. But Kes, an Ocampa, would be fortunate to see her ninth birthday.

Nine years had seemed like a lot, at one time. Now, it didn't seem like much at all. She felt compelled to try new things, to take on responsibilities no Ocampa her age would have dreamed of. To pack as much into her brief existence as she could.

With that came a certain eagerness. A certain impatience. As much as she had attempted to tone it down, knowing how irritating it could be, she wasn't always successful.

Now was a good case in point.

The Doctor didn't seem to be any closer to a cure than when he'd begun his think-session a couple of hours earlier. Yet he didn't seem ruffled or concerned. Obviously, he believed there was plenty of time in which to accomplish his task.

Kes, on the other hand, couldn't help but worry. She couldn't help but feel time was running out.

And the worst part, the part that made it almost intolerable for her, was that the Doctor's labor was a one-man operation. Talented as she was as a physician, she didn't have the empirical knowledge to expedite the process. She couldn't be of any assistance whatsoever.

All she could do was stand here. And watch the patient's biosigns. And fret. And wait.

Suddenly, out of the corner of her eye, she saw movement in the Doctor's office. Glancing in his direction, she saw him turn to her. And *smile.*

A cure, she thought excitedly. He's found a cure.

Janeway tossed and turned in her bed, caught in a limbo between waking and sleeping, troubled by an awareness of something dark and terrible prowling the starless night.

At first, she thought the dark thing was after *her.* Then she realized it wasn't interested in her at all. It was after Torres and Kim. But it was she who'd let it out. She who'd released it to prey on her officers—her friends. And she was the only one who could send it back the way it came.

Or *could* she? Wasn't it already too late for her to do anything? Hadn't she had her opportunity and failed? She wanted to believe otherwise, but—

Suddenly, Janeway sat up in bed. Her skin was clammy and her mouth was dry and her heart was slamming against her ribs.

A nightmare, she concluded. Just a damned nightmare. She took a breath, let it out. Another. And another. Gradually, her heart rate slowed to something approaching normal.

And she had the distinct feeling that someone was waiting for her to do something. Not Torres and Kim, as in her dream, but *someone.* She looked around her quarters, at the vague, shadowy contours of her furnishings. There was no one there, of course. Still . . .

She ventured a response: "Janeway here."

"Captain," said a familiar voice over the intercom. "Sorry to wake you, but sensors show the approach of a Kazon cruiser. Its weapons are powered up and it seems to be on an intercept course."

Doing her best to shrug off her cobwebs, Janeway tossed aside the covers and padded across the room on bare feet. "Acknowledged, Chakotay. I'll join you on the bridge in a minute or so. In the meantime, go to red alert. Then hail the Kazon and see what happens."

"Aye, Captain," came the commander's reply.

Opening her closet, Janeway took out a hanging uniform. Then, tossing it on her bed, she removed her nightgown and slipped into it. Finally, with practiced dexterity, she pulled her hair back and clipped it up.

By then, she could hear the whooping voice of the klaxons signaling the red alert. It reminded her that there were worse ways to wake up than getting a call in the middle of the night.

In a matter of seconds, the captain was emerging into the corridor, her destination the nearest turbolift. The klaxons were louder out here and the lighting was a bloody shade of red. Crewmen were hurrying up and down the hallway, heading for their posts—just as she was.

Janeway still felt a little groggy, but that couldn't be helped. She had a job to do—and no dark and terrible pursuer was going to prevent her from doing it.

CHAPTER 7

JANEWAY EMERGED ONTO *VOYAGER*'S BRIDGE, SECURE IN the knowledge that the ship's shields had been raised and her weapons powered up. What's more, she was surrounded by Chakotay, Tuvok, and Paris, the officers she trusted most. If the commander of the approaching Kazon cruiser was going to try something, he would find her prepared for anything.

Turning to Tuvok, she asked, "Any response to our hails?"

The Vulcan shook his head. "None, Captain. It would seem—" He stopped in mid-sentence, then inspected his monitors and arched an eyebrow.

"What is it?" Chakotay inquired.

"The Kazon have chosen to respond," Tuvok noted simply—though it was difficult to conceal his surprise.

"Well," said the captain, "open a channel, Lieutenant. We wouldn't want to keep our Kazon friends waiting."

At his helm station, Paris chuckled at the ironic nature of the remark. Ignoring the human's response, Tuvok worked his controls. A moment later, the image of a tall, bony-faced Kazon filled the viewscreen.

The captain lifted her chin. "This is Captain Kathryn Janeway of the Federation starship *Voyager.*"

"We know who you are," the Kazon blurted. "I am called Lorca, second Maj of the Kazon-Ogla."

"Why are you here?" she asked.

The Kazon laughed. "To destroy you as you destroyed our sister ship, the *Barach'ma.* Did you think we would let our comrades go unavenged? Or their slayers unpunished?"

Janeway frowned. Signaling to Tuvok, she had him cut out the audio portion of her transmission.

"Any idea what he's talking about?" she asked Chakotay.

The first officer frowned back at her. "Judging from the Kazon's course, he's already been to the place we're headed for. I guess he didn't like what he found there."

"A ship," she said. "Probably another cruiser, if Lorca's calling it his sister ship. And according to him, it was destroyed."

"Could it be," asked Tuvok, "that this *Barach'ma* was waiting for the smaller vessel we've been pursuing? Could the Kazon have been planning a rendezvous between the two?"

"Makes sense," Chakotay replied. "But then . . ."

He didn't have to finish his question. They all knew what the first officer was wondering. If the *Barach'ma* was supposed to take custody of Torres and Kim, and it had been destroyed . . . did that mean Torres and Kim had been destroyed as well?

The captain thought for a moment, then signaled for the audio portion to be restored. Her eyes narrowed as she faced second Maj Lorca.

"We haven't destroyed anything or anyone," she said sternly. "Though we might have been justified in doing so, considering the way you and your people stole my officers."

Janeway let the implied threat hang in the air, hoping she wouldn't have to back it up. It seemed to work. Lorca didn't flinch—but he didn't say anything hostile either.

"But," the captain added, softening her voice, "I would much rather join forces with you, in an effort to determine who *did* destroy your vessel—and if they took my officers off first. After all, there might have been Kazon who survived and were taken prisoner as well."

The second Maj considered Janeway for what seemed like a long time. Then he nodded. "For the time being, I choose to believe you, Captain. But we of the Ogla will continue to monitor your movements. If you are lying, we will be back in force."

"And what about the possibility of survivors?" Janeway asked.

Lorca made a gesture of dismissal. "I have no

interest in risking my ship for a handful of failures," he told her.

"Failures?" she echoed.

"If they were *true* Kazon," he explained, "they died in battle defending their vessel. And if they were *not* true Kazon, they are no longer worth saving."

The captain sighed. Lorca's logic was impeccable—at least from the Kazon point of view. She wasn't going to get anywhere arguing with it.

"Then we will continue our investigation alone," she announced stubbornly. "Janeway out."

Taking his cue, Tuvok severed the communication. Once more, the viewscreen displayed an image of the Kazon ship.

For a second or two, it hung in space, still a threat. Then it described a tight loop and retreated. When it had put sufficient space between itself and *Voyager,* the vessel went to warp speed and vanished.

The captain breathed a sigh of relief. It appeared they were free to pursue the search for their missing crewmen—though when it came to the Kazon, one never knew.

Even when it was Kim's turn to keep an eye out for them, B'Elanna didn't sleep very well. It wasn't that she didn't trust her colleague. It was just the Klingon in her.

Thanks to her mother's bloodlines, her instincts and senses were still tuned to the world of predator and prey. The lieutenant was cued in to sounds and smells at a level Kim could only dream about.

Every so often, she bolted upright with her heart pounding and her lips pulled back over her teeth—primitive, ready for anything. But each time, her readiness was wasted. There was no threat—or at least none she could discern in the darkness of the cargo hold.

B'Elanna was actually relieved when it was time for her watch. That way, she could do away with the pretense, with the wearisome drifting in and out. In a funny way, she could *relax.*

Unlike her, Kim slept like a baby. But then, he was human—*completely* human—far enough removed from his barbaric forebears to pretend he was somewhere safe.

Of course, the lieutenant could only guess where that might be. Home, maybe, back on Earth? Or perhaps his quarters on *Voyager?* But in any case, a place where people weren't thinking about killing him.

By contrast, their neighbors in the cargo hold were almost as wakeful as the lieutenant had been. Some of them, it seemed to her, only pretended to sleep to keep their guards happy. Others drifted in and out as she had.

One thing B'Elanna noticed was that the Nograkh never cast wary glances at each other—only at those of other races. Despite their violent natures, despite the fact that a murder had been committed among them, the brutes seemed to trust one another when it came to their slumber time. To cease hostilities.

Just as well, B'Elanna thought. She'd seen enough hostilities to last her for a while.

She had barely completed her thought when a squad of Nograkh guards opened the door to their prison and barged in with their blasters at the ready. B'Elanna's instincts told her their ship had arrived at its destination. The mining station, if Teeg'l had guessed right about that.

Kim raised his head, trying to blink away the cobwebs. "We're there," he said, echoing her thoughts.

"Looks that way," she agreed.

With a series of harsh, guttural commands, the guards rousted everyone out of the hold and ushered them into the corridor beyond. There were rustlings of discontent, but not many. Also, furtive glances among the prisoners—but not many of those either.

Whoever didn't move quickly enough was poked mercilessly with the narrow barrel of a guard's weapon. Perhaps needless to say, none of them needed to be poked twice.

B'Elanna tried to stay close to Kim and vice versa. For a while, it worked. Then the corridor twisted, and their fellow captives were shuffled along by the guards, and before she knew it the lieutenant was lucky to catch a glimpse of her companion.

In a matter of minutes, they came to a pentagon-shaped air lock, bigger than the others they'd seen. It was open already, with more armed Nograkh on the other side. The prisoners were rushed through unceremoniously. Then the air lock door was closed behind them with a clash of metal on metal.

The sound had a finality to it, B'Elanna mused, a sense that, for her and all her fellow prisoners, that door would never open again. Teeg'l had certainly led her to believe that.

But no matter how grim things looked, she wasn't about to throw in the towel. Nor was Kim, judging from his earlier comments. Maybe that's why they'd become friends so easily. They were both optimistic by nature—inclined to hold out some hope, no matter how slim it might be.

The corridor on this side of the air lock was a lot like the corridor on the other side—except for a humming sound that seemed to come from everywhere at once. B'Elanna guessed it had something to do with the ore refinement process—again, based on what the Kazon had told her.

But she wasn't going to find out right away, it seemed. After the corridor jogged right and then left, they came to a large chamber with a narrow opening for an entranceway. Then, though it wasn't even remotely necessary, the guards began shoving them inside.

That's when Teeg'l appeared to lose his mind. After being stun-blasted and robbed of his ship, after being bumped and tossed about the Nograkh vessel, B'Elanna would have thought the Kazon had learned to endure rough treatment. She would have imagined his skin had thickened a bit.

Obviously, she hadn't known Teeg'l as well as she'd thought. As the third Maj was sent sprawling into the prisoners ahead of him, something seemed to snap inside him. His expression went from one of tolerance to blind, unreasoning fury.

Giving in to his instincts, he lashed out—and tore a blaster rifle out of the hands of the nearest guard. Then he turned it on the Nograkh who had humiliated him and pressed the trigger.

The blue-white blast caught the guard square in the chest, sending him pinwheeling through the air. Slamming into a bulkhead, he slumped to the deck in a tangle of heavy limbs. Even before she saw the angle of the Nograkh's broken neck, B'Elanna knew how dead he was.

For the space of a heartbeat, there was silence. Then, like air rushing in to fill a vacuum, time seemed to accelerate—first to its normal rate and finally well beyond it.

There were shouts of anger and cries of defiance and bodies flying every which way. More blue energy blasts, more fallen guards. And fallen prisoners as well, because neither Teeg'l nor his brutish captors seemed to give a damn about bystanders.

B'Elanna flung herself to the floor to avoid the beams, trying at the same time to catch a glimpse of Kim. Instead, she caught a glimpse of the other Kazon—the one whose name she had never learned.

As she watched, he wrestled a guard for his rifle. It seemed he was winning, too. Gaining the upper hand.

Then the weapon went off and the Kazon was flung high in the air. When he came down and hit the deck, it was with the loose-jointed posture of a rag doll. And he didn't move again.

Other prisoners fell as well—those who had tried to put up a fight of their own, or who had been unlucky enough to find themselves too near a panicky guard. In a matter of moments, the nature of the melee changed. The tide of battle ebbed and died.

Instead of several struggles going on all at once, there was just one. Instead of a scattering of insurgents, there was a single figure, left naked and alone. And that figure was Teeg'l.

As he roared at his captors, spraying them with burst after burst of blue-white energy, he had to know he was doomed—had to know they were drawing a bead on him. But it didn't seem to daunt him. He was too caught up in his outrage and his anger to stop himself.

So the Nograkh did it for him.

What seemed like a dozen azure beams hit him all at once. He spun in one direction, then the other, his weapon flying out of his hands. Then another stream of energy hit him sharply in the temple—and toppled him.

After that, he lay still. As still as death, B'Elanna thought.

And she'd thought *she* was having a bad Day of Honor.

One of the guards collected Teeg'l's borrowed rifle and tossed the third Maj of the Kazon-Ogla over his shoulder. Then, without even looking at the other prisoners, the Nograkh jerked his head.

"Against the wall," he growled.

The survivors did as they were told, gathering by the bulkhead the guard had indicated. While they watched, the other guards roused their colleagues—

except for the one Teeg'l had killed when it all started. That one they just dragged out the door.

The guard carrying Teeg'l departed as well. That left the rest of the prisoners—both those who were standing and those who were unconscious. And no one bothered to wake the latter variety.

No longer required to stand by the bulkhead, B'Elanna picked an empty corner of the chamber and beckoned for Kim to follow her. Warily, he complied. Corners, after all, were easier to defend. She had learned that as a member of the Maquis.

"Some welcome wagon," she said as she and her companion hunkered down together.

"A barbecue would have worked just as well," he commented drily.

There was silence for a moment. "Hard to believe Teeg'l cracked so easily," the lieutenant added.

Kim glanced at her. "Maybe not."

"What do you mean?" she asked.

"He knew what we had to look forward to. Maybe he figured it was better to get it over with."

B'Elanna wished she had an answer for that. Unfortunately, that wasn't the case.

Kes looked at the Doctor. "Now?" she asked.

"Now," he confirmed.

They were standing on either side of the biobed, where their patient still lay sleeping. There was no evidence of her injuries, no sign of the burns that had covered a good part of her body.

Pressing the control padds on the bed, the Ocampa

eliminated the electromagnetic field that had protected the woman since her arrival in sick bay. Then she cut off the flow of sedatives into the patient's blood and introduced a mild stimulant, no more powerful than smelling salts, to bring her out of her medicated sleep.

A moment later, the woman opened her eyes. Kes saw they were a startling shade of blue. For several seconds, they drifted in and out of focus. Then they seemed to lock onto the Doctor's face.

"Who . . . who are you?" she asked.

"I have no name," the Doctor explained, "unusual as that may seem. However, I do have a description. I am the emergency medical program for the starship *Voyager*. This physical manifestation you see is only a hologram, which allows me to interact with sentient organisms—much as I am doing now."

Their patient's brow creased down the middle. "I . . . see," she said tentatively. She turned to Kes. "And are you a hologram as well?"

The Ocampa smiled and shook her head. "No, I'm a flesh-and-blood organism, just as you are."

Kes resisted using the word "real" to distinguish between herself and the Doctor, since she considered him every bit as real as she was. After all, he was capable of independent thought, even feelings. The only significant difference was his lack of biological functions.

"How are you feeling?" she asked the woman.

Their patient seemed to take stock of herself for a moment. "Well," she concluded. "Very well." The crease in her brow deepened. "But on the ship, I was exposed—"

"To a significant amount of radiation from your damaged engine core," the Doctor noted. "Fortunately, we were able to counteract the effects of the exposure. As you can see, there will be no permanent scarring."

The woman nodded. "I'm grateful." Tentatively, she sat up. Examining her arms and legs, she began to smile. "You've performed a miracle."

The Doctor shrugged. "All in a day's work," he told her. Then, without another word, he retreated to his office.

Their patient watched him go for a second, then turned to Kes. "My name is Pacria," she said. "Pacria Ertinia."

"Kes," the Ocampa replied. "Good to meet you. Though, of course, I wish it were under better circumstances." She frowned. "We weren't able to save the others on your ship."

Pacria's expression became one of regret. "We ran into a subspace anomaly. Never knew what hit us."

Abruptly, the Doctor emerged from his office with a hypospray in his hands and held it against the woman's arm. "This won't hurt," he said reassuringly. "And more importantly, it'll save your life."

Pacria pulled her arm away. "What do you mean?" she asked.

"I'm introducing a vaccine to cure you of your disease." The Doctor explained where he had gotten it. "If you'll hold still, it'll take just a moment."

"I cannot allow that," Pacria told him.

The Doctor looked at her. "I beg your pardon?"

The muscles in the woman's temples worked furiously. "I said I cannot allow that," she told him.

Kes shook her head. "I don't understand. The Doctor has developed a vaccine that can save you from a fatal ailment—and you're refusing it?"

"That's right," Pacria insisted.

"But why?" asked the Ocampa, as gently as she could. "Why would you want to die when you can live?"

The patient turned away from her. "Please," she said, the protuberances on her jaw swelling and turning red. "I have my reasons."

Kes couldn't accept that. "If you shared your reasons with us, there might be something we could do to change your mind."

Pacria glared at her with unexpected anger. "I don't want my mind changed. I just want to be left alone."

The Ocampa swallowed. She wasn't used to being the object of such fury. "All right," she conceded. "Whatever you say."

"Indeed," said the Doctor. He scowled—first at Kes, then at Pacria. "Though I, too, would like to hear your reasons," he told Pacria, "your decision is yours and yours alone. For me to intrude on it would be a violation of my oath as a physician."

"Thank you," their patient replied. "Now if I can make arrangements for my passage home . . ."

"I'll speak to our captain about it," the Doctor promised. "However, a couple of our crewmen have been abducted and we are currently in the process of attempting to recover them. I expect it'll be a while before we can turn our attention to getting you home."

Pacria nodded, even though she had to know she probably wouldn't last that long. Kes bit her lip. What had the Doctor given the woman? A week?

"That's reasonable," the patient said.

But it wasn't reasonable, the Ocampa told herself. None of this was. And though she respected the Doctor's principles, she couldn't see the wisdom in them this time.

After all, life was so precious. So fleeting. It was a crime to throw it away when it could be preserved.

The Doctor held his hand out to Pacria. "Since it appears your treatment here is over, there's no reason for you to remain in sick bay. I'll see to it you're given appropriate quarters."

"Thank you," the woman told him. "Again."

Taking his hand, she swung her legs around and eased herself off the biobed. Then she followed him into his office.

Kes sighed. Was this why she'd maintained her lonely vigil over Pacria? Was this why the Doctor had worked so hard to find a cure? So she could spurn the gifts they'd given her?

And the worst part was she wouldn't even say *why*.

CHAPTER 8

KES STOOD BY THE DOOR TO THE HOLODOCTOR'S OFFICE and watched him circle sick bay, hands clasped behind his back. No doubt, he felt as if they were tied there.

"Clearly," he said, "Pacria has her reasons for refusing the treatment. And of course, it's her right to refuse it." He frowned. "It's also her right not to tell us those reasons, if she doesn't want to."

"I suppose so," the Ocampa replied. "But I can't help wishing it were otherwise."

"Neither can I," the Doctor admitted. He heaved a sigh. "This is the first time a patient has ever thanked me for not saving her life. And you know what? I don't like it—not one little bit."

Kes understood. He had been programmed to save

lives, not watch them dwindle away without doing a thing about it.

"We've got to find out why Pacria's made this decision," she decided.

The Doctor's eyes narrowed. "Not if she doesn't want us to. As physicians, we must respect her right to privacy."

Kes thought for a moment. "Look," she said at last, "would it violate her right if I just asked her again? Nicely? Maybe now that she's had a while to get used to her surroundings . . ."

He regarded her. "You'll have to be *very* nice. I won't have anyone harassing my patient. Not even you."

"I promise," she told him. "I'll be discreet."

Then she left sick bay and headed for Pacria's quarters, already playing out the scene in her mind.

Tom Paris stared at the main viewscreen from his helm position. It was just as bad as he'd feared. Just as bad, in fact, as second Maj Lorca had led them to believe.

There was debris spread across space as far as the eye could see. Pieces of metal, mostly, according to the sensor report on his monitor. And whatever else was out there, he didn't want to know about it.

In any case, they knew two things for certain. First, that there had been a Kazon vessel here, if the alloys they'd detected were any indication. And second, that it had been destroyed.

What they didn't know was who had done it and

why. Apparently Lorca hadn't known that either, or he wouldn't have accused *Voyager* of it. Most importantly, they didn't know if Harry and B'Elanna had been on the *Barach'ma* when its adversary blew it up.

Maybe they had gotten here after the encounter, and seen what *Voyager* was seeing. Maybe, Paris told himself, they had altered their course and found another ship to rendezvous with. Maybe this, maybe that.

Funny, he thought. Not so long ago, he'd considered his comrades' captivity a terrible thing. Their situation had seemed about as grim as it could get.

Now, it seemed a lot grimmer. He would've given his right arm to know they were in one piece—on a Kazon vessel or anywhere else.

Abruptly, Tuvok spoke up. "I have isolated another ion trail," he told the captain. "However, it is different from the trail we followed here. Clearly, it did not originate from a Kazon form of propulsion technology."

"That rules out another Kazon sect," Chakotay observed. "But it leaves the door open for a host of other possibilities."

Janeway looked at the Vulcan. "We can follow it, can't we? Just as we followed the other trail?"

Tuvok shrugged. "It will entail a recalibration of our instruments, but that should not take long."

The captain nodded. "Good. See to it, Lieutenant."

Tuvok assured her he would do that and set to work. Unlike the rest of the crew, unlike even Janeway herself, he never seemed to tire. It was a good thing, too, considering the Vulcan could do things no one else could—and in half the time.

Turning back to the viewscreen, Paris regarded the field of debris again. It could well be that his colleagues had bought the farm here. But clearly, the captain wasn't accepting that possibility. She was doing everything she could to find them and get them back.

He liked that. Because if it were he out there, lost and alone, he would want to know his friends hadn't given up on him.

B'Elanna was up and alert with the first sharp sound of footsteps inside the rest chamber. Glancing at the entrance, she saw several armed guards enter the room—and her heart leaped into her throat.

A reprisal for Teeg'l's outburst the day before? An object lesson, just in case his death and that of the other Kazon weren't enough?

Those were the possibilities that came to mind first. And wouldn't they have been right in line with her Day-of-Honor luck? Before long, however, the lieutenant realized her fears were groundless. The guards weren't just rounding up a *couple* of prisoners—they were rousting *all* of them, jerking their heads in the direction of the exit.

And, she asked herself, what would be the sense of killing the whole bunch of them? Especially since it would leave no one to benefit from the Nograkh's object lesson.

Of course, the guards might simply be taking

them somewhere else, where they could conduct a little seminar on the value of rebellion. But B'Elanna didn't think so. The Nograkh seemed to her a particularly brutal and expedient people. If they intended to kill someone, to make an example of him, they would have done it then and there.

As she got to her feet, she looked at Kim. He looked wary of the guards' intentions as well.

"Where do you think we're going?" he asked as he stood.

"Nowhere we want to be," she assured him.

But they both knew the answer to his question—at least, the one Teeg'l had supplied them with. And if he was wrong, the lieutenant mused, they would find that out soon enough as well.

A hurried walk down a long corridor later, they found themselves in another chamber, maybe three times as big as the other one. Except this one wasn't so sparsely furnished.

An entire bulkhead was lined with a series of small, open hatches, through which chunks of rock were emptying into two-handled metal containers via heavy-duty conveyor belts. Apparently, the station was receiving a new load of raw material at that very moment.

On the other side of the room, there were massive, dark machines with monitors and control consoles, and more of the same kind of conveyor belts running in and out of them. Also, several more of the metal containers, waiting to transport the processed ore.

"Seems Teeg'l was right," she commented.

Kim grunted. "But he didn't do the place justice. It's much more oppressive-looking than I imagined."

A guard approached them and pointed to one of the hatches, where a container was almost full of debris. "Bring it to the processing unit," he told them. "And see you don't spill any."

They did as they were instructed. The other prisoners were given their orders at the same time—either to transport the incoming rocks alongside B'Elanna and Kim or to familiarize themselves with the processing controls. Either way, the lieutenant observed, it would be difficult to avoid exposure to the radioactive ore.

B'Elanna had never seen anyone who'd been a victim of radiation poisoning, but she'd heard about it. Apparently, there were quicker and less painful ways to die.

But the lieutenant wasn't going to think about dying just yet. She was going to think about *Voyager* tracking them down and getting them out of here. And she was going to do whatever it took to make that possible.

Before long, the prisoners settled into a routine under the watchful eyes of their guards. B'Elanna, Kim, and a handful of others dragged the containers full of rocks. Others worked the processing units, which separated the valuable ore from other debris. And still others dragged the containers full of ore out of the room for storage elsewhere in the station.

The debris was dumped in containers as well. But these were allowed to pile up until they took up too much room, then dragged off in another direction. More than likely, to be shoved out an air lock, the lieutenant thought.

This went on for hours. It wasn't long before B'Elanna experienced the first effects of the radiation. Her head felt light and her skin felt dry and raw. Judging by Kim's expression, he was enjoying the working conditions even less than she was. And still their captors kept them at it, until the last of the ore had been processed and put in storage.

Then they were herded back into the first chamber, where they slumped against the walls. The lieutenant felt a growling in her stomach, but somehow she didn't feel hungry.

Radiation will do that to you, she remarked inwardly. That and a whole lot more.

But she would have to eat sometime. Otherwise she'd become useless to her captors and get herself tossed out an air lock with the rest of the debris.

And wouldn't *that* make it a Day of Honor to remember?

The Nograkh prisoners sat on the other side of the rest chamber. Tired as they were, it didn't stop two of them from trading remarks—or getting into a pushing match. Almost as quickly as that other fight B'Elanna had seen—the one that had ended in the death of one of the combatants—this one escalated, too.

In a heartbeat, the pushing had turned into bone-jarring blows. No one, not even a healthy Nograkh, could have held up long under that kind of pounding.

Nor did the lieutenant have to guess which Nograkh would buckle first.

After all, one of the brutes was considerably bigger than the other—and his superior strength was already staggering his opponent. Before long, she told herself, another Nograkh would be lying on the floor, his skull crushed or his neck broken.

B'Elanna couldn't let that happen. It didn't matter if this was someone else's fight, someone else's culture. She had to act.

A look from Kim told her he felt the same way. He was leery of what they'd be getting themselves into, but not so leery he wasn't willing to try.

They started for the combatants. But before they could get very far, a chorus went up from the other Nograkh. And it had a very distinct tone of disapproval about it.

Immediately, the two engaged in the fight stopped and looked around. They seemed to be searching the faces of the other Nograkh. Whatever they found there didn't seem to please them. Then the one with the scar on his face spoke to them.

B'Elanna wouldn't have expected him to play peacekeeper, considering how he'd murdered his fellow Nograkh in the last melee. Nonetheless, his comments sealed the deal.

With a last, hostile glance at one another, the combatants backed off and melted into the ring of spectators. For a little while, they spat and gesticulated and complained volubly—the bigger one in particular. Then even that subsided.

B'Elanna looked at Kim. He shrugged.

"Looks like our services aren't needed anymore, Maquis."

"No objections from me, Starfleet."

By then, a couple of the guards had poked their heads in to see what was going on. They seemed disappointed that the fight hadn't gone further. Still, they appeared to find some humor in the situation, and grinned with their wide, cruel mouths.

That was one sight she wouldn't miss when they were reunited with *Voyager,* the lieutenant decided. And they *would* get back—somehow.

She wouldn't accept any other outcome.

As the door to Pacria's quarters slid aside, Kes peered inside. The woman was seated at a computer terminal, its glare illuminating her alien visage and her impossibly blue eyes.

"Kes," she said.

It wasn't a greeting—not really. There was no warmth in it, certainly. Only suspicion.

Wonderful, thought the Ocampa. I haven't even opened my mouth and I already feel like I'm prying. Still, she had come here for a reason, so she went ahead with it.

"How are you feeling?" she asked.

Pacria leaned back from the terminal and shrugged. "Fine. Except for the virus, of course. But that's to be expected." She indicated a chair on the other side of the room. "Won't you have a seat?"

Kes nodded. "Thank you."

Taking the chair, she saw Pacria swivel to face her. She was about to broach the subject of the woman's reasons for turning down the vaccine—until Pacria herself broached it.

"You want to know why I'm doing this," she said.

The Ocampa leaned forward. "If you don't want to tell me, you don't have to. The Doctor takes that part of his programming very seriously."

"And you?" asked Pacria, her eyes narrowing. "Don't you take it seriously as well?"

"I'm not a doctor," Kes explained. "But I've been taught to respect people's rights. If you want to keep your reasons a secret, that's your prerogative." She paused. "Only . . ."

"Yes?" the woman prodded.

"Only I wish you would share them with me. You see, the average lifetime for one of my people is only eight or nine years. We see life as something to be treasured. And it's difficult for me to see why anyone would—"

"Waste it," Pacria suggested.

"I didn't say that," Kes pointed out.

The woman considered her. "No," she conceded at last. "You didn't. And maybe I'm being a little harsh on you. After all, you *did* save my life—you and your friend the Doctor. And, contrary to what you might think, I cherish the extra days you've given me—painful though they will be."

The Ocampa smiled sympathetically. "You're obviously a courageous person. I admire you for that."

Pacria grunted. "You won't gain anything by flattery." Her features softened. "But maybe I do owe you an explanation."

"I don't believe you *owe* me anything," Kes clarified. "But I'd still be glad to hear it."

"All right," said the woman. "I'll tell you, then. But to understand why I'm doing what I'm doing, you must first understand the history of my people. We call ourselves the Emmonac."

Pacria described the Emmonac—their devotion to learning, to the arts, to wisdom in general. And their invasion by the Zendak'aa, a haughty race of conquerors from a neighboring star system.

The woman's voice took on a husky tone. "The Zendak'aa enslaved the Emmonac—and worse. Entire clans were selected at random and herded into camps, where they became the subjects of all kinds of experiments. Terrible experiments, involving mutilation and misery—but all in the name of science." She swallowed. "One of those experiments concerned a disease."

"The one you're carrying around inside you?" Kes asked.

"Not exactly," Pacria replied. "It was a disease restricted to the Zendak'aa. But what I have is very much like it. So similar, in fact, that what the Zendak'aa developed to fight their own virus would be an effective vaccine against it.

"The problem," said the Emmonac, "is it was bought with the blood of my people. That makes it monstrous to me. It makes it evil. To use it would be to honor the Zendak'aa who developed it—and that is too hideous an idea for me to even contemplate."

Kes looked at her. "I see."

There was silence for a moment. Then Pacria said she was tired, and wondered if she might not have some privacy.

And Kes had little choice but to grant it to her.

CHAPTER 9

JANEWAY PUSHED BACK FROM THE COMPUTER TERMINAL in her ready room and rubbed her eyes. She'd been at it for hours now, on and off—though it felt even longer.

With Tuvok in charge of tracking the ion trail of the Kazon battleship's mysterious destroyer, and her other officers busy with their own details, the captain had taken it on herself to more thoroughly analyze the sensor data on the debris field. What's more, it had yielded some interesting results.

First, she'd found there was more mass in the field than could be attributed to a battleship alone, but nothing with a Starfleet signature—nothing to indicate that the Kazon scout ship had definitely been destroyed at those coordinates as well.

Second, she'd been able to identify the sort of energy beam employed by the destroyer. Unfortunately, it hadn't come from any kind of weapon with which she was familiar. And when she'd asked Neelix about it, the Talaxian couldn't shed any light on the question either.

However, to this point, Janeway hadn't discovered what she was *really* looking for—some indication of where the destroyer had gone, some sense of its destination. Because if they knew that, they would be a big step closer to learning the fate of their missing crewmates.

The captain stretched her arms, feeling resistance from the cramps in her neck and shoulders. Somewhere in that mass of data, she told herself, was a clue. And she was determined to find it, with or without Neelix's—

Abruptly, she stopped herself. Neelix wasn't the only local guide they had aboard—not anymore. Their guest . . . what was her name? Pacria, wasn't it?

She came from this part of the Delta Quadrant. Odds were she knew it better than Neelix did.

And from what she'd heard, Pacria had recuperated enough to leave sick bay and occupy an empty suite. And, at her own request, the woman had been granted limited access to ship's computer, so she had to be pretty alert.

Alert enough to entertain a visitor, the captain hoped.

* * *

By the time the guards brought them some food, B'Elanna's appetite had improved considerably. But it went downhill again when she saw what they were serving for dinner.

The *plat du jour* was a thin, yellowish gruel with lumps of something vaguely meatlike in it. The guards maneuvered it into the room in a huge pot, not unlike the containers they used in the ore-processing chamber—except the pot had wheels to make the going easier.

The prisoners were told to line up. Then each one was given a plateful of the stuff. After B'Elanna and Kim got their fair shares, they returned to their place in the corner.

The ensign swallowed as he inspected his meal. "You know," he said, "I'm starting to appreciate Neelix more than ever."

"So am I," she agreed. "At least when he was serving something inedible, he knew how to disguise it."

Her companion looked at her. "I thought Klingons could eat *anything.*"

The lieutenant shook her head. "I'm only *half*-Klingon, remember? And the other half is pretty discriminating."

She smiled wanly, remembering how the Talaxian had tried to please her a few short days ago. She was glad she'd had a chance to apologize to him. If that was the last she and Neelix saw of each other, at least he'd have something good to say at her funeral.

No, she reminded herself. No funeral—not for a

good long while. She'd be tasting Neelix's food again before she knew it.

In the meantime, she noticed, the other prisoners didn't seem to appreciate the gruel they were being served either. Not even the Nograkh, whose needs it was no doubt designed to fulfill.

There was considerable grumbling. Sounds of discontent. Nothing new in this place, of course. B'Elanna herself had been tempted to grumble a little now and then.

One alien seemed to be complaining a little more loudly than the others. He had a single eye in the middle of his brow, right where the bridge of his nose would have been if he'd been human. He was dark—very dark, actually—and hairless as far as she could tell, and he had pale blue striations running down either side of his neck.

What's more, he towered over the prisoners on either side of him. In fact, he towered over everyone in the chamber, even the largest of the Nograkh. As B'Elanna watched, he turned his eye her way.

No, the lieutenant thought. Not her way, not exactly. It seemed to her he was scrutinizing the ensign beside her.

"Heads up," she whispered.

Kim looked up at her. "What?"

The alien's single eye narrowed and the striations on his neck turned a darker shade of blue. Letting his plate drop to the floor, he crossed the room. And he was headed in the ensign's direction.

"Trouble," she said, answering Kim's question.

The ensign's eyes slid to one side, but he didn't turn his head. He just frowned a little.

None of the other prisoners exercised that kind of restraint. They stopped eating and followed One-Eye's progress with great interest. And their interest heightened even more when he came to a halt in front of Kim.

One-Eye spoke in a voice surprisingly thin and reedy, as if someone had damaged his vocal cords somewhere along the line. "You," he said to the human. "Kazon-lover."

B'Elanna watched Kim's reaction. Or rather, his lack of one. The ensign didn't acknowledge the other prisoner's presence. He just scooped another dollop of gruel out of his bowl and deposited it in his mouth.

"Didn't you hear me?" asked One-Eye.

Still no response, at least from Kim. But B'Elanna could feel her pulse starting to race. The Klingon in her didn't like insults—regardless of whether they were directed at her or her friends. And when there was an implicit threat of violence in them, she liked them even less.

"I called you a Kazon-lover," One-Eye persisted.

It wasn't what he had said, really. It was the way he had said it—the taunt in his voice, so much like all the taunts B'Elanna had endured since her arrival here.

She could feel the anger rising inside her. She could feel her hands clenching into fists. But she told herself she wouldn't do anything drastic—not unless Kim was in danger.

The ensign didn't look at his tormentor. He just

said, "I don't love the Kazons any more than you do. It was just a coincidence that we were captured with them. In fact—"

Suddenly, the alien reached down and grabbed the front of Kim's uniform. Almost effortlessly, he dragged the ensign to his feet, causing his plate of gruel to fall out of his hand.

"You think you can deceive me?" he rasped. "You think you can lie your way out of this? The Kazons raided my world—killed my nestlings. Who's going to pay for that, eh?"

Kim wasn't making a move to save himself. But then, maybe he didn't think he needed saving. Maybe he was hoping this would all boil over if he just kept his mouth shut from here on in.

B'Elanna disagreed. Without considering the consequences, without considering *anything* except the danger her friend was in, she got up and belted One-Eye across the mouth as hard as she could.

The alien staggered backward, releasing Kim in the process. The ensign retreated to a spot beside his benefactor.

"You shouldn't have done that," he told her. "I could have handled it."

"Like hell," she spat.

Recovering, One-Eye growled and wiped his mouth with the back of his hand. It came away red with blood.

"You will be sorry you did that," he told her, a bestial grin spreading across his face. "You will be *very* sorry."

He signaled to the clot of prisoners gathered behind

him. Two of them got to their feet, large specimens in their own right. One, a being with a pinched face and horns like a ram's, rubbed his powerful hands together in anticipation of what was to come. The other, a leathery-looking bruiser with faceted yellow eyes, slammed a massive fist into his palm.

The lieutenant could feel her heart pounding. She could feel the surge of fire in her veins. *Klingon* fire.

Over the years, she had learned to deal with her battle lust—to channel it into more useful endeavors. Now, it seemed, the most useful thing she could do was tear her enemy's throat out. Anything less and he would probably do the same thing to her.

B'Elanna wished it hadn't come to this. But then, hadn't it seemed inevitable to her from the beginning? Neither she nor Kim had any friends here, only each other. And with the stigma of the Kazon on them, their status as scapegoats had been assured.

The Day of Honor was lasting a little longer this year.

"I'll take the two on the right," Kim told her. He assumed a fighting stance, no doubt one he'd learned at the Academy and hadn't used since.

The lieutenant grimaced. "Take what you can handle," she advised him, "and leave the rest to me."

Then their antagonists were on top of them, and there was no more time for strategy. There was only time for kicking and ducking and jabbing for all she was worth.

But right from the beginning, it was clear it wouldn't be enough. One-Eye wasn't just powerful, he was deadly quick. And he had help from his friend with the ram's horns.

Together, they maneuvered B'Elanna into a corner, where her own quickness wasn't as much of an asset. Then they took their shots at her, one after another, until she couldn't elude them anymore and they started landing with bone-jolting frequency.

Still, her thoughts were for her companion, who was matched up against the leathery prisoner with the yellow eyes. She tried to steal a glimpse of Kim even in the midst of her own peril, but what little she could see wasn't very encouraging.

Like her, the ensign was backed into a corner. But unlike her, he didn't have the wherewithal to deal with it. His face was bloody, his legs barely able to hold him up. Any more such punishment and he'd be a dead man.

Not that B'Elanna could do anything about it. In fact, she probably wouldn't last much longer than her friend would.

Then something happened. At first, she wasn't sure what—only that there was an uproar from the other prisoners, the ones who hadn't seen fit to participate in the slaughter. And a single shout that came through the general outcry, sounding very much like a challenge.

One-Eye didn't seem to be able to ignore it. Pausing to look back over his shoulder, he gave B'Elanna the chance she needed to slip past him.

That's when she saw what was going on. Kim was slumped in his corner, bloody but still alive. And in his place one of the Nograkh was fighting the prisoner with the leathery skin. Surprisingly, it was the killer—the one with the scar.

As the lieutenant looked on, the Nograkh blocked a roundhouse blow with one hand and launched one of his own with the other. There was a crack, and the leathery one toppled, senseless.

But no sooner had he hit the deck than One-Eye and Ram's Horns were charging his assailant. The Nograkh whirled, ready to take them both on. And for a little while, that's just what he had to do.

He didn't do badly, either. He wasn't very agile, but he was immensely strong. And what he couldn't elude, he could ward off. Of course, it was still two against one, and he couldn't have held out forever.

That's why it was so important for B'Elanna to rejoin the fray—to literally jump into it with both feet. Getting a running start, she leaped at just the right moment and plowed into the small of One-Eye's back.

Her adversary snarled with pain and sank to his knees, clutching the point of impact. In the meantime, no longer outnumbered, the Nograkh buried his fist in Ram's Horns' belly. And when Ram's Horns doubled over in pain, his adversary launched an uppercut that lifted him off the floor.

By the time he came down again, Ram's Horns was unconscious. That left only One-Eye to deal with, and he was still bent over from the blow to his back. The Nograkh crossed the floor and stood menacingly above him.

When he spoke, his voice was gravelly and his tone full of rancor. "An uneven fight," he told One-Eye, "is dishonorable. My people don't *like* dishonorable fights."

With a tilt of his head, he indicated the other Nograkh in the room. They were each as intent on One-Eye as he was. From B'Elanna's point of view, it looked like any of them would have performed the same kind of rescue—except the one with the scar had beaten them to it.

"They came in with the Kazon," One-Eye hissed. He pointed a long, gnarled finger at B'Elanna. "They deserve to die."

"I hate the Kazon as much as anyone," the Nograkh snarled. "But they aren't Kazon. As far as I can tell, the only one who deserves to *die* here is *you*."

And he pulled his fist back for what B'Elanna feared was a deathblow.

"No!" she yelled. "Let him be!"

Without thinking, she took a couple of steps toward the Nograkh. He stopped, looked at her and then Kim.

"You'd spare his life?" he asked them.

"Yes," the lieutenant said quickly.

The ensign nodded. "Yes."

The Nograkh hesitated. Then, with a shrug, he turned and rejoined his comrades. And he didn't look back.

B'Elanna made her way to Kim's side, just in case One-Eye decided he wanted to resume hostilities. But he didn't do that. He simply returned to where he'd been sitting, grumbling and holding his injury.

"How about that?" Kim mumbled, a swollen lip getting in his way.

The lieutenant checked him to make sure he hadn't sustained any serious damage. "Yes. How about that."

She glanced at the Nograkh with the scar. He was exchanging comments with his comrades.

"Apparently," the ensign said, "we didn't give his kind enough credit. He could just as easily have watched us get hung out to dry."

"I guess," B'Elanna responded.

Despite all their belligerence, despite the cruelty that seemed part of their nature, there seemed to be a code of honor among the Nograkh. She wouldn't have thought it possible.

And yet, she'd seen it with her own eyes.

"It just goes to show you," Kim said. "Things aren't always what they appear to be."

B'Elanna glanced again at the Nograkh. This time he noticed, and glanced back at her. "Spare me the platitudes, Starfleet—at least until we find a way out of here."

Janeway stood outside Pacria's door and waited for the woman to give the captain entry to her quarters. A moment later, the door slid aside.

Pacria was sitting on a chair in front of a computer terminal much like the one Janeway had just left. The lines of her face were drawn tight. Like the gates of a citadel, the captain thought.

And she hadn't even asked a question yet.

"Captain Janeway," said Pacria, acknowledging her host.

"How are you feeling?" asked Janeway.

"Better," the alien told her.

It was a guarded remark if the captain had ever heard one.

"Don't tell me," Pacria went on. "Kes asked you to speak with me."

The captain smiled, seeing that she had inadvertently intruded on some controversy. "Actually, no. I came of my own accord."

Pacria's expression changed—became vaguely apologetic. "I'm sorry. Perhaps I jumped to the wrong conclusion." She indicated a chair on the other side of the room. "Please. Sit down."

Janeway accepted her offer. "The reason I came," she explained as succinctly as she could, "has to do with our search for a couple of our officers. They were abducted by the Kazon—"

"I've heard of the Kazon," Pacria responded, sounding a little impatient.

The captain nodded. "As I was saying, the Kazon took our people. But we came across what appears to be the wreckage of the Kazon ship—where we picked up the ion trail of another vessel entirely."

Janeway rubbed her hands together. "We've got a problem. We're hoping our friends were seized and spirited away by the destroyer, but we don't know where they were taken."

"But you said there was an ion trail," Pacria pointed out.

This time the captain was certain of the woman's impatience. Maybe Pacria hadn't gotten her strength back as much as the Doctor believed—though as far as Janeway knew, the Doctor had never been wrong before.

"That's true," the captain conceded. "But ion trails aren't always a hundred percent reliable. And they have a habit of petering out before you get to the end of them."

Pacria frowned. "What is it you wish me to do?"

"Take a look at the data," Janeway told her. "See if there's anything about it—either the ion trail or the weapons residue or anything else—that might tell you who destroyed the Kazon."

The woman looked at her for a moment. "All right," she agreed. "Give me access to it and I'll take a look. It's the least I can do, considering what your doctor did for me."

The captain smiled. "If you can tell us anything at all about our officers' whereabouts, it's *we* who'll be indebted to *you.*"

CHAPTER 10

B'ELANNA'S SECOND DAY OF WORK WAS PROBABLY NO harder than the first—but it *felt* much harder. She knew that was due to the radiation. It sapped her strength and burned her skin and made her head ache.

When all the ore had been processed, she and the other prisoners were allowed to return to their rest chamber. In the corridor en route, she felt a hand on her shoulder. It was Kim's.

"At least we get some exercise," he gibed. He was pale, drawn, waxy-looking. "And on Friday nights, I hear there's a concert. I may be called upon to play my clarinet."

The lieutenant looked at him. "You're out of your mind, Starfleet."

The ensign grunted, touching two fingers to the cut

over his eye, which had grown red and puffy. It looked like an infection had set in.

"Don't I wish," he replied. "Then I wouldn't have to put up with this torture." He lowered his voice. "B'Elanna, if the captain were on our trail, don't you think she would have—"

"I don't think anything," she told him. "I just wait and watch for a chance to get out of here. That's all either of us can do."

Kim nodded. "Right."

As they filed into the rest chamber, they passed a bunch of burly Nograkh, who had already begun to hunker down in their usual spots. One of them was the prisoner with the scar on his face—the one who had come to their aid when One-Eye and his friends attacked them.

The one who had likely saved their lives.

The lieutenant paused for a moment. Kim stopped, too.

"What is it?" he asked.

"I'd like to thank our unexpected benefactor," she told him. "It seems like the right thing to do."

The ensign glanced at the Nograkh in question. "Are you sure? I mean, I get the feeling there wasn't anything personal in what he did. He just felt . . . I don't know, *compelled* to do it."

"All the more reason to express our gratitude," B'Elanna asserted.

Kim frowned. "I'll go with you."

"Not necessary," she said. "Besides, one of us may be less threatening than two."

The ensign thought for a moment. "All right," he

decided. "But I'll be right over there if you need me." He indicated a bulkhead with a jerk of his head. "I'll be the one slumped wearily against the wall."

The lieutenant smiled. "Acknowledged."

Then she walked over to the Nograkh. He saw her coming, but didn't move in response.

Taking a breath, she extended her hand to him.

He looked at it with his small silver eyes. So did the other Nograkh. But none of them seemed to understand what B'Elanna was up to.

"It's a gesture of friendship," she explained. "You grasp it."

The Nograkh looked at her and her hand for what seemed like a long time. Then he spoke.

"Why would you want to be my friend?" he asked.

B'Elanna kept her hand extended. "You came to our aid. Maybe saved our lives."

"It was an uneven contest. If it hadn't been me," he said, "it would have been one of the others."

"But it wasn't," she insisted. "It was you."

The Nograkh pondered that. Reaching out, he took her up on her offer—though he probably didn't use all his strength when he clasped her hand.

He looked at her sullenly, perhaps seeking assurance that he was performing the gesture correctly. She nodded.

Then he released her hand. And patted the deck beside him, indicating that she should sit down.

As she complied, the other Nograkh moved away a bit—though some grumbled about it. They were giving their comrade some privacy, the lieutenant realized.

"My name is B'Elanna," she told him. She smiled, though it was hard to work up much enthusiasm when she ached so much. "B'Elanna Torres."

The Nograkh grunted. "They call me Tolga." And then he added, "You are not from any world I have ever heard of."

"That's true," she said. "My people were brought here by a phenomenon we still don't quite understand. Our worlds are far away—so far, in fact, it could take a lifetime to return to them."

If one *had* a lifetime, she added inwardly. At the moment, hers looked rather inadequate. But she didn't say that. What she said was, "I want to thank you."

Tolga looked away, his face a stony mask. "It was nothing. Only what honor demanded of me."

Honor, thought the lieutenant. It was a word the Klingons used as well. And often, if her mother was any indication.

Abruptly, he turned to her again, his silver eyes catching the light. "How did you come here, anyway?"

Obviously, he was curious about her. And she had no reason to hold anything back—though she resisted an urge to mention her mother's holiday.

"We were kidnapped by the Kazon-Ogla," she explained. "Then their ship was attacked by the one that brought us here. When the Ogla were taken prisoner, so were we."

Tolga's mouth twisted as if he had a bad taste in it. "Too bad," was his only comment.

He looked down at his big, powerful-looking hands. For a while, he seemed interested in nothing else. Then he looked up and spoke again.

"You must have wondered what we Nograkh are doing here. Why we were thrown into this hole with you and the others."

"The question occurred to me," she admitted.

"Most often," Tolga told her, his mouth twisting again, "if a Nograkh is brought to a place like this, it's because he is a criminal. A thief or a murderer or a defiler of holy places. You're familiar with such people?"

The lieutenant said she was. She had met several of them when she served with the Maquis. Hell, she'd stolen a few things herself in the name of freedom from the Cardassians.

"Is that what you did?" she asked. "You took a few things that didn't belong to you?"

Tolga made a derisive sound deep in his throat. A profoundly bitter sound, B'Elanna thought.

"No. None of us here did anything like that." He paused, as if searching for words. "We were rebels. We tried to overthrow the government on our homeworld."

"I see," she said. "So . . . you're political prisoners."

He tried the notion on for size. "Yes, you could say that." A pause. "For a long time, our world was enslaved by the Zendak'aa—just like a lot of other worlds. Then we rose up against them and smashed their control over us. For those of us who had risked our lives to see the Zendak'aa gone, it was like a dream. We never expected to know oppression again."

The lieutenant saw where he was going with this. "But that wasn't the way it worked out?"

"No," he said, his eyes fixing on something she couldn't see. "It didn't work out that way at all. We had just exchanged a Zendak'aan tyrant for one who looked more familiar to us. And for some of us, like myself, the fight began all over again."

It sounded familiar. B'Elanna told him so.

"Except we fought on behalf of many different worlds—many different peoples," she said. "And our enemy," she added, unable to keep the venom out of her voice, "was a race called the Cardassians."

Tolga nodded. "Then you know what it's like. To strike and escape, then strike again. To know it's only a matter of time before you're discovered and sentenced to death."

"Actually," she said, "it was a toss-up as to what would do us in first—the Cardassians or the ships we cobbled together. But yes, I know what it's like to be on the run."

He frowned deeply, staring off into some imagined distance again. "Seven nights ago, we sabotaged a weapons factory on one of our moons. Blew it up. I suppose we didn't retreat quickly enough. We were stunned, every last one of us. The next thing we knew, we were on a ship—the one where we first saw you and your friend there." He indicated Kim with a thrust of his chin.

"No court of law?" asked the lieutenant. "No trial, no sentencing?"

His expression said she had just made a miserable excuse for a joke. "None," he said. "When there's a need for workers on the stations, Nograkh justice can be swift."

B'Elanna understood. Klingon law could be the same way. Quick, merciless, and often irrevocable. Or so she had heard.

Tolga's nostrils flared with anger. "I wish I were free again," he said. "Just for a little while. I would have done more to weaken the tyrant." The muscles worked savagely in his temples. "I would have done a great many things."

There was silence in the wake of his comment. Then her curiosity got the better of her.

"I hope I won't offend you by asking," she said, "but that Nograkh you killed—was his death really necessary?"

Tolga nodded. "Honor demanded that as well. He was someone who had betrayed me years ago, before I joined the rebellion. There's nothing more onerous than betrayal. It can't be tolerated. That's the Nograkh way."

"Later on," she said, "there was another fight. But you didn't let that one continue."

He shrugged. "That, too, was a case of betrayal. But the combatants weren't evenly matched. The bigger one will have to find someone the size of the smaller one to fight for him."

B'Elanna absorbed the information. "I see." Silence again. "Well, it was good talking to you." She got up.

Tolga looked up at her. "You fight well," he observed. "I think you'll survive here as long as anyone."

She smiled at the dark-edged nature of his comment. Then, with the same understated irony in her voice, she said, "Thank you."

And she crossed the room again to join Kim.

Tolga intrigued her, the lieutenant acknowledged. While there was no question about his bitterness or his potential for cold-blooded violence, she couldn't help but feel there was a certain nobility about him as well—an unswerving fidelity to his own ethical code.

In fact, he'd risked his life for what he believed in. And if that wasn't nobility, she didn't know what in the universe *was.*

Kes leaned back in her chair and eyed the Doctor across his desk. "So that's the problem," she said.

"Pacria believes the cure for her disease came at the cost of her people's misery and degradation."

"Yes," she confirmed with a sigh. "And that's why she won't let us use it to save her life."

The Doctor's brow furrowed. "I don't understand. If Pacria's people hate this vaccine so much, why was it included in their ship's data base?"

The Ocampa nodded. "That's a good question. Apparently, all Emmonac vessels—including Pacria's, which was on some kind of stellar research mission—access and use scientific data gathered by the Zendak'aa. After all, in most fields of endeavor,

Zendak'aan research wasn't conducted at the expense of the Emmonac."

"Only in the biological sciences," the Doctor inferred.

"Exactly," said Kes. "And where it *was* gathered at the expense of the Emmonac, it was left there anyway—for historical purposes, to remind Pacria's people of what they endured at the hands of their oppressors."

The Doctor frowned. "I see."

There was silence for a moment, as they considered the situation from their respective points of view. Kes was the first one to break that silence.

"It's insane," she concluded.

The Doctor harrumphed. "I agree. There's an old Earth expression about cutting off one's nose to spite one's face. I believe it has some relevance in this case."

"Ultimately," said the Ocampa, "research is research. Data is data. And if it can save a life, especially your own, it seems silly not to use it."

"Again," the Doctor said, "I concur wholeheartedly. But it really doesn't matter what you and I think. The only opinion that matters is Pacria's. And as far as she's concerned, the cure I offered her is tainted."

"Tainted with her people's blood. I know. But," Kes went on, "if she dies, it'll just mean more blood. More misery. At least if she lives, her people's sacrifice will have meant something. It will have had some value."

The Doctor shrugged. "Not in Pacria's estimate.

And for all we know, the Emmonac who died in Varrus' clinic might have looked at this the same way she does. Since they're dead, there's really no way to know."

The Ocampa bit her lip. "There's got to be a way to help her."

"We don't have the right to decide that for her," the Doctor rejoined. "We can only help her if she *wants* to be helped. And from what I've seen so far, I wouldn't be too optimistic on that count."

Kes turned to him, her frustration flaring into uncharacteristic anger. "But you're a *physician.* How can you just sit there and watch someone die—without trying to do something about it?"

The Doctor remained calm. "In fact," he said, "I *am* going to do something about it. I'm going to seek a cure that is not based on Zendak'aan data." He sighed. "Of course, given my lack of familiarity with Pacria's disease, I'm not confident I'll find a cure in time."

"But you'll try," Kes noted. She shook her head apologetically. "I'm sorry. I didn't mean to become angry with you. None of this is your fault."

The Doctor acknowledged her remarks with a nod. "Make no mistake," he told the Ocampa. "It pains me to watch Pacria suffer. It pains me even worse to know she'll perish soon. But I'm a doctor. I can't force my patients to do what I believe is best for them. I can't make choices *for* them. I can only present a range of options and hope for the best."

"Even if the best is death?" Kes wondered.

He regarded her grimly. "Even then."

Intellectually, the Ocampa could appreciate the Doctor's position. He had been programmed to adhere to a strict code of ethics, and he couldn't diverge from that programming.

She could even see the sense in those ethics. If she were a patient, she would want the right to make decisions about her treatment. She would want to be able to decide her own fate.

But what Pacria was doing just seemed wrong to Kes. No matter what the Doctor said, she just couldn't sit still and watch the Emmonac die. There had to be a way to help Pacria despite herself.

And if there was a way, the Ocampa would find it. She promised herself that as sincerely as she'd ever promised anyone anything. But where was she to start? What was her first step?

Abruptly, it came to her. She got up from her chair. "I'll see you later," she told the Doctor and headed for the exit.

"Kes?" he called after her. "Where are you going?"

"To speak with the captain," she told him.

CHAPTER 11

PACRIA HAD PROMISED CAPTAIN JANEWAY SHE WOULD GO over the data they'd accumulated at the scene of the Kazon ship's destruction. And, to the best of her ability, she meant to keep that promise.

First, she looked at the ion pattern the destroyer had left behind. Though propulsion systems were hardly her specialty, the Emmonac knew enough about them to identify the technology that had created the trail.

It was Zendak'aan, of course. But that didn't tell her much of anything. Half a dozen races in this sector used Zendak'aan technology or some close variation on it.

Next, Pacria looked at the molecular decay patterns in the debris, to see what kinds of weapons had been employed. There, too, though she was not a military tactician, she detected the legacy of the Zendak'aa. But again, there were at least six or seven races currently in possession of that weapons technology—maybe more.

After that, she checked for organic debris, though surely Captain Janeway had done that as well. Pacria found only trace amounts, certainly not enough to identify the victim or victims, much less the manner in which they had perished.

Knowing how fond the Truat Nor were of ejecting memorial dust after a battle, she checked for the stuff. There was none in evidence. That ruled out the Truat Nor.

Pacria then combed the sensor data for gaps in the debris spread or indications of graviton particles. Either one would have made her suspect the Taserrat, who liked to use their tractor beams to snare trophies from the remains of their enemies.

As it happened, she found neither gaps nor gravitons. That meant the Taserrat were probably not the culprits either.

Beyond that, Pacria knew, there was little she could do. She would have liked to contact Captain Janeway and tell her she had located her colleagues. Or at least offer her some assurance they had survived the Kazon ship's destruction.

She wished she could leave these people a gift for all their kindness to her. However, it didn't appear she would get the chance.

* * *

Kes stood outside the door to Captain Janeway's ready room and waited for the computer to alert the captain to her presence. After a moment or two, the door slid open.

The captain was seated on the other side of her desk. She looked tired. Still, she managed a smile.

"Kes. What can I do for you?"

The Ocampa took a seat across the desk from Janeway. "It's about Pacria," she began.

The captain's brows knit. "Don't tell me she's suffered a setback? I just saw her in her quarters."

"Actually," Kes said, "she's recovering nicely. At least, as far as her injuries are concerned. But . . ."

"Yes?" Janeway prompted.

"She has a disease," the Ocampa explained.

The captain's eyes narrowed. "It's not contagious, is it? A danger to the crew?"

"No, nothing like that."

"Then what?" Janeway asked.

Kes described the illness in some detail. Having been trained as a scientist herself, the captain listened patiently and with great interest. Also, with great sympathy.

"Then it's fatal," she concluded.

The Ocampa nodded. "But," she added quickly, "we can help her. The doctor found a cure."

Janeway looked at her. "Then . . . what's the problem?"

Kes told her.

"What about an alternative cure?" the captain asked.

"The Doctor's working on it," the Ocampa noted. "But without success."

Taking a deep breath, Janeway settled into her chair to give the matter some thought.

"I see now," she said, "why Pacria didn't mention any of this earlier. She wanted to keep it to herself." The captain paused. "The Doctor is right, of course. You can't force Pacria to accept the cure. And it doesn't sound like any amount of arguing is going to change her mind."

Kes leaned forward, her hands clenched in her lap. "But I can't let her die. Not when we can prevent it."

Janeway smiled a sad smile. "I know how you feel. And believe me, I feel the same way. It goes against my grain to stand by and do nothing. But it's Pacria's life. It's up to her what she does with it."

Kes looked away. She had hoped the captain would be of more help—that she would come up with some fresh perspective, some brilliant insight, and therefore a way to keep Pacria alive.

Then Janeway spoke up again. "How much do you know about the Zendak'aa?" she asked.

Kes shrugged. "Only what Pacria's told me. That they were conquerors. And that they conducted hideous experiments."

"But there's information on them in our data files—correct?"

The Ocampa nodded. "All the data we downloaded from Pacria's vessel. But what does . . ." Her voice trailed off.

"But what's that got to do with your patient? And

her decision to let herself die?" the captain asked. "It may have everything to do with it. If we can learn more about the Zendak'aa and the kinds of experiments they were conducting, we may obtain a better understanding of why Pacria's doing what she's doing."

The Ocampa's eyes lit up. "And maybe find a way to change her mind?"

"Yes," said Janeway, though her expression wasn't nearly as exhuberant as Kes's. "At least, that's one possibility. The other is that, after coming to understand the Zendak'aa better . . . you'll come to agree with her."

The Ocampa looked at her. The captain wasn't joking. "I don't believe that will happen," Kes replied.

Janeway smiled that sad smile again. "Perhaps not. In any case, I guess you'd better get a move on. From what you've told me, our friend Pacria doesn't have much time."

"No," said Kes. "She doesn't." She got up and moved to the door, then turned around again. "Thank you," she said to the captain.

Janeway regarded her with obvious sympathy. "Don't thank me yet," she advised the Ocampa.

As Kes departed, the captain sighed. She wished she had known about Pacria's condition before she had put her to work.

She looked up at the intercom grid hidden in the ceiling. "Janeway to sick bay."

Abruptly, the holodoctor's face sprang to life on her monitor, replacing the sensor information the captain had been studying. "Yes?" he replied.

"Doctor," she said, "I just learned of Pacria's condition from Kes."

He frowned. "You would have learned of it sooner if you'd kept up with the reports I've been sending you."

"No doubt," the captain conceded. "In any case, not knowing about the disease, I gave Pacria an assignment. Nothing arduous, of course. I just asked her to look over some data for me—something that may help us find Torres and Kim. Any problem with that?"

The Doctor thought for a moment. "I don't suppose it can hurt," he decided. "Besides, she might welcome the distraction."

Janeway nodded. "Good. Keep me posted. And from now on, I'll take the time to read your reports."

The Doctor lifted his chin, only mildly pacified. "Acknowledged," he said. A moment later, he disappeared, giving way to the sensor data the captain had been studying earlier.

Propping her face on her hands, Janeway tried to concentrate on the information. She knew her work would have little value at this point, since she'd already gleaned about everything she could. If there were any other insights to be drawn from it, it would have to be Pacria who drew them.

And yet, she couldn't stop poring over the information. It was her only link to B'Elanna—and of course, to Kim. Her only way of reaching out to them. That made it hard for her to put it aside.

Pacria could no longer remain in her quarters studying the debris field data. She felt compelled to get out, to move around.

After all, she didn't have long to live. And even if *Voyager* was populated with a slew of unfamiliar faces, they were still sentient beings. They had the potential for happiness and sadness, just like her own people. Because of that, their presence was comforting to her.

As she found herself growing hungry as well, she headed for the ship's mess hall, expecting she could satisfy both her needs there—for company as well as for food. Nor was she disappointed.

As she walked in, she smelled something wonderful—so wonderful, in fact, it made her salivate. Winding her way past tables full of crewmen, she traced the smell to a cooking alcove of some sort. Inside it was a man with yellowish skin, golden eyes and a feathery tuft of hair that ran from his crown to the back of his neck.

He looked up as he saw her coming. And smiled at her, in a way no one else on the ship had done. It was an easy smile, an unassuming smile, that placed no demands on her. It simply told her she was welcome here, without limit or qualification, and always would be.

"Excuse me," she said. "I'm new here. My name is Pacria."

The man nodded. "Yes, I know. I'm Neelix. I run

this place." He tilted his head to indicate a pot of stew. "Care for some?"

She didn't ask what it was. It smelled so good, it didn't matter to her. "Yes," she said. "I would. Please."

Neelix picked up a ladle that he'd hooked onto the lip of the pot and stirred the stew a bit. Then he fished up a chunky assortment of ingredients, emptied them onto a plate, and turned it over to Pacria.

"There," he said. "And if you'll wait a moment, I'll join you."

Repeating the process with obvious pleasure, Neelix prepared a second plate. Then he gathered up some implements and a couple of cloth napkins with his free hand and emerged from his alcove with them.

There was an unoccupied table just a few feet away; he took it. Pacria sat down opposite him. There were a beverage container and glasses on the table. Neelix poured some out for her, then himself.

"Thank you," she said.

"Well?" he replied, looking at her expectantly. "Dig in."

He didn't have to tell her twice. The stew was just as flavorful and satisfying as she'd anticipated. Neelix didn't start to eat right away.

"You like it?" he asked.

Pacria nodded. "Very much."

He grinned. "Good." Then he had a few mouthfuls himself. He seemed to enjoy it as well, if the look of bliss on his face was any indication.

"You know," she said, "it's very pleasant to meet a man who loves his work as much as you do."

Neelix shrugged. "What's not to like? People come to me with a need and I satisfy it. They come in frowning and leave with a smile."

"I'm not surprised," Pacria told him. "Especially if everything you make is as wonderful as this stew."

He shook his head. "I'm not talking about the food—though, of course, that fills a need as well. I'm talking about the camaraderie. The fellowship. When you're far from home, in a strange quadrant, it's important to know there's a place where you can sit down and unwind—maybe share an experience or two with someone who cares. Or failing that, with the cook."

"I see," she said, smiling at his joke. "But you *do* care. It's obvious."

Neelix became more pensive. "These people have become my family. That's why it's so hard to lose one of them. Or, in this case, two."

Pacria knew immediately whom he was referring to. "You mean the crewmen you're trying to recover."

"Yes." He sighed. "You know, I had a little tiff with one of them. But she had the decency to come in before she left and apologize. I'm glad she did, too. I would have hated to think her last thoughts of me—"

Neelix stopped himself, apparently too choked up to go on. Then he dabbed at one of his eyes, where he'd secreted some liquid.

"I shouldn't be acting this way," he said at last. "I'm the morale officer on the ship. I should be assuring you they'll be back in one piece, safe and sound. It's just that I've got this feeling. This *bad* feeling . . ."

"It's difficult to lose someone," Pacria agreed. "I know. I lost a whole ship full of colleagues. Nearly twenty of them."

Neelix's brow furrowed. "That's right. You did, didn't you? And here I am, crying over a couple of casualties that haven't even happened yet. I guess that was pretty insensitive of me."

"No, it wasn't," she insisted. She put her hand on his. "We're not talking about numbers here, Neelix. We're talking about people's lives. And every life is important."

He looked at her. "Yes," he said softly. "I suppose you're right."

Suddenly, Pacria realized what she had said. *Every life is important.*

Every life.

Every life.

Even her own.

Pacria looked at her plate. In the course of the conversation, she had finished her stew. She slid her chair back.

"I ought to be going now. I told Captain Janeway I'd help her with something."

Neelix nodded. "Come by again," he told her. "As often as you like. On Monday, I'm making my famous root and tuber casserole."

Monday. Three days from now, she thought.

"We'll see," she said.

Pacria would have liked to give him an outright yes. However, as she might not be alive on Monday, it was a promise she was loathe to make.

CHAPTER 12

THE SECOND NIGHT ON THE MINING STATION WAS DIFFERent from the first. But it wasn't an improvement by any stretch of the imagination.

B'Elanna wasn't able to stand watch. She was too damned tired, too feverish from her prolonged exposure to the radioactive ore. Too full of pain inside and out.

Kim was no better off. He fell asleep as soon as his head touched his forearm, One-Eye or no One-Eye. But there didn't seem to be any danger of attack from One-Eye or anyone else. Like the Starfleet officers, the other prisoners were too fatigued to keep their eyes open.

Nonetheless, B'Elanna's sleep wasn't restful. It was shot through with flashes of pain, echoes of real-life aches deep in her bones.

Then she felt another kind of pain, sharper than the others. Again. And a third time. She opened her eyes and saw a Nograkh guard standing over her. He was poking at B'Elanna with his free hand. In the other one, he held a rifle pointed at the ceiling.

"You," said the guard.

"Me?" she responded.

"You," he confirmed. He jerked his thumb at the exit. "I've got an ore container that needs to be moved in the processing room."

There was another guard standing behind him, and two more at the door. They were all watching her. But all the other prisoners were asleep. Or if they weren't, they were doing a good job of faking it.

It was still lights-out on the station. A strange time for her to be lugging containers around—especially when she was the only one. Not that she had much choice in the matter.

But as she got up and started for the exit, she heard a scraping on the floor. Turning, she saw Kim scramble to his feet.

"I'll give you a hand," he said, still rubbery-limbed and bleary-eyed but obviously awake.

"No," the guard barked, raising his weapon until it was aimed at the ensign's chest. "Not you. *Her.*"

There was a look in his eye that B'Elanna didn't like. Still, she couldn't let her friend die trying to help her.

"It's all right," she told him.

Kim shook his head, never taking his eyes off the guard. "No," he whispered. "It's not all right. B'Elanna, can't you see what—"

"I said it's all *right,"* the lieutenant rasped. "That's an order."

Her companion snorted disdainfully. "Right now, that doesn't mean much. A court-martial is the least of my worries."

B'Elanna admired him for his chivalry. Quiet as he might be, Harry Kim had never been one to let down a friend. But it didn't change anything. She still couldn't let him sacrifice himself.

"Stay here," she begged him. "Please."

As she said it, she looked deep into his eyes, trying to speak to him without words. For a moment, he didn't seem to understand what she was trying to tell him. Then, finally, he got the message.

Satisfied he wouldn't make a fuss, B'Elanna crossed the room and went out into the corridor, with the guard close behind. Without speaking, they made their way to the ore-processing chamber.

Sure enough, there was a container full of ore there. But she didn't know how that could be. Hadn't Tolga and some of the others lugged all the ore containers to the storage room before they left?

No matter. It wasn't as if she could argue that this wasn't her job. She had to do whatever they told her to do. Approaching the container, she took hold of its handle. Then, following the guard's gesture, she dragged it across the floor.

Kes leaned back in her chair. Her research had given her much to think about. However, it hadn't given her a clue yet as to how she might convince Pacria to accept the Doctor's cure.

Abruptly, a beeping invaded the silence. There was someone out in the corridor. "Come in," she said, swiveling around to face the door.

It slid aside, revealing Commander Chakotay. He smiled, though not with a great deal of enthusiasm. "Captain Janeway told me about your problem," he said. "Or, more to the point, Pacria's problem."

The Ocampa glanced at her monitor, which was filled with information about the Zendak'aa. "I've been trying to follow the captain's advice and find out more about the Zendak'aa. But I haven't gotten anywhere. At least, not yet." She sighed. "Would you care for a seat?"

Chakotay shook his head. "Thank you, no. I've got to get back to the bridge." He folded his arms across his chest. "Unfortunately, I don't have any special insight to share with you when it comes to the Zendak'aa. But I do have some advice."

Kes leaned forward in her chair. "I'm listening," she told him, so attentive she was almost childlike.

"When I was a teenager," he said, "my father took me on several hunting trips. At his insistence, we often hunted with bows, as in the old days on Earth. Remarkably enough, we were pretty successful.

"One time, we took my friend along on the hunt. This friend was a good shot, but not very patient. The first animal he saw was big and strong and my friend became overeager. He shot without aiming properly—without looking around to make sure it was safe."

Chakotay grimaced a little. "The shaft hit my father in the arm. I rushed to his side, intending to pluck it out—but he shooed me away. Then my uncle came over. Apparently, he'd had some experience with such things. Instead of pulling the arrow out, he pushed it in even deeper. So deeply, in fact, that it came out the other end."

By then, Kes was grimacing, too. "It must have hurt a great deal," she said. "Your father was a brave man."

Chakotay smiled, remembering. "He was very brave. And wise, too. Wise enough to know that you've often got to make something hurt more before you can make it hurt less."

The Ocampa's eyes narrowed. "You're speaking of Pacria's problem?"

"Yes," he said. "I don't know what it is you can tell her that'll make her change her mind. But I know *you,* Kes. I know how compassionate you are. How *kind* you can be. And I hope you won't let that kindness stand in the way of what you're trying to accomplish."

Kes considered what he'd told her. After a while, she nodded. "I understand. At least, I think I do."

"Good," said Chakotay. "Then I'll be going. But keep me posted, all right? And let me know if there's anything I can do."

The Ocampa assured him that she would do that.

B'Elanna gritted her teeth and strained against the weight of the metal container.

The thing was heavy enough by itself, but full of ore it was even heavier. She'd never seen one of them dragged by fewer than two workers, and sometimes it took three.

Still, she did the best she could. And slowly but certainly, she made progress. After a lot of groaning and struggling, she reached the opening that led into the corridors beyond.

On her way out, she imagined that Kim was still watching her—still worried about what she was walking into. But he'd decided to trust her when her eyes said she knew what she was doing.

And did she? B'Elanna asked herself. She sorely hoped so.

Once out in the corridor, she looked to the guard again. After all, she had never participated in the storing of the ore; she didn't know where the stuff was supposed to go.

The Nograkh pointed to her right with the emitter end of his weapon. "That way," he told her.

Once again pitting her strength against the weight of the container, she wrestled it down the corridor, its metal bottom scraping against the pocked metal deck. The guard followed her at a distance, his silver grey eyes crinkling at the corners. He seemed amused by her struggles.

That made the lieutenant angry, but she was careful not to show it. Subduing her Klingon sense of pride, she drew only on her Klingon strength. Little by little, sweat streaming down her neck until it soaked what was left of her uniform, she pulled the container along.

They passed a storage chamber, full of other containers like the one B'Elanna was dragging. But the guard signaled for her to keep going.

After what seemed like a long time, she reached

another room—another storage chamber, but smaller than the first one. And this one had a door, which slid aside at B'Elanna's approach.

Peering inside, she could see a couple of other containers full of ore. Outside of that, the place was empty.

"Inside," the guard snapped.

Light-headed from her exposure to the ore, hands chafed raw, arms cramping, B'Elanna wrestled the container into the chamber. The guard followed her in. And a moment later, the door slid closed behind him.

The Nograkh grinned savagely, his teeth gleaming in the uneven light. The lieutenant just looked at him, her chest heaving violently as she tried to catch her breath.

"The life of a slave," he growled, "is a hard one. Sometimes a deadly one. I can make it easier for you. Safer . . . if you let me."

It was just as Kim had warned her, B'Elanna told herself. It wasn't just work the guard wanted from her. It was something a lot more intimate.

And if she didn't give it to him, he would no doubt attempt to take it from her by force. After all, no one was likely to hear her calls for help in this secluded storage chamber. And even if they did, who was going to come to her rescue? One of the other guards?

"Well?" the Nograkh prodded.

B'Elanna wished she hadn't spent so much of her strength dragging the container. She wished she could lift her arms without pain, or slow the beating of her thunderous heart. But wishes weren't going to help her.

Biting her lip, she nodded. "Go ahead. Do what you want with me."

The very words were like gall in her mouth. But when one was fighting for one's life, one did what was necessary.

His grin widening, the guard propped his rifle against the wall and advanced on her. Big and powerful-looking, even for a Nograkh, he was easily a head taller than the lieutenant and twice her weight. And he hadn't been lugging around a container full of ore.

But then, strength wasn't everything. Had he been a Klingon, he would have known that.

Clenching her teeth against the acrid odor of his sweat, B'Elanna stood her ground as the guard reached out and grasped a lock of her hair. With a tug, he drew her to him, bringing her face within a couple of inches of his own. His breath stank even worse.

"Now," he grunted, "show me I've chosen well."

"Whatever you say," she breathed promisingly.

Bringing her knee up into the Nograkh's groin as hard as she could, she elicited a cry of pain and doubled him over. Then she interlocked her fingers and clubbed him over the back of his neck, drawing on the strength she'd inherited from her mother.

The guard fell to one knee, but didn't lose consciousness. It took two more blows, each louder and more vicious than the one before it, to knock the behemoth out entirely.

Without a moment's hesitation, B'Elanna scooped

up the rifle he'd leaned against the bulkhead and peeked out the door. No one there. Lucky for them, she thought, and made her way out into the corridor.

She didn't really have a plan in mind. She just knew that this was a chance—maybe the only one she'd get. And she'd be damned if she wasn't going to take advantage of it.

It didn't take long to get back to the main chamber. No surprise there, she thought. It was a lot easier to run without a container full of ore dragging behind her.

It was only when she came in sight of the guards at the door that she slowed down. And even then, it was only long enough to take aim and fire her stolen rifle.

The first guard never knew what hit him. But when he went flying across the floor, it warned the second guard that something was amiss. He whirled, mouth agape with anger and surprise.

Not that it mattered. Another bolt of blue energy and he was laid out as well. Two down, she told herself, and one to go. And the best way to meet that last obstacle was the same way she'd met the first two—head-on.

Otherwise, she would let herself in for all kinds of problems. After all, the chamber was full of prisoners. It would be too easy for their Nograkh captors to use them as shields.

Without breaking stride she raced past the entrance, rifle at the ready. She could see the prisoners turning their heads as she appeared, stunned by the sudden turn of events. But no guard—at least not yet.

Then, suddenly, there he was. But he was prepared,

tracking her with his weapon even as she took aim at him. They fired at the same time.

One of them cried out and was flung backwards, knocked unconscious by the force of a direct hit. Fortunately for B'Elanna, it wasn't her.

Of course, there was still a need for caution. Just because there'd been three guards there when she left didn't mean there'd be three now. But as she poked her head in past the threshold and took a quick look around, she couldn't see any other watchdogs.

She knew that could change—and quickly. Though there weren't any surveillance devices she could see, that didn't mean the Nograkh didn't have a way of detecting an uprising. Come to think of it, she mused, wasn't there a changing of the guards in the middle of the night?

Spurred on by the fear of getting caught, she darted into the chamber and found Kim. He looked just as amazed as any of the other prisoners, though he'd known what she was up to when the guard took her away.

He smiled at her with undisguised admiration. "Good going, Maquis."

B'Elanna looked around for Tolga—and found him. For a moment, their eyes met, and she imagined she'd gained some new respect in those silver orbs as well.

Then she turned back to Kim. "Let's go, Starfleet."

Together, they headed for the exit. As they ran past one of the fallen guards, the ensign helped himself to the Nograkh's rifle. Now both B'Elanna and her fellow officer were armed.

Nor were they the only ones. Tolga and the rest of the prisoners were right behind them, scooping up the remaining blasters.

Kim checked his weapon. "The odds are getting a little better, Maquis."

"Looks that way," she breathed.

But B'Elanna's optimism was tempered with a healthy respect for what they were up against. They still had a number of guards to get past—no one knew how many. And they also didn't know what internal safeguards might be used against them.

Motioning for the others to stop short of the doorway, she gritted her teeth and placed her back against the bulkhead. Then she stuck her head past it, to see if there was any sign of reinforcements.

It was almost her last act among the living. No sooner had she shown herself than the corridor was illuminated with blue energy beams. Cursing out loud, she pulled her head back.

"They're onto us," she told Kim.

"I figured that out," he replied.

"We'll rush them," said one of the Nograkh. He pounded his massive fist against the bulkhead. "They can't take down all of us."

"Yes, they can," B'Elanna barked, silencing the prisoner for the moment. "If we leave the chamber, we're as good as dead."

She could feel her anger getting the better of her as she sensed her opportunity slipping away. It was the Klingon in her, muddling her judgment, urging her to face her enemies head-on.

But she wasn't going to do that. She was going to

think this through. There had to be a way out of here short of suicide.

"Wait!" snarled Tolga. "What about the ceiling?"

B'Elanna followed his gesture. The surface above them was made of individual plates, held in place by a suspended framework. If they could knock out one of the plates, they might find a crawl space beyond it. At any rate, she thought, it was worth a try.

Two of the Nograkh ran to the door, armed with rifles. They were going to give the lieutenant the time she needed to check out Tolga's suspicion.

Training her weapon on the ceiling, she blasted out a couple of the plates. Then she signaled for Tolga and one of the other Nograkh to hoist her up—which they were only too glad to do.

B'Elanna looked around. There was a crawl space, all right. And it showed her an opening that seemed to lead beyond the boundaries of their prison. She beckoned for the others to follow.

Kim came next, followed by a couple of the smaller prisoners. Lacking the luxury of waiting until everyone took to the ceiling, the lieutenant made her way toward the opening on hands and knees.

It didn't take long. Not with adrenaline pumping through her body like high-energy plasma. Not with the smell of freedom in her nostrils.

The opening turned out to be an abbreviated power conduit—though there was no evidence of the power that once ran through it. What's more, it wasn't as dark as it should have been. There was a dim, grey light up ahead.

Lucky me, thought B'Elanna. She crawled inside it.

"Harry?" she rasped, wanting to make sure he was still with her.

"Right behind you," he assured her softly, his voice nonetheless echoing in the narrow confines of the conduit.

At its far end, the conduit terminated as abruptly as it had begun—emptying into another crawl space. B'Elanna didn't know what kind of room was below it, but she didn't have time to think about it. All she could do was blast out a ceiling plate and find out.

As she approached the egress she had created, she exhaled softly. They were over one of the storage chambers for the separated ore. Giving Kim her rifle, she took hold of the metal frame that had supported the plate, swung down, and landed on the floor.

Then she looked up. One at a time, the ensign dropped their rifles to her. Then he came down after them.

Returning Kim's weapon to him, the lieutenant crossed to the door, which was wide open. Looking back, she saw several other prisoners drop down from the ceiling as well.

She didn't stop to count how many. That would depend on the Nograkh who'd volunteered to guard their retreat. Her job was to keep forging ahead.

Taking a breath, B'Elanna came closer to the door—and darted a glance out into the corridor. There weren't any guards apparent in either direction. At least, not yet.

Emerging from the storage room, she made a quick decision. A left would take them back to the air lock through which they'd entered the station—but it would also take them past the rest chamber. She opted to go right.

Heart pounding, she made her way down the corridor as quickly as she could. She didn't have any idea of what was ahead, of course. For all she knew, she was running into a dead end. But she went on in the hope she was getting closer to a way out.

That hope died as she heard the pounding of footsteps up ahead, where the corridor made a sharp turn to the right. Keeping her eyes forward, B'Elanna stopped and signaled for the others to retreat. It seemed they would have to go back past the rest chamber after all.

Then that option was taken away from them as well. Hearing a cry, then another, the lieutenant whirled and saw a flash of blue-white energy. Before her eyes, the prisoner she'd dubbed One-Eye toppled and crashed to the floor.

He wasn't stunned, either. Half his chest had been torn away by the force of the blast.

B'Elanna clenched her teeth at the sight, then turned again. The sound of footsteps was getting louder in back of her. Closer. Pinning herself against the right bulkhead, she raised her weapon and waited for the guards to show themselves.

They didn't disappoint her. They came out firing—and so did she. Except her beams bounced off an invisible shield—the kind the Nograkh had used in their takeover of the Kazon scoutship.

Great, the lieutenant thought. As if the odds hadn't been stacked against the prisoners to begin with. Clearly, they were in bad straits. Unless something went in their favor, and quickly, the escape attempt was doomed—and so were they.

As it happened, *nothing* went in their favor. Little by little, the guards whittled away at them from behind their transparent barriers. Prisoners fell all over the place, clogging up the corridor.

She didn't have time to take a head count, but she had the sense there were fewer than a dozen of them still standing. Then fewer than half a dozen. B'Elanna saw Tolga glance off a bulkhead, propelled there by a directed-energy barrage. Kim was knocked off his feet.

She did her best to blast away at the guards, but it was no use. They had the damned shields. They just grinned at her.

It couldn't end this way, she told herself. Not after all she'd been through. Not when they had come so close.

Then they cut *her* down as well.

CHAPTER 13

TUVOK WAS STUDYING HIS CONTROL CONSOLE WHEN MR. DuChamps approached him. "Sir," said the junior officer, "I've got a problem."

The Vulcan nodded. "I am aware of it, Lieutenant. I have been attending to the same matter myself, after all. And if I am not mistaken, we have come to the same conclusion."

DuChamps glanced in the direction of Janeway's ready room. "I guess I should tell the captain." He seemed unenthusiastic about the prospect. Nor was it difficult to understand why.

"It is all right," Tuvok told him, letting him off the proverbial hook. "I will inform Captain Janeway myself."

The human nodded. "Whatever you say, sir."

Looking grim, he returned to the station customarily occupied by Ensign Kim.

Tuvok sighed. There was no point in delaying the matter. Without another word, he rose from his seat and went to see the captain.

B'Elanna was surprised to find herself still alive. She had a nasty bruise over one eye and a soreness she attributed to incipient radiation fever, but she was still in one piece.

Quickly, she looked around. Kim was lying a few meters away, grimacing—but clearly, he had survived as well. Apparently, not all the guards they'd faced in the corridor had had their weapons set to kill.

It made sense, now that she thought about it. The Nograkh had gone to so much trouble to acquire their prisoners, why mow them all down out of spite? Why not preserve them so they could give the last of their strength to the ore-processing center?

The lieutenant heard something down the hall. The approach of footsteps—a great many of them. She crawled across the floor, grabbed Kim's arm, and roused him. His eyes blinked open.

"What's going on?" he groaned.

"I don't know," she told him. But in the back of her mind, she wondered if it had something to do with the escape attempt.

The footfalls got closer and closer. Other prisoners started to lift their heads as well, no doubt hearing the same thing. They exchanged looks but didn't say anything.

Abruptly, a squad of guards entered, walking past

the pair at the threshold. At the same time, the lights came up, so brightly it made B'Elanna wince and shade her eyes. Beside her, Kim did the same.

"Up," said one of the guards. He pointed to a bulkhead with the barrel of his energy rifle. "Over there."

The lieutenant's mouth went dry. Getting to her feet, she complied with the guard's instructions. Kim moved along beside her as the prisoners formed a line against the wall.

Yes, she thought. This was *definitely* about the escape attempt. But that was all she knew, though she wished she knew more.

When the last of the prisoners was in place, the guards turned to the door. As B'Elanna watched, someone entered the room.

It was a Nograkh she hadn't seen before. Though he looked much like the others, big and ruddy and heavy-browed in his dark bodyarmor, there was an unmistakable air of authority about him.

Clearly, he was higher up in the station heirarchy than the guards were. Perhaps he was in command of the entire facility. In any case, he didn't allow the lieutenant much time to speculate.

"My name is Ordagher. I am the Overseer of this station. As such, I hold your lives in the palm of my hand."

He paused, eyeing each of the prisoners in turn. When he came to B'Elanna, he seemed to linger for a moment—but only for a moment. Then he went on.

"There was an escape attempt," Ordagher continued. "Like all escape attempts, it was a failure. Still, I cannot permit such things. They are wasteful, and waste is to be avoided at all costs." The Overseer's wide mouth twisted savagely. "I want to know who led the attempt, and I want to know it without delay."

B'Elanna's heart began to beat harder in her chest. This was it, she told herself. She shifted her eyes from one side to the other, curious as to who would finally give her away.

But no one did. In the wake of the "commander's" demand, there was silence. That is, except for the throb of heavy machinery that seemed to pervade the place at all times.

Ordagher's eyes narrowed under his overhanging brow. "I am not a patient man," he growled. "Again, I ask—who led this attempt?"

As before, his question was met with silence. B'Elanna swallowed. How could this be? She wasn't surprised that Kim would stand up for her—or maybe even Tolga, with whom she had established some kind of bond.

But the other prisoners? They didn't owe her a thing.

Nonetheless, they didn't point B'Elanna out. They didn't move at all. They just looked straight ahead in defiance of the Overseer, ignoring their instincts for survival.

What's more, Ordagher didn't get as angry as the lieutenant expected. He didn't even seem entirely surprised. But then, he was a Nograkh as well.

"You choose to be stubborn," observed the Overseer. He clasped his hands behind his back. "Very well. I know how to deal with stubbornness." He turned to one of the guards who stood behind him.

There was no order. Apparently, none was necessary. Without comment, the guard advanced to within a meter of one of the prisoners. A fellow Nograkh, as luck would have it.

Raising his energy weapon, the guard placed its business end under the prisoner's chin. Then he pushed it up a little, forcing the Nograkh's head back in response. For his part, the prisoner said nothing—did nothing. He just stood there, eyes fixed on oblivion.

Ordagher eyed the others. "Once more, and for the last time, I ask you who led the escape attempt. If I do not receive an answer, your fellow prisoner will die in the ringleader's place."

None of the Nograkh said a word. They seemed content to let their comrade perish for them. Maybe that was their way—but it wasn't B'Elanna's.

"Me," she said, loudly and clearly.

The Overseer turned to her. "You?" he replied, his brow furrowing. Obviously, there was some doubt in his mind.

"Me," the lieutenant confirmed. "I was the one who led the escape attempt." She searched inwardly for a way to back up her claim—and decided some facts might help. "One of your guards tried to rape me, and I grabbed his weapon. The rest just happened."

Ordagher shook his head. "No," he concluded.

"I swear it," she told him. She took a deep breath.

"If you're going to kill someone, it should be me. No one else."

She could feel the eyes of her fellow prisoners on her. Tolga's, Kim's. And those of the guards as well. The prisoner whose chin rested on the guard's energy weapon was probably eyeing her, too.

The Overseer considered her a moment longer. Then he tossed his head back and began to laugh. It was a hideous sound, like the sucking of a great wound. Without looking, Ordagher pointed to the prisoner whose life hung in the balance.

"Kill him," he snarled.

Before B'Elanna could do anything, before she could even draw a breath, the energy weapon went off. There was a flare of blue-white light under the prisoner's chin, and a sickening snap.

Then his eyes rolled back and he fell to the floor, lifeless.

B'Elanna's hand went to her mouth. The suddenness of it, the horror and the injustice—it threatened to overwhelm her. She could feel tears taking shape in the corners of her eyes.

The Nograkh had accepted his fate impassively, unflinchingly. He hadn't said so much as a word in his defense. And all for a being he barely knew.

"Take him away," said Ordagher, with a gesture of dismissal. "And watch the rest twice as closely," he told the guards, "or the next neck that snaps will be your own." Then, glaring one last time at the other prisoners, he turned his back on them and left the chamber.

The guards took their spots at the exit. The lights

dimmed. One by one, the prisoners drifted to their customary sleeping spots.

But not B'Elanna. She remained where she was, trying to get a handle on what had just happened. Trying to understand what she was supposed to do about it—what she was supposed to think.

The lieutenant felt someone's touch on her shoulder. Numbly, she turned to Kim. He looked white as candlewax.

"Are you all right?" he asked her.

She shook her head from side to side. How could she be all right? How could she just accept what had happened and go on?

Caught in the grip of unexpected anger, she looked for Tolga. Found him at the other end of the chamber, where he always took his rest. And stalked him like an animal seeking its prey.

As she approached, his back was to her. Still, the closer she got, the more he seemed to notice. Finally, he glanced at her over his powerful shoulder, his silver eyes glittering in the light from the doorway.

"You," she said, her lips pulling back from her teeth like a she-wolf's, her voice little more than a growl.

Then she made a fist of her right hand and hit him as hard as she could. Tolga's head snapped around and he staggered back a step.

She tried to hit him with her left, but the Nograkh managed to grab her wrist before she could connect. And a moment later, his hand closed on her right wrist as well. Finally, he kicked her legs out from under her and pinned her with his considerable weight.

Left with no other weapon, B'Elanna spat at him. "You could have saved him," she rasped. "You could have said something, but you just stood there and let him die for me!"

Narrow-eyed, Tolga took in the sight of her. "Should I have interfered with Manoc's sacrifice?" he asked. "Am I a barbarian, that I should have stained his honor?"

"It was me who should have died," she railed, hardly bothering to struggle. "Me! I led the escape!"

The Nograkh nodded slowly. "Yes. When circumstances allowed, you did what was in you to do. And Manoc did what was in him."

B'Elanna shook her head. "It should have been me," she moaned. "It should have been me."

Tolga didn't say anything. He just watched her expend her outrage and her sorrow. Then he got off her and let her get to her feet.

Kim had been standing nearby, ready to try to intervene if it became necessary. But it never reached that point. At no time had the Nograkh seemed willing to hurt her, even in his own defense.

Massaging her wrists, the lieutenant looked up at Tolga. "Why didn't they believe me?" she asked softly. "Why did they laugh like that?"

The Nograkh shrugged. "Ordagher didn't believe a female could lead a rebellion." He paused. "But then, he does not know you as I do."

B'Elanna nodded. Before this was over, she vowed, she would show the Overseer just how frail she really was.

* * *

Janeway was sitting behind the desk in her ready room, still poring over the debris field data, when a chiming sound told her there was someone waiting outside her door.

"Come in," she said, leaning back in her chair.

A moment later, Tuvok entered with a data padd in hand. His expression didn't give anything away, but the captain had known the Vulcan a long time. She knew when he was about to give her bad news.

"What is it?" she asked softly.

Tuvok frowned ever so slightly. "I regret to report that the ion trail has dissipated beyond our ability to recognize it. We can no longer follow it with any assurance."

Janeway bit her lip. "Can't we extrapolate a course based on the information we've accumulated so far?"

The Vulcan took his time answering. "That is not a promising strategy," he said finally. "There are any number of reasons why a vessel might diverge from its long-range course as it draws closer to its destination."

"I agree," the captain said, "it may not be promising. But unfortunately, Mr. Tuvok, it's the only strategy we've got." She leaned forward. "I would like you to create a computer model based on available data and come up with a likely course."

The Vulcan's nostrils fluttered, but he nodded. "As you wish," he replied. And without further comment, he left to fulfill that wish.

For a while, after the door closed behind Tuvok, Janeway sat and weighed the exigencies of their situation. It was something the captain had done a dozen times already since B'Elanna and Kim had disappeared.

Sighing, the captain looked to the intercom grid in the ceiling and summoned her exec.

"Commander Chakotay."

"Here," he replied.

"I would like to speak with you in my ready room," she told him.

"On my way," he said.

After all, Torres was one of the Maquis he'd commanded long before he'd even laid eyes on *Voyager*. Even if he weren't the first officer, he would have deserved to know what was going on.

CHAPTER 14

ALLOWING THE GRAY METAL DOORS TO SLIDE OPEN IN front of her, Pacria stopped and surveyed the place her hosts called sick bay. It seemed smaller and brighter than she remembered, even though it had been only a couple of days since she left.

The Doctor was waiting patiently for her inside. "Won't you come in?" he asked cordially.

Pacria entered. She looked around and saw that they were alone. Kes, then, was elsewhere. She found herself sorry to discover that. Despite the Ocampa's intrusiveness, Pacria had enjoyed her company.

"If you'll lie down on the bed," said the Doctor, "this will only take a few seconds. I just need to check your biolevels, perhaps take a few more esoteric readings. Of course, I can tell just from looking that you're not experiencing any setbacks with respect to tissue regeneration." His expression became a more sober one. "It's really just the virus I'm concerned about at this point."

When the Doctor had contacted her regarding this checkup, Pacria hadn't really seen the sense in it. After all, she was dying. That fact wasn't going to change, regardless of what shape her vital signs were in.

Then the scientist in her had chimed in, reminding her that knowledge had a value all its own. It was possible the Doctor's inquiries might help him refine the antigen, or at least gain a better understanding of what he was up against. And someday, that might save the life of someone less particular than Pacria about the origins of her cure.

In Pacria's estimate, that would be a good thing. She was all for saving lives. She just couldn't bear the thought of buying back her own with the coin of misery and degradation.

As the Doctor had requested, she lay down on the bed. He used a handheld device to examine her. And as he had indicated, it took only a few seconds. Then he looked up from the device.

"Thank you," he told her. "You may sit up now."

Again, Pacria complied. "I take it there are no surprises?"

"Only a small one," he told her. "It seems your exposure to so much radiation has slowed the virus down—if only marginally. Another such exposure might slow it down even more."

"How much?" she asked.

The doctor shrugged. "A couple of days, perhaps. Unfortunately, it would take almost that long to recover from the exposure."

"So nothing would be gained," Pacria concluded.

He regarded her. "Extremely little. I only wanted you to be aware of the full range of options."

Was that a note of sarcasm in his voice? Or a note of regret, because he hadn't found a way to heal her that she could accept? Either way, she decided to ignore it.

"I'm grateful," she told him.

"Think nothing of it," the Doctor replied. "Incidentally, I have something for you."

Returning to his office for a moment, he took something off his desk. Then he brought it out to her.

"I didn't know if it had any value, sentimental or otherwise," the Doctor explained. "And you weren't awake for me to ask, so I took the liberty of having it cleaned in one of our laboratories. It was coated with a considerable amount of radioactive debris, you understand."

Pacria took the object from him—and smiled. It was a flat, oblong brooch made of platinum. The raised symbol on its face was meant to represent two birds ascending in harmonious spirals.

"My badge," she said. She turned it over in her hand. "I received it less than a year ago."

Eight months later, Pacria realized she had contracted the virus. At the time, she had wondered how her crewmates would take the news of her impending death. She hadn't expected to outlive them, even in her wildest dreams.

Running her finger over the birds rendered on the badge, she made a decision—and gave it back to the Doctor. "Here," she said. "I want you to have it. For saving my life."

He looked at her askance. "I would like to say how much I appreciate the gift. However, as I've informed you, I am simply a holographic program. I have no need of possessions."

"Nor do I," Pacria reminded him. "I'll be dead soon. But your program will still exist."

The Doctor frowned and accepted the badge. "Very well, then," he said. "I will keep it . . ." He paused. "On my desk?"

She nodded her approval. "An excellent choice. That way, you won't have cleaned it for n—" Pacria stopped in midsentence, her mind churning. "Gods," she muttered. "How could I have been so stupid?"

The Doctor regarded her. "Stupid? About what?"

"I've got to get back to my quarters," she told him hurriedly, and bolted for the exit.

The doors slid aside just in time. She ran for the nearest turbolift as fast as she could, her breath coming in gasps from excitement as much as from exertion.

The captain, she thought. I've got to tell the captain.

No, another part of her—the scientist—insisted. First, she had to confirm her suspicions. *Then* she would contact the captain.

* * *

Paris was pushing some of Neelix's latest concoction around his plate when he saw Chakotay walk into the mess hall. The first officer looked as if he had lost his best friend.

Paris sighed. He knew the feeling.

As he watched, Chakotay picked up a tray and some utensils and walked past Neelix's serving area. Receiving a few hearty dollops of the same thing Paris was eating—or not eating—he proceeded to an unoccupied table.

To be alone with his thoughts? Paris wondered. Or because he didn't feel he'd be very good company right now?

The helmsman drummed his fingers on his tray as he considered joining the first officer. The risk, of course, was that he'd intrude on some private thought, some personal meditation.

But wasn't that what a person's quarters were for? If Chakotay had wanted privacy, he could've stayed in his room.

Casting discretion to the winds, Paris picked up his tray and made his way toward the first officer. What the hell, he mused, the worst he can do is convene a court-martial.

Once, the helmsman and Chakotay had been like two fighting fish in a glass bowl—ready to tear each other apart at the drop of a snide comment. It was a hostility that had its roots in their razor-edged days with the Maquis.

After all, Chakotay had left Starfleet and joined the rebel group on principle, to defend his home colony from the Cardassians. Paris, on the other hand, had screwed up as a cadet and never even made it into Starfleet.

Wandering from place to place, taking whatever jobs offered themselves, he'd steadily lost his self-esteem. He'd descended so low, in fact, he would have worked for anyone who could pay his bar tab.

In Chakotay's eyes, that made the younger man the worst kind of mercenary—someone entirely without ethics or attachments. And of course, that was no more than the truth.

Then, on the Caretaker's planet, Paris had risked his life to save Chakotay's. Though the older man had never actually acknowledged the debt, it was there nonetheless.

Perhaps because of that, their relationship had gradually become one of mutual respect—if not affection. And while Chakotay hadn't treated Paris any better than other crewmen, he also hadn't treated him any worse.

Then, one day, Janeway had called Paris into her ready room. Tuvok was standing there as well, looking even more solemn than usual. Apparently, the captain had said, there was a traitor on board. And Paris was going to go undercover to try to flush the bastard out.

The ploy was a simple one. He was going to be what everyone had believed him to be when he'd first signed on. A malcontent and a screw-up. Someone who couldn't be trusted to do his job. It had worked, too. And out of the entire crew, Chakotay had swallowed the bait the quickest.

Which was fine, at the time. It had made Paris's act that much more convincing. And in the end, they'd accomplished what they'd wanted—they'd identified the officer who was sending information to the Kazon.

For a while afterward, Chakotay was angry. After all, he hadn't been let in on the scam. It was as if the captain hadn't trusted him—though, of course, that wasn't her thinking at all. And the fact that she'd confided in Paris, of all people . . . well, that had to have hurt a little.

But to his credit, the first officer had gotten over it. Hell, he'd *more* than gotten over it. It seemed to Paris he'd found a new respect in Chakotay's eyes. In lieu of affection, it would have to do.

The helmsman stopped in front of the first officer. "Mind if I sit down?" he inquired.

Chakotay looked up suddenly, as if roused from a deep reverie. "No," he answered at last. "Of course not. Please, have a seat."

Paris sat. For a moment, neither of them said a thing. Then the helmsman broke the silence.

"So, what do you think?" he asked.

Chakotay looked at him. "About what?"

"About whether our friends are still alive."

The first officer shrugged. "I think they are."

"You don't sound very certain," Paris observed.

The other man frowned. "If you're trying to cheer me up, Lieutenant, you're not doing a very good job."

Paris smiled. "Sorry. It's hard to keep from being a

little bitter about it." He paused. "You know, I felt responsible for Harry from the moment I met him. He was such an easy mark."

One that may already have met his end, the helmsman thought. But he didn't say it out loud.

"Where did you meet B'Elanna?" he asked.

Chakotay's eyes lost their focus. "Kaladan Three, not long after the Federation withdrawal from the border worlds. A group of Maquis there had gotten their hands on a load of phaser rifles. My job was to pick them up and pass them along."

Paris pushed his food around some more. "Even though the Cardassians were thick as flies there at the time?"

"Even though," the other man agreed. "As you can imagine, everything had to go like clockwork. Our people on the planet were awaiting us. I sent out the signal, dropped our shields, and gave the order to beam the rifles aboard." He chuckled. "But the rifles weren't all we beamed up. There was a humanoid in the midst of them. One you'd recognize, in fact."

"B'Elanna?" the helmsman asked—although the answer was pretty obvious already.

"In the flesh," said Chakotay. "Apparently, she felt her talents were wasted on Kaladan Three. She had some Starfleet training, so the leader of the cel there let her go. Good thing, too. We had barely taken off when a Cardassian caught sight of us."

Paris looked at him. "B'Elanna helped?"

"Did she ever. We were smaller, more maneuverable, but we couldn't match the Cardassian's speed—or his firepower. It looked like we were goners. Then B'Elanna started reprogramming our transfer conduits—funneling everything into the weapons array for one, big barrage.

"To me, it looked like suicide. Our engines were barely capable of warp eight. How were we going to generate enough force to punch through the Cardassian's shields? B'Elanna insisted there was no time to explain. I would have to trust her, she told me.

"By rights, I should have dismissed her idea and focused on evasive maneuvers. But there was something in her eyes, in her voice, that convinced me to go along with her." He grinned at the memory. "Of course, she had an ace up her sleeve. While on Kaladan Three, she'd spent her time researching and identifying Cardassian shield frequencies."

"Researching . . . ?" the helmsman asked.

"From Maquis ships' logs—what there were of them. The information had been there since the rebellion began. It was just a question of digging it up and having the ability to make some calculations."

Paris leaned forward, enthralled by the story. "But how did she know which frequency to go with?"

"She didn't," said Chakotay. "She had to pick the most popular one and keep her fingers crossed. Fortunately for us, she picked right. Our barrage pierced the Cardassian's shields as if they were never there.

"Before they knew it, they'd sustained massive

damage to half a dozen systems. In the end, they were too busy trying to hold their ship together to worry much about us getting away."

The helmsman grunted. "A promising start."

Chakotay nodded. "Lucky, but promising. Unfortunately, the Cardassians eventually figured out we had their shield frequencies and changed them. But B'Elanna always seemed to stay a step ahead of them."

Again, there was silence. The first officer's lips compressed into a straight line. "I should have sniffed out the Kazons' trap in advance. I should have . . . I don't know, seen it coming somehow."

Paris looked at Chakotay disbelievingly. "You think you could have prevented this?"

The muscles worked in the other man's temples. "I'm the first officer. I'm responsible for what happens to my crew—good or bad."

The helmsman shook his head. "They're not children, Commander. You can't protect them from everything—not in space or anywhere else."

Chakotay turned to him, his dark eyes full of pain. "I understand what you're saying, Lieutenant. I understand it perfectly. But making myself believe it . . . that's another story entirely."

Yeah, thought Paris, *another story. And unfortunately for Harry and B'Elanna, it doesn't look like it's going to have a happy ending.*

Janeway had decided to go out onto the bridge when she heard her name called over the intercom system.

"Captain Janeway? This is Pacria."

"What is it?" the captain asked.

"I've got to speak with you," came the reply. "I may have found something in the debris data."

"I'm on my way," Janeway told her.

CHAPTER 15

A FEW MOMENTS LATER, THE DURANIUM PANEL SLID ASIDE and revealed Pacria sitting at her workstation, the graphics on her monitor reflected in her eyes.

"What is it?" the captain asked, moving to the Emmonac's side.

"This," Pacria replied, pointing to the screen.

Janeway looked over her guest's shoulder and saw an analysis of the debris field—one of the dozens she had studied so intently she'd almost committed them to memory. It showed a chemical breakdown of each fragment present.

Nothing jumped out at her. The captain looked at Pacria. "I don't see it."

Pacria tapped a control padd and magnified a particular piece of debris. It filled the whole screen. At first glance, it didn't seem any different from the other fragments. The same composition, the same thickness, and so on.

Then Janeway noticed a dusting of red dots. At least, they appeared red in the graphic. "Radioactive particles," she concluded.

The Emmonac nodded. "That's right."

The captain looked at her, still not seeing the significance of it. "But couldn't the destroyer's weapons have caused that?"

Pacria shook her head. "Only one race in this part of space has that kind of weaponry—and that's my own. And we don't go around annihilating enemy vessels the way this one was annihilated."

Janeway thought for a moment. "So the radioactive particles had to come from somewhere else."

"Yes," Pacria agreed. "And if we take an even closer look at them . . ." Again, she tapped a control padd on her board. And again, the magnification jumped significantly. ". . . we see that they're made up of a particular kind of radioactive material. Orillium, to be precise."

"I've never heard of it," the captain confessed.

"It's found in only one place that I know of," Pacria told her. "An asteroid belt mined by the Zendak'aa when they were in power—perhaps a dozen light years from the coordinates of the debris field."

"Let me get this straight," said Janeway. "You're suggesting the orillium came from a mining operation? But how did it get *here?* Why wasn't it scoured off when the ship entered warp?"

"Most of the vessels in this sector were either built by the Zendak'aa or incorporate Zendak'aan design principles—and Zendak'aan shields don't fit the lines of a ship the way *Voyager*'s do. There's a considerable pocket between the deflector surface and the hull. When the shields are lowered and then raised again, debris is often trapped in that pocket."

The captain nodded. "Then a vessel could have lowered its shields in the vicinity of a mining facility, raised them, lowered them again where we discovered the debris field—and left some radioactive dust behind."

"Precisely," said Pacria.

"But it wouldn't be the Kazon," Janeway decided. "They're nomads. They wouldn't get involved in that kind of mining."

"True," the Emmonac confirmed. "At least, from what I've heard of them. But there are other races who would be only too glad to take over a Zendak'aan mining facility. The Torren'cha, for instance. Or the Nograkh."

Something else occurred to the captain. "If this dust got there the way you think it did, it means the destroyers had to lower their shields. But why would they have done that?"

Pacria shrugged. Obviously, she hadn't thought the matter through that far. "To allow a reconnaissance vessel to leave the mother ship? Perhaps to loot the vessel it had just victimized?"

"Or to take prisoners," Janeway suggested hopefully.

The Emmonac considered the possibility. "It could be." She looked up at the captain. "Then your comrades may still be alive."

"Yes," Janeway replied, trying to keep a rein on her excitement. "Pacria, can you give me the location of that mining facility?"

"Not the *exact* location," the woman said. "However, I *can* point you in the general direction. Unfortunately, my people's knowledge of that area isn't extensive."

Then she studied the screen and came up with some approximate coordinates. And added, "I wish you luck, Captain."

Janeway wanted to get up to the bridge, to tell her officers what she'd learned. She wanted to get their course corrected as soon as possible. But she restrained herself for just a moment.

Just long enough to say, "Thank you."

Pacria smiled a faint smile. "You're welcome."

Haunted by the Emmonac's expression, hoping Kes would find a way to change the woman's mind, Janeway made her way to the nearest turbolift.

As the turbolift doors slid open, Chakotay glanced at them. It was Captain Janeway, he noted. And she was clearly excited.

"What is it?" he asked as he met her at her center seat.

"A breakthrough," she told him—and explained what she meant by that.

The first officer took it all in. Before long, he was excited, too.

Unfortunately, someone had to play devil's advocate here. Someone had to question Pacria's findings and Janeway's confidence, and it looked like he was elected.

"What if that's not the only asteroid belt in the sector?" he asked.

"It's the only one Pacria knew of," the captain replied. "And her expertise is in stellar cartography."

Chakotay frowned. "But who's to say the destroyer returned to the mining station? What would it be doing there, anyway?"

Janeway considered the possibilities. "Mining stations need laborers, especially when they deal with hazardous materials. That might have been the destroyer's job—to acquire workers for their mining operation."

"Or for half a dozen other uses," the first officer commented. "As soldiers, for instance. Or to supplement the ship's crew."

"Perhaps," the captain rejoined. "But we've established that the destroyer had a link to the asteroid belt. It seems likely it would return there. At least to me, it does."

Chakotay looked at her. Janeway couldn't give him any real assurances. All she could do was guess. But in the time they'd served together, he had come to value her opinions. Her judgment.

And vice versa, apparently.

"All right," he said at last. "I'm sold."

The captain turned to Paris. "We're making a course adjustment, Lieutenant." And she gave him the coordinates.

"Aye, Captain," came the helmsman's response.

Chakotay eyed the viewscreen with its flow of stars. He desperately wanted this course correction to do the trick. But he wouldn't do any rejoicing until they had found B'Elanna and Kim.

Her clothes ragged and torn, her skin burned and blistering, Kes stood in the midst of the bustling Kazon-Ogla camp and contemplated her surroundings. They were spartan, to say the least.

The sun above her was a searing, blinding ball of fire. And though she stood in the shade of a simple tent, it offered no protection from the heat reflected up at her from the ground.

While the camp was made up largely of such tents, they weren't the only structures around. The bone-white, partially buried ruins of ancient structures were scattered about as well, bitter reminders of their mortality. And to the east, there were a half-dozen Kazon scoutships.

But that was it. No sprawling public squares, no cool blue fountains. No soaring ceilings or graceful thoroughfares or thoughtful works of art. And certainly no smiling faces.

Not in this place. Not in the desert, where the terrain outside the camp stretched as far as the eye could see in every direction, unobstructed by hills or vegetation or other camps. Only scrub plants and tiny lizards and insects lived on that barren surface, though even they could hardly be said to thrive there.

The Kazon-Ogla didn't thrive either. They were devilishly low on water, and their cracked, parched lips bore testimony to the fact. The sect only lingered to mine the ground for rare minerals, which they could then trade to other Kazon sects.

Though they told her they were her masters, they weren't dressed much better than she was. Nor were they nearly as well fed.

Kes heaved a sigh. She recalled the curiosity, the spirit of adventure that had driven her from her home underground. She remembered, too, the ferocity of the Kazon men and women who had seized her almost as soon as she'd emerged from her tunnel—then kicked her and reviled her when they realized it had somehow sealed itself after her.

Living among them had been hellish. She had served as a bearing maid, dragging about loads too heavy for her slight frame. And when she failed to pull the loads quickly enough, she had been beaten for her laziness.

The Ocampa remembered her misery here. Her shame at being treated like an animal. Her despair of ever seeing her loved ones again.

It hadn't been easy for Kes to program this holodeck recreation. Or, for that matter, to step inside it. It was so real, so visceral, she could almost imagine that her stay on *Voyager* was the dream, the illusion, and this the stark reality.

She had to keep telling herself that she was no longer a slave of the Kazon. That Neelix and the crew of *Voyager* had rescued her from her captivity. That she was safe.

In a sense, it was good that she was scared. In fact, it had been her goal to scare herself—to remind herself of the most frightening situation and the cruelest people she had ever faced. And to heighten the experience, to make it seem even more authentic, she had lifted the holodeck's built-in safeguards against user injury.

That way, she had hoped, she could empathize with Pacria. She could gain some insight into the woman's abiding hatred for the Zendak'aa. And, as Chakotay had advised, she could perhaps find the hard thing that would ease Pacria's pain.

"Ocampa dog!" bellowed someone behind her.

Kes whirled just in time to put her arms up, to protect herself from the attack. But even then, the Kazon's fist struck her a glancing blow. She tasted blood and felt herself spinning.

Abruptly, the ground came up to meet her. It slammed the wind from her chest and jarred the teeth in her mouth. Knowing her attacker was standing over her, ready to strike again, she got her hands underneath her somehow and pushed, arms trembling. But before she could prop herself up, she was seized from behind and wrenched about.

Suddenly, she found herself looking into the face of Maj Jabin, unquestioned leader of the Kazon-Ogla. It was a face twisted with anger and resentment.

She should have expected this, the Ocampa told herself.

Jabin was part of the program she'd created. She'd wanted the recreation to be as painful as the memory that inspired it. And Jabin had been a big part of her pain.

"Don't you have anything better to do than lounge about?" the Kazon railed, a string of spit stretched across his mouth.

Then he struck her again, backhanded her across the mouth. Her knees buckled, but somehow she managed to keep her feet.

"Or do you think work is beneath you?" he rasped.

Grabbing her by the hair, he brought her face close to his. It hurt terribly. But she endured it.

Jabin's eyes were smoldering. "Maybe you'd rather put your feet up and watch the *Kazon* work instead?"

His lips pulled back and he struck her again. And again. And once more, until her mouth was swollen and bleeding and there was no strength left in her limbs. No strength even to plead for her life.

But the Maj didn't kill her. Why would he do that when he could take his frustrations out on her? When he could make himself feel better by making her feel worse?

No, he wouldn't kill her. But he could make her wish she were dead. Gracing her with a choice Kazon curse, he kicked some dirt on her, spat, and walked sullenly away.

Kes turned to look at him, her tears hot rivers of

shame on her sunburned cheeks. She remembered it all now. The Ocampa always taught their children not to hate, but she had come closer to hatred in that moment than ever before in her young life.

By what right had Jabin held her against her will? she demanded silently. By what right had he made a burden beast of her, assaulted her body and trampled her dignity?

She would have liked to get up and tell him what she thought of him. She would have liked to wipe the savage smile from his face.

But she didn't—and not just because it would have meant an even harder beating. She held her tongue because she didn't want him to know how badly he'd hurt her. She didn't want to give him the satisfaction of—

Kes stopped herself in mid-thought. There was something there, she told herself. The kernel of an idea.

The satisfaction, she repeated inwardly.

The *satisfaction.*

Slowly, painfully, Kes got to her feet. She looked up at the sky, where the sun beat down on her mercilessly. It was also where she imagined the main controller mechanism for the holodeck to be.

The Kazon-Ogla were all staring at her. Pointing at her. Cursing her and laughing at her. And Jabin, her greatest tormentor, was laughing harder than any of them.

"End program," she instructed, though the swelling in her mouth made it difficult to speak.

Immediately, the Kazon and their camp and the surrounding desert disappeared. Mercifully, a yellow-on-black grid took its place.

The Ocampa believed she knew a way to deal with Pacria. But first, she would have to visit sick bay and ask the Doctor for some help. In this condition, she wouldn't be of much use to anyone.

CHAPTER 16

JANEWAY WENT OVER TUVOK'S LATEST UPDATE ON THEIR progress. The news wasn't good, she reflected. Not good at all.

They had come within sensor range of the coordinates Pacria had guessed at, and there was no mining station to be detected. In fact, at this point, there appeared to be no man-made structures at all.

It seemed their hopes had been dashed yet *again.*

Given the finite nature of their supplies and the uncertainty of their mission, the commonsense approach was to abandon their search. To pull the plug, as it were . . . and live with the consequences.

And the captain was an avowed fan of the commonsense approach. She had demonstrated that over and over again to her crew.

"Janeway to Commander Chakotay," she said out loud.

"Chakotay here."

"I would like to see you, Commander. In my ready room."

Silence for a moment. "I'll be right there," he told her.

When the chimes sounded again, the captain gave him permission to enter. He looked like a man expecting the worst.

"Tuvok gave you his report," Chakotay noted.

"He did," she confirmed.

The muscles worked in the first officer's jaw. "We can't give up on them," he argued. "That's one thing we were clear about in the Maquis. No matter what, we didn't give up on anyone."

Janeway sighed and indicated the chair across her desk. "Please, Commander. Have a seat."

He sat. But it didn't diminish the determination in his posture or in his expression.

The captain swiveled her desk monitor around so Chakotay could see it. The first officer scanned the screen, saw the state of their food and water stores, then looked up.

"We're low on supplies," he said. "It doesn't change anything. At least, not for me. B'Elanna and Harry are still out there somewhere and we've got to find them."

"I don't wish to give up on our friends any more than you do," Janeway said quietly. "That's why I asked Lieutenant Tuvok to extrapolate a course when that ion trail petered out. It's also why, when he told me about the sensor scan, I didn't give the order to come about."

Chakotay's eyes narrowed. "But?"

The captain leaned forward. "I'm not giving up on them, Chakotay. You can set your mind at ease about that. I won't stop looking, supplies or no supplies."

He looked at her, surprised. Obviously, he'd expected to have a fight on his hands. "Then . . . why am I here?"

She leaned back in her seat again. "Two reasons. First, we have to impose a ration system if we're going to go on much longer. I don't think you'll get any argument from the crew on that count. There's not one of them who wouldn't rather go hungry if it means continuing the search."

"Acknowledged. And the other reason?"

Janeway frowned. "While we all hope B'Elanna and Harry are still alive, we've got to face the possibility that they're not. And both of them were important personnel on this ship."

Chakotay nodded. "In other words, we've got to plan for a transition. Just in case."

"Just in case," the captain echoed. "I'd like you to head down to engineering and lay the groundwork. So if it becomes necessary, the changeover will be as smooth as possible." She told him exactly what she wanted him to do. "I'd say we owe that much to the crew."

Her first officer smiled a little sadly. "Yes," he said, "I suppose we do." He got up. "If that's all?" he asked.

"That's all," she confirmed. "Dismissed."

The first officer started for the door, then stopped and looked back at her. "Thanks," he told her.

"For what?" Janeway asked. "They're my friends, too."

Chakotay stood there for a moment, speaking without words. Then he left the room.

Alone again, Janeway swiveled around to glance at her monitor. It didn't look any better than it had before. Common sense still dictated that they turn around and look for a Class M supply world.

And she was still a fan of the commonsense approach. But not this time. Not when two of her people were depending on her to find them.

Janeway and her crew had no one to depend on but each other. She wasn't about to forget that. And as she had told Chakotay, she wasn't going to call off the search while there was a ghost of a hope B'Elanna and Harry might still be alive.

Despite the difficulty of her shift, despite the considerable weight of her fatigue, B'Elanna couldn't sleep. Everything hurt, her throat most of all. Slowly but surely, the radiation was getting to her, drawing the strength out of her body.

She looked at Harry, who was dozing in and out of slumber just a few feet away from her. There were dark hollows under his eyes and his color was terrible. If she'd had access to a reflective surface, she was sure she wouldn't have looked any better.

Of course, they'd had their chance to escape this slow death, a better chance than any of them would have dreamed. But they had blown it sky-high. And they weren't likely to get another one.

The lieutenant saw someone stir on the other side of the rest chamber, where the Nograkh prisoners customarily congregated. It was Tolga. And he was headed her way.

She didn't say anything. She just watched him hunker down beside her, as if he had grown tired of his old sleeping place and was seeking a new one. His back was to the doorway, his eyes alive—though their sockets were beginning to look hollow.

"B'Elanna Torres," he whispered, "I need your help."

The lieutenant looked at him. "To do what?"

Tolga looked around, then whispered a little louder. "To escape this pit of a prison."

B'Elanna couldn't believe what she'd heard. Surely the Nograkh had uttered something else. "What did you say?" she asked.

He frowned and repeated himself. "To *escape.*"

The lieutenant looked at him as if he'd asked her to play dom-jot with the Kai of Bajor. That's how absurd the idea seemed to her.

"We tried that already," she reminded him. "As I recall, we didn't do so well."

"Last time," he said, "I didn't know what I know now."

B'Elanna sat up a little. "Which is?"

"That there's a secondary control location down the corridor."

"Secondary control," she murmured.

The lieutenant tried to recall seeing something of

that nature as she was charging headlong through the hallways. Unfortunately, nothing came to mind.

"I spotted it before the guards stopped us," Tolga went on. He spread his hands out almost as far as they would go. "It looked like a door, this big and gray, with a couple of studs set into it. The controls are behind it. From such a location, a single warrior can shut down every hand weapon on the station." He paused. "At least, I think he can."

B'Elanna grunted. "You're not sure?"

"Until now," he said, "my experience has been limited to battle cruisers, each of which has at least two secondary control units. But what I saw here looks like the same thing. I'm willing to bet it performs the same function."

The lieutenant thought for a moment. There was a similar centralized override on Federation starships, to keep hand phasers in the possession of the overzealous from poking holes in the hull.

But this wasn't a Federation ship. It wasn't a Nograkh battle cruiser either. If Tolga was wrong about that big, gray door . . .

"If we can reach it," he told her, his whisper becoming harsher as his voice charged with excitement, "we can disable the guards' weapons. And since there are more of us than there are of them—"

"We can overwhelm them," B'Elanna noted.

"Yes. And when the next mining ship arrives, we grab it—and get out of here. No one will know there's a problem on the station for hours—maybe even days, if we're lucky." He leaned closer to her. "The

Nograkh would follow *me,* but the others wouldn't. They have no love for my kind. But an outsider *like you* . . . one who has already earned their respect . . ."

She sighed. "I don't mind the idea of leading. But what if the gray door isn't what you think it is?"

Tolga shrugged. As he had pointed out, it was a gamble. And they would be wagering nothing less than their lives.

Of course, the alternative was to die by inches—and the lieutenant's confidence in the possibility of rescue was waning fast. She still believed *Voyager* would manage to track them down—but she was starting to doubt she'd be alive to see the ship arrive.

Tolga's mouth twisted. "I do not wish to rot in this place—to wither from radiation poisoning. This way, the worst that will happen is we will die fighting. For a warrior, that's not so bad . . . is it?"

B'Elanna considered the question. "No," she conceded. "It isn't."

"Then you'll lead us?" he asked.

"I'll lead you," she confirmed.

The Nograkh nodded his hairless head and moved away. That gave the lieutenant a chance to wake Kim and tell him what she had agreed to.

As Chakotay entered engineering, he looked around. Without a doubt, a change had taken place there.

It wasn't anything he could put his finger on. Certainly, everyone seemed to be going about his or her assignment with the same efficiency as before. A glance at a control console told the first officer that all systems were functioning within normal parameters.

And yet, he thought. *And yet.*

"Can I help you, sir?" said a voice.

Turning, Chakotay saw Lieutenant Carey approaching him. The redhead gave the unfortunate impression of a mother bird defending her young.

But then, in a way, Carey saw the engines as his babies and the engine room as his nest. That had been all too apparent in his brief stint as head of engineering, after the death of *Voyager*'s first chief engineer and before B'Elanna's assumption of the post.

"I need to speak with you," the first officer told him.

Chakotay ushered the man to an unpopulated corner of the engine room. Then he looked Carey in the eye and forged ahead.

"While we're continuing the search for Lieutenant Torres and Ensign Kim," he said, "we have to prepare for the possibility that we won't find them. In that event, Mr. Carey, the captain wants you to take over here as chief of engineering."

The man nodded. "I'd heard the search wasn't going well."

"That's true," Chakotay confirmed.

Carey looked down at his hands. "You know," he said, "there was a time when I might have taken this differently. Not that I ever wished anything terrible would happen to Lieutenant Torres—I wasn't *that* petty. But you'll recall we had our differences."

The first officer recalled it vividly. In one altercation, B'Elanna had even broken Carey's nose. In several places, apparently.

"At first," the engineer confessed, "I thought she was just a Maquis hothead, with no appreciation for protocols or regulations. But I found out otherwise." He looked up. "No offense, sir."

"None taken," Chakotay assured him.

Carey went on. "I've served under a good number of chief engineers, as you know from my service record. None of them was as bright or innovative . . . or as well loved as Lieutenant Torres."

The first officer swallowed. "Yes," he said. "I know. And I appreciate your saying so, Mr. Carey. But we have to carry on."

The redhead nodded. "Aye, Commander. You can depend on me."

Chakotay managed a smile. "That's what I was hoping you'd say. Keep up the good work, Lieutenant."

"I'll try," Carey said.

Taking his leave of the man, the first officer headed for the exit. He still held out the hope that his officers were still alive, and that Carey wouldn't have to take over engineering after all.

But that hope was a slim one. And, the spirit-guides help them, it was growing slimmer by the minute.

CHAPTER 17

JANEWAY WALKED OUT ONTO THE BRIDGE, NOT AT ALL looking forward to what she had to do. After all, she'd been so hopeful about Pacria's hunch. They'd *all* been hopeful.

But the course they'd been pursuing hadn't been a fruitful one. They'd expended time and effort—and more important, precious resources—and they hadn't found a thing.

They had to regroup, go back to their previous plan—the one based on Tuvok's data extrapolations. Janeway didn't feel good about it, but it seemed to be their only other option.

And she was in command of this vessel. If she didn't make the hard decisions, who would?

Reaching her captain's chair, she sat. Then she turned to her helmsman. "Mister Paris?"

He turned in his seat, obviously with an inkling of what was coming. "Aye, ma'am?"

"Lay in a change of course," Janeway ordered. "Bearing two-three-four-mark-two."

"Acknowledged," said Paris, containing what had to be considerable disappointment. He turned back to his controls and made the necessary adjustments. "Coming about," he announced, in a voice that was dutiful but devoid of animation.

"Captain," said Tuvok.

Janeway glanced at him, wondering what he wanted to say to her. Surely, he wasn't having second thoughts about his advice to her.

"What is it, Lieutenant?"

The Vulcan's features remained as passive as ever. However, there was a gleam in his eye that told her he was on to something.

"I have detected something on the long-range sensor grid," Tuvok explained. "I believe it is a station of some sort."

The captain took a few steps toward him, her heart leaping in her chest. "A station?" she repeated. *The* station?

"Yes," he confirmed. "And while there is nothing to indicate that our comrades may have been taken there, it does seem to be the only fabricated body in this sector."

Janeway nodded. "Can you give me a visual, Lieutenant?"

"I will try," he replied.

A moment later, the viewscreen filled with the image of an unmoving starfield. It was only by concentrating that the captain could make out a small, gray shape in the midst of it—a man-made facility surrounded by a thick swarm of asteroids.

Asteroids. *Mining,* she thought. It was looking better and better.

The station seemed whole and in working order. And with any luck, they would find Torres and Kim there—also whole and in working order. Janeway fervently hoped so.

"Captain," said Chakotay. "We've got to check it out."

"I agree," she told him. Her eyes narrowing with determination, she turned to her helm officer. "Mister Paris? Belay that last order and resume our previous course."

The helmsman smiled at her. "I would be happy to," he responded, his fingers dancing over his console with unbridled enthusiasm.

Beside the captain, Chakotay muttered something in his Native American dialect. Though all but unintelligible to her, it was unmistakably a declaration of hope.

Janeway smiled at him. "Best speed," she added.

After all, the station was still a long way ahead of them. And truth be told, she was every bit as eager as the others were to get there.

No. *More* so.

B'Elanna woke with someone's hand on her arm. Fortunately, she had the presence of mind not to voice her surprise or lash out—at least until she saw whose hand it was.

As it turned out, the hand was Kim's. And it took the lieutenant only a moment to gather her faculties and remember why he would be waking her. Getting up on one elbow, she looked around.

Most of the prisoners were awake. And those who weren't were being prodded by those who were. There was an air of expectation in the room, like a silent predator coiling for an attack.

The trio of guards standing outside the rest chamber didn't seem to realize there was anything afoot. That was good. If the guards had suspected, her ruse wouldn't have stood a chance.

B'Elanna eyed Tolga. He noticed her scrutiny and returned it. One way or the other, he seemed to be saying, they had worked their last shift in the station's ore-processing center. One way or another, they had seen the last of this place.

That was fine with her. But the lieutenant was determined it would be *her* way. In other words, *alive.*

"It's time," Kim whispered to her.

"High time," B'Elanna agreed.

She waited until everyone seemed alert. Then she looked to Ogis, one of the Nograkh. The warrior nodded, got up and made his way to where Ram's Horns was hunkered down. Ram's Horns did his best not to make it obvious he knew what was coming.

The Nograkh mumbled something, then gave Ram's Horns a shove with the heel of his boot. Grabbing Ogis's foot, Ram's Horns toppled the Nograkh. Then Ram's Horns pounced on him.

That drew the guards' attention. They looked at each other and smiled. True to form, they came inside the rest chamber but remained aloof and apart from the fight, more entertained than concerned.

If all went as planned, thought the lieutenant, that would prove to be a mistake. A *big* mistake.

Meanwhile, Ram's Horns and the Nograkh were going at it as if they really meant it. And by then, maybe they did. Despite their dedication to a common goal, their instincts had to be crying out for them to defend themselves.

That was also fine with B'Elanna. It would only make their performances more convincing.

Finally, the guards had seen enough. While one waited by the threshold, the other two moved to break up the fight. There was a moment when B'Elanna and Kim and the other prisoners seemed to hold their collective breath. Then they boiled over into quick and brutal action.

Tolga moved first, delivering a kick to the arm of the nearest guard. As the Nograkh dropped his weapon, another prisoner grabbed it and a third tackled him at the knees.

The second guard spun around, bringing his weapon up. But someone latched onto its barrel and forced it toward the ceiling. And before he could get off a blast, he was swarming with prisoners eager to repay him for his kindnesses.

The only problem was the guard at the door. B'Elanna saw him hesitate, uncertain of whether to intervene or go for help. In the end, he decided to intervene.

Raising his energy rifle, he barked out a warning. It had no effect on the prisoners, who were still contending with the other guards. Snarling, the guard at the door got off a shot.

It hit one of the Nograkh prisoners in the back. Crying out a curse, he spun and hit the floor, a seething black hole where the energy beam had speared him. The guard fired again and laid waste to another prisoner.

By then, B'Elanna had crossed the room and was gathering momentum. The guard must have noticed her, because he whirled in her direction. But it was too late.

Hurtling across the space between them, the lieutenant reached for the Nograkh's throat. Her fingers closed on it and squeezed, cutting off his air supply. Hanging onto his weapon with one hand, he tried to tear her arms away with the other—but she held on.

Then someone else grabbed the guard from behind, and a third person ripped his weapon out of his hand, and he went down under a mountain of angry prisoners. What's more, B'Elanna couldn't find it in her heart to feel sorry for him.

Their captors had laid down the ground rules. She and the other ore-slaves were just playing by them.

Kim joined her. "Are you all right?" he asked.

"Never better," the lieutenant lied.

Tolga tossed her a weapon he'd stripped from a guard. "This way," she cried, raising the weapon like a banner.

Advancing to the entrance, B'Elanna peeked out into the corridor to make sure there weren't any guards lying in ambush. Seeing that the corridor was empty, she beckoned for the others to follow.

Then she bolted from the rest chamber in the direction of the secondary control center, with Kim and the others right behind her.

For a long time Janeway had remained in her captain's seat, regarding the image of the station up ahead of them. Gradually, almost imperceptibly, the facility and its accompanying asteroid field had loomed larger and larger, until they had nearly filled the screen.

Now they were only minutes away from their objective, and Janeway could feel butterflies in her stomach. It was one thing to search for days on end. It was quite another to face the moment of truth that would tell them if all their efforts had been in vain.

Nor was the captain the only one who had found the station of unavoidable interest. Chakotay had been intent on it as well. Tuvok, too. And Paris, who had found a family on this ship and must have hated the idea of leaving some of it behind.

Sighting the station had given them a second chance, Janeway reflected. A chance to buck the odds and bring their friends home. And it wouldn't have been possible without Pacria, who had herself been given a second chance when *Voyager* found her on her doomed research vessel.

Kindness for kindness. Measure for measure.

If the scales of Justice were in working order in the Delta Quadrant, they would find their friends Torres and Kim alive and unharmed. And the two of them would have a chance to meet the stranger who'd made the key contribution to their rescue.

The captain didn't know whether Kes would be successful in her attempts to preserve Pacria's life. She didn't know what Kes would try or how the Emmonac would react. But she hoped with all her heart that Pacria would be rewarded for all her hard work.

In whatever way she valued the most.

Janeway had barely completed her thought when she saw something new on the viewcreen. She leaned forward.

"Ships," she said out loud.

"Indeed," Tuvok confirmed. "Six of them, to be precise."

The captain studied the vessels. "They're too small to be of any tactical use," she decided. "They must be transports."

As she watched, the ships began to dock along the flanks of the larger structure. They looked like grim, gray babies trying to get nourishment from an equally grim-looking mother.

That made sense. A mining station would need raw materials brought in and pure ore taken out. And since these people had no access to transporter technology, they had only one other option.

Chakotay moved to her side. "We don't know what those ships are capable of. In the Maquis, we had transport vessels that packed quite a wallop. And they may be faster than they look as well."

Janeway glanced at him. "You're saying we should stop here and wait until they leave?"

The first officer frowned. "I guess I am. Believe me, Captain, no one wants to get to that station sooner than I do. But I can be patient if it improves our chances of getting our people back."

Janeway took that into account. "All right," she said after a moment. "We'll do it your way, Chakotay. At least for now."

She turned to her helmsman. He was already looking at her, awaiting the captain's instructions.

"All stop, Mr. Paris. We're going to give those transports some time to discharge their business and take off."

But not forever, she added silently.

B'Elanna raced through the darkened corridor ahead of the other prisoners, trusting that each step was bringing her closer to freedom and the chance to be reunited with *Voyager.*

Suddenly, a squad of Nograkh guards spilled into the corridor up ahead, blocking their path. And, judging by the looks on their faces, they weren't taking any prisoners this time.

After all, this was the second escape attempt in as many days. In Overseer Ordagher's mind, this batch of laborers had to have become more trouble than it was worth.

The guards and the prisoners fired at the same time, illuminating the corridor with their firefight. Combatants sprawled and toppled on both sides, the sounds of their dying echoing from one bulkhead to the other.

Fortunately for the prisoners, the guards didn't seem to have the personal forcefields B'Elanna had seen earlier. In their haste, they probably hadn't been able to access any. But the bastards still had a decided advantage—they were better armed and they had a narrow space to defend.

And they didn't have to advance the way the prisoners did. All they had to do was hold their ground until reinforcements arrived.

Both sides fired at will, barrage after blinding barrage. The corridor was filled with cries of rage and pain. More bodies fell. One of them was a Nograkh prisoner beside B'Elanna, wisps of smoke twisting from the bloody ruin of what had been his head.

Picking up his energy rifle and tossing it to a comrade, the lieutenant sent a vicious burst at the guards. Then she slammed herself flat against the cold, metal wall to avoid their return fire. When it missed her, she squared and fired again.

Her second shot hit a guard and sent him sprawling, leaving one of his colleagues wide open. Taking advantage of the opportunity, B'Elanna pressed the trigger and fired again. The other guard went flying as well.

Her fellow prisoners were finding their targets also. Punching holes in their enemies' ranks. Before she knew it, there were only three guards standing. Then two. Then one.

Then none.

The corridor before them was littered with bodies, but not one of them was any kind of obstacle. And, just as important, the guards' weapons were lying there for the taking.

The lieutenant looked around. Tolga was still standing. So was Kim—and he'd picked up a weapon. But nearly a dozen prisoners lay dead at their feet, having paid the ultimate price for their freedom.

If they didn't want to join them, they would have to get a move on. As before, B'Elanna led the way. The others paused only long enough to pick up energy rifles from the fallen guards.

Then, like a riptide in a dark river, the whole pack of them moved down the corridor. The secondary control center couldn't be much farther now.

CHAPTER 18

B'ELANNA HELD HER WEAPON AT THE READY AS SHE negotiated a curve in the corridor—and caught sight of a big, gray door with two studs set into it. It was just as Tolga had described it to her.

Pulling up alongside her, Tolga handed his weapon to one of his fellow Nograkh and flipped the cover off one of the studs, revealing a keypadd. Without hesitation, he punched in a code.

A moment later, the door swung open. There was a small room beyond it—packed with control consoles. Gesturing for the other prisoners to stand guard, Tolga entered it.

Kim moved to the lieutenant's side. "How did he know the code?" the ensign asked her.

B'Elanna shrugged, intent on the section of corridor before her. "He served on a Nograkh warship. Maybe the code is the same all over."

Kim grunted. "Doesn't seem like much of a security measure to me."

"You're not a Nograkh," she reminded him. Obviously, they had a different way of looking at things.

Suddenly, she heard the clatter of approaching footsteps. Signaling to her fellow prisoners to brace themselves, she trained her rifle on an intersection perhaps twenty meters away.

Then a squad of guards exploded into the corridor, bristling with weaponry, silver eyes slitted with violent intent. They took aim as soon as they spotted the prisoners, meaning to obliterate them.

But B'Elanna and the others got off the first barrage, choking the corridor with a blue-white display of destruction. Then they plastered themselves against bulkheads and floors, hoping to avoid the return volley.

But there wasn't any. Not at first, at least. And much to her chagrin, the lieutenant saw why.

The Nograkh's shields—the ones she'd seen for the first time on the Kazon scoutship. They were crawling with crepuscular energy strands, though the protective surfaces themselves were still invisible.

Behind them, the guards were laughing with their wide, cruel mouths. They were still grinning as they raised their weapons and prepared to pick off the prisoners at their leisure.

And Ordagher was among them, grinning the widest of all. The prisoners had been nettlesome to him, an annoyance. But now he would see that annoyance swept away.

That was what he seemed to expect, anyway. And B'Elanna was hard-pressed to believe in any other outcome.

After all, the prisoners didn't have any shields. They were sitting ducks, as the human saying went. And they couldn't retreat—or the guards would see what Tolga was up to.

So they stood their ground and fired again, hoping to blind the guards if nothing else. But some of them fell anyway—and most of them Nograkh, because they moved forward to shield B'Elanna and the other prisoners.

Not with personal force fields, because they didn't have any. Instead, they used the flesh and bone and blood of their bodies, sacrificing themselves so the others might live.

Absorbing burst after blue-white burst. Writhing in agony as the energy consumed them, cell by cell.

It was horrible to watch. B'Elanna cried out in protest. Kim, too. But before they could stop it, the guards' attack came to a halt.

The lieutenant's eyes had been dazzled by the fire of the battle, so it took her a few seconds to see the expressions on the guards' faces. They weren't the smiles of exhilaration she'd seen there earlier. They weren't the sneers of those whose victory was assured.

Not at all. There was doubt in their expressions now. There was trepidation, even a hint of fear. Something had happened—and the guards didn't seem to understand what it was.

But B'Elanna knew. The guards' weapons, even their shields, were no longer in operation. They'd been turned off. Disarmed. Made useless by Tolga, whose observation had begun to pay off.

As she thought that, she saw Tolga emerge from the control center. His expression was cold and deadly, less triumphant than determined. As he came forward, undaunted by the presence of the guards, he reached down and relieved a fallen comrade of his rifle.

"This won't fire any longer," he grated, suffused with righteous anger. "But it will still break a few heads." And with that, he turned it over in his hands so he was grasping the barrel instead of the stock.

Ordagher couldn't have risen to the rank of Overseer without being shifty, scheming, and manipulative. But there was no guile in the guttural cry that tore from his lips. There was no deceit in the savagery with which he charged at Tolga, brandishing his energy weapon like a club.

The two of them met in the center of the corridor like rival beasts vying for supremacy, their weapons clashing with a loud, resounding clang. Then the rest of the prisoners came charging after Tolga, intent on taking down the unarmed and outnumbered guards.

To their credit, the guards didn't retreat. They withstood the charge as best they could—but their best wasn't good enough. The prisoners rolled over them like a targ trampling a colony of pincered yolok worms.

B'Elanna was in the thick of the action, uppercutting a guard with the barrel of her weapon and then—

when he staggered backward—smashing him across the face. As he collapsed to his knees, however, he was still conscious—so she felled him with a blow to the back of his head.

Beside her, Kim was battling another guard, rifle to rifle, as if they were fighting with quarterstaffs. But the ensign didn't have the Nograkh's strength or his stamina. Weakened by fever and exertion, he couldn't keep his weapon from being knocked out of his hands.

For a single, sickening moment, B'Elanna saw her friend stand there helplessly, his arms his only protection as his adversary raised his rifle for a death blow.

Nor was there anything the lieutenant could do about it. She and Kim were separated by too many clawing, struggling bodies. All she could do was watch and curse.

Then Ram's Horns came out of nowhere and slammed Kim's adversary into the bulkhead. Somehow, he found the strength to wrench the guard's weapon out of his hands. And with a fury not even a Klingon could muster, Ram's Horns beat the Nograkh senseless with it.

After that, the fight seemed to go quickly. In the end, the prisoners' numbers prevailed and not a single guard was left on his feet. And when B'Elanna looked back, gasping for air after her exertions, she saw Tolga had won his contest as well.

He was standing over a beaten and bloodied Ordagher, clutching a fistful of the Overseer's tunic in one hand while he hefted his rifle-club menacingly with the other.

But there was no longer any need for it. Ordagher was dead, his skull caved in just above one eye.

Tolga allowed Ordagher to fall to the deck. Then he turned to B'Elanna, awaiting her orders.

She pointed to the weapons that lay on the floor unclaimed. "Gather the rifles," she said—not just to Tolga, but to all the surviving prisoners. "When we've got them all in hand, I'll activate them from the control center. Then we can keep the guards at bay until a transport arrives."

Abruptly, there was a flashing of red and blue lights from inside the control center. A moment later, it was followed by a ringing.

B'Elanna looked at Kim, then at Tolga. She smiled a ragged smile. "I think a transport is here."

Tolga darted into the control center, B'Elanna and Kim on his heels. The Nograkh consulted one of the instrument panels for a moment. Then he shook his head.

"Not a transport," he said. He glanced at the lieutenant. "That is, not *just* one. There are *six* of them."

Six, thought B'Elanna. "And all of them full of Nograkh who won't be pleased to see us escape."

Tolga nodded. "But they don't know what's happened here yet. If we hurry, we can catch them by surprise." And he set to work reactivating the weapons they had seized.

A couple of seconds later, the lieutenant could feel a surge of power in her rifle as its energy cell came back to life. They were armed now—at least most of them were. And, as Tolga had pointed out, the transport crew wouldn't be expecting a problem here when they docked.

But it would be too hard to take on all those transports at once. They would have to focus their efforts on one or two of them and hope they could get away before the other crews caught on.

B'Elanna said as much. Said it out loud so everyone could hear. "We'll take the first two transports that try to dock. Strike hard and fast, and we should succeed."

Tolga eyed the other prisoners from beneath his jutting brow. "I know these ships. I'll pilot the first craft. And the other . . ."

He turned to B'Elanna, but she shook her head. "Kim. He's a better pilot than I am."

Tolga regarded the man. "Kim, then," he confirmed.

The muscles worked in the ensign's temples. "I'll do what I can," he told them, his voice strong despite his pallor.

Satisfied, Tolga slammed the door of the control center and led them all in the direction of the docking ports.

Janeway was growing impatient. She and *Voyager* had been maintaining their position for nearly an hour and the transport ships were still clustered around the station.

"I'm getting antsy," she confessed to Chakotay, who was still standing by her side.

"You're not the only one," he confessed in turn.

The captain chewed the inside of her cheek. "They could remain there for hours. A day. Even several."

"And when they leave," the first officer noted, "they may take more than just ore."

Janeway looked at him. "You think they transport prisoners from place to place? Say, from this mining facility to another?"

"If casualties have been greater in the other one?" Chakotay shrugged. "Stranger things have been known to happen. And if we were to scan the station *after* B'Elanna and Kim had been taken off . . ."

"And not find them . . ." she said, picking up the thread.

"We wouldn't know whether the ships had taken them away or they'd never been there in the first place."

The captain shook her head. That way lay madness. Trying to guess where they'd gone wrong, what they might have done differently—wondering which of the transports, if any, had whisked their friends to another facility.

Of course, there was a way to avoid all that.

"I think I've changed my mind about waiting," said the first officer.

Janeway nodded. "Me, too." She raised her voice so Paris could hear. "We're going in, Lieutenant. Warp six. Drop to impulse when we get within two million kilometers of the asteroid belt."

"Aye, ma'am," came the response.

"Red alert," called the captain. "All hands to battle stations. Mister DuChamps, I'll need a tactical analysis of—"

She found herself stopping in mid-command, her mind riveted on what was going on around the station. Suddenly, a couple of the transports had begun to move—to depart. But not in the leisurely way she'd expected.

They looked like they were running *away*.

B'Elanna stood on one side of the air lock, Kim on the other. The white light on the bulkhead showed them the transport outside was in the process of docking. Or anyway, that's what Ogis had told them.

And Ogis was in a position to know. Like Tolga, he had served on a Nograkh battle cruiser.

Suddenly, the light on the bulkhead turned red. The two Starfleet officers hefted their weapons and looked to Ogis.

"How long?" asked the lieutenant.

"A minute," said the Nograkh. "Maybe less, maybe more."

Ram's Horns was with them also. He nodded. "It depends on how eager they are to off-load their cargo."

As it turned out, the Nograkh couldn't have been *more* eager. It only took ten seconds for the air lock door to open from the outside and discharge the commander of the transport. That left him a perfect target for the prisoners pressed against the bulkhead on either side.

According to plan, Ogis took out the commander with a single burst of blue-white energy fire. Then B'Elanna, Kim, and Ram's Horns, who were considerably quicker than their fellow prisoners, rushed through the air lock to take care of the transport's crew.

There were two of them in the main cabin. B'Elanna took one down. Kim blasted the other. But there were supposed to be five Nograkh aboard—again, according to Ogis.

The lieutenant and the ensign charged in to dig out the two remaining crewmembers, with Ram's Horns right behind them. B'Elanna turned right and went forward. Kim turned left and went aft.

B'Elanna found a Nograkh at the helm. He was obviously surprised to see her. Before his confusion could wear off, she stunned him with a beam to the middle of his chest.

Then she turned in time to see a flare of blue-white light in the rear compartment. There was a short, strangled cry. Kim came out with a grim semblance of a smile on his face.

"Never knew what hit him," the ensign reported.

The lieutenant grunted. "Fortunately, none of them did."

The next step was to clear out the unconscious bodies of the crew, a task they accomplished in a matter of seconds. After that, they shut the doors to the station air lock—both inner and outer—as well as the door in the hull of the transport itself.

Kim slipped into the pilot's seat. B'Elanna took her place behind him. Ram's Horns claimed the weapons station. Everyone else piled into the main cabin or the smaller rear compartment.

They were ready to roll.

"What about Tolga?" asked Ogis.

The lieutenant shook her head. "We can't wait for

him—or he for us. But once we're underway, we can scan for his ship."

Something happened then that made B'Elanna's blood run cold. Something she was totally unprepared for. She heard a *voice.*

"Ebra? Are you there?"

It hadn't come from anyone in the transport. In fact, it sounded as if it had come from all around them. Cursing beneath her breath, B'Elanna looked up at the ceiling, where it was customary to conceal communications grids in Starfleet vessels.

The intership communications system had been activated accidentally. Or maybe the Nograkh she'd stunned had managed to press a padd while still conscious. Either way, they had an open—and unwanted—channel to one of the other transports.

And it wasn't the one Tolga had gone after. That was the one thing of which the lieutenant was certain.

"Answer me, Ebra!"

Ogis signed for Kim not to make a move. Then he approached the controls and made an adjustment. Finally, he looked to the ceiling and spoke.

"This is Ebra. As you can hear, we're experiencing some communications problems, some static. What is it you want?"

For a moment, there was silence on the other end. B'Elanna crossed her fingers, hoping Ebra would fall for Ogis's ruse.

Unfortunately, it didn't work out that way. They could hear someone in the other ship shouting urgent orders to his crew. Then the communications line went dead.

Clenching her teeth, the lieutenant turned to Kim. "Get us out of here, Ensign. And I mean *now.*"

Kim was staring at something through the vessel's forward observation port. B'Elanna hunkered down and saw what it was. An asteroid belt.

Abruptly, she remembered what he'd told her about Paris's holodeck program. Damn, she thought. An *asteroid* belt.

"You want me to take over?" she asked.

The ensign shook his head. "No. I can handle it."

The lieutenant bit her lip. For everyone's sake, she hoped he was telling her the truth.

CHAPTER 19

MY GOD, HARRY THOUGHT AS HE GUIDED HIS TRANSPORT forward. It figures, doesn't it?

They were surrounded by an asteroid belt, of all things. A big, dense *monster* of an asteroid belt.

Now he knew where the station got all its raw materials. They were all around it in plentiful supply. *More* than plentiful.

An asteroid belt, he repeated inwardly.

The kind in which he'd already proven his piloting skills to be woefully inadequate. The kind he'd told Paris he'd probably never encounter in a million years. And just for good measure, a bunch of enemy ships would soon be on his tail, spurring him to new heights of urgency.

Not to mention a raging fever, reflexes that had been slowed by radiation exposure and an ache in his bones he couldn't ignore. His hands were wracked with pain as they worked the controls.

Worse yet, his helm panel was different from the kind he'd learned on in Starfleet shuttles, so he couldn't operate on instinct alone. He had to watch everything he was doing or take a chance on smashing the ship into a big hunk of ore-laden rock.

One thing was the same. The monitor on the console was located on his right, just where he would have expected it in a shuttle console. And the sensor arrangement must have been similar as well, because the asteroids up ahead were represented as blips of white light.

But this wasn't a holodeck exercise. This was real life. If they cracked up, there would be no rebooting the program. They'd be dead, finis, kaput. End of the line.

As Harry studied the monitor, he shivered—and not just because of his fever. There wasn't any clear-cut path among the asteroids. Even at impulse speed, it was going to be a toss-up as to whether they'd make it out of this place alive.

He felt a hand grip his shoulder. He didn't have to look to know it was B'Elanna's. "How are we doing, Starfleet?"

"Couldn't be better," Harry said, albeit with a confidence he didn't feel. He swallowed hard. "Piece of cake."

That's when he saw a series of blue-white energy bolts strike the asteroid up ahead of him, annihilating an entire quadrant of the thing in an explosion of light and debris. What's more, the bolt had missed Harry's transport by only a few short meters.

Switching his monitor to rearview for a moment, he saw where the attack had come from. The other transports were giving pursuit. And for them, pursuit meant trying to knock the prisoners out of space.

Janeway leaned forward in her chair and followed the movements of the ships in the asteroid field with more than casual interest.

They looked for all the world as if they were trying to escape the station. No—not all of them, Janeway realized. Two of them were doing that. The others seemed to be in pursuit.

There was a flare of light. And another. The transports were firing at each other, for god's sake.

"What's going on?" asked the captain, hoping one of her bridge officers could shed some light on this.

Naturally, Tuvok was the first to answer her—though all he could do was state the obvious. "We seem to be witnessing an altercation."

It could have been a squabble among the operators of the station—one that had evolved into violence. But Janeway sensed it was something else. Something along the lines of a jailbreak.

"It's Harry!" blurted Paris.

Janeway traded glances with Chakotay and came forward. "How do you know?" she asked the helmsman.

Paris pointed to the viewscreen, where they could see the transport ships weaving their way through the asteroid belt. One of the ships seemed to be leading the way, blazing a torturous trail despite the energy beams slicing space all around it.

"Look!" he said, as if that were explanation enough. Then he added: "It's Harry, dammit! We were practicing those moves on the holodeck!"

The captain looked up and saw the conflict on the screen in a new light. It wasn't just *any* jailbreak, she told herself. Not if it was Kim on that ship—and maybe B'Elanna as well.

"Two million kilometers," Chakotay announced.

"Dropping to impulse," said Paris, knowing a cue when he heard one. His hands danced over the helm controls with practiced ease. "Heading two-three-two-mark-eight."

There were a couple more flares of light in the asteroid belt. But the escaping transport avoided them somehow.

Janeway gripped the armrests of her chair. Come on, she thought, silently urging her ship forward. She hadn't come all this way to watch her officers vanish in a barrage of energy fire.

One of Harry's pursuers seared the void with another barrage. This time, he had to pull his craft to starboard to avoid it. As before, the errant bolts smashed into a rock formation and took a chunk out of it.

"Who's at the weapons console?" B'Elanna barked, though she knew full well who it was. "Show them *we've* got some teeth, too!"

As Ram's Horns moved to comply, a deeper voice

surrounded them. It was the communications system again. "This is Tolga."

"Tolga!" someone exclaimed. "He made it, then."

"For now," someone else commented.

"We'll do better if we split up," Tolga advised. "We'll meet on the other side of the belt."

"Agreed," said B'Elanna.

The other side, Harry thought, switching to forward view again. If I make it that far. If we don't run into a rock or an energy blast and become part of the scenery. If—

Suddenly, he seemed to hear a voice in his ear. Paris's voice, just as if they were back in their holodeck simulation.

"You can do it, Harry."

The ensign grunted softly and wiped sweat from his eyes. *"What makes you think this time is going to be different from the others?"* he asked in the privacy of his own mind.

Paris gave him the same answer as last time. *"I've got a feeling. Pay attention now, Harry. Those asteroids are coming up fast."*

As the first rock loomed, the ensign gritted his teeth and pulled the mining transport hard to port. Then, to avoid a second rock, hard to starboard. And again to port.

And each time he tensed a little, expecting to feel the impact of a well-placed energy beam. But nothing hit them.

Maybe the other transports were having trouble drawing a bead on him. Maybe they had their hands full just trying to keep up. Or maybe Ram's Horns was making life difficult with some well-placed shots of his own.

No matter. Harry couldn't worry about any of that. He had to stay focused on the job at hand.

A precipitous dip. A sharp turn to starboard. Another dip and a tight squeeze to port.

A rise, another dip. A torturous corkscrew maneuver to avoid a series of smaller rocks that made the deck plates shiver and groan. The next turn had to be a hairpin tack to starboard.

Harry engaged the thrusters and watched the rock ahead of them veer to port. But it didn't veer quickly enough. He had to decelerate, give the thrusters more time to work. And even then, they cleared the asteroid by only half a meter.

Harry took a breath and let it out. Squinting through the haze of his fever, he sent them hard to starboard, then to port again. Up over a big, misshapen boulder and down below another one.

A quick switch to rearview showed him the ore transports were still hot on his trail. But not all of them—just three. The fourth must have gone after Tolga's vessel.

Back to forward view. Harry estimated they'd gone through half the asteroid field. Halfway home and still unscathed.

Turn, dive, ascend, turn. Dive, ascend, twist, and dive again. Slowly but surely, they were nearing the finish line.

Harry's eyes felt hot and swollen. He blinked. Just a little farther, he promised himself. Just a little farther and they'd be out of this. Then they would be in open space and he could *really* maneuver.

He worked his controls with infinite patience, infinite attention to detail. One crag after another slid out of sight, another looming up ahead to take its place each time.

"Not bad," he heard Paris say in his head.

"I'm not out of the woods yet," Harry reminded him.

He wasn't, either. Because just as he negotiated a massive rock to starboard, he felt a jolt from behind that jerked his head back. And another, even worse than the first.

"What the *hell* is going on?" he snapped out loud.

But he knew the answer. Their pursuers had gotten a couple of clean shots at them. So far their shields were holding, but they wouldn't last long under that kind of punishment.

Harry bent over his board and got them past the asteroid to starboard, ignoring the cold spot between his shoulder blades where sweat had moistened his uniform shirt. Then he climbed sharply to avoid another rock and slid to port to dodge a third.

They were almost at the limits of the belt. As the ensign circumvented another asteroid, it erupted with a directed-energy hit. Better a rock than us, Harry thought, and got his first look at the next set of obstacles.

His jaw dropped. There were two asteroids ahead of him, almost side by side. If there were five meters between them, it was a lot.

It was just as it had been in the holodeck sequence. Well, maybe not exactly—but close enough. And the last time he'd tried this maneuver—hell, *every* time he'd tried it—he'd botched it royally. He'd blown up his ship and killed his crew.

The ensign looked around for another option, but there wasn't any. The asteroids in every other direction were too densely packed. He would have had to backtrack, weave his way in and out until he found another means of egress—and with those transports breathing down his neck, he would be blasted to bits if he even tried.

His Nograkh pursuers must have known he was headed for this—which was why they hadn't sent barrage after desperate barrage after him. No matter how deftly he piloted his craft, no matter how many asteroids he avoided, they knew they would have him cornered in the end.

Harry concentrated on the pass ahead of him again and began to rotate his craft. It wasn't rolling as quickly as the shuttle had in the holodeck. Gritting his teeth, he tried to compensate with a few extra bursts from the thrusters as he watched the opening loom before him.

He heard Paris' voice. *"You can do it, Harry."*

But the maneuver wasn't working. Harry wasn't getting the rotation he needed.

He was going to crash into one of the asteroids, maybe both of them. And they were all going to die, he and B'Elanna and everyone else in his craft, just a few meters short of freedom.

Unless . . .

He whirled to face Ram's Horns and barked an order. "Fire forward! I need a chunk taken out of that asteroid to port!"

Ram's Horns hesitated—but only for a fraction of a second. Then he targeted the asteroid just as Harry had demanded. And with a tap of a control padd, sent a blast of blue-white fury at it.

Instantly, the asteroid's nearest quadrant blew apart, pelting the transport with a thousand tiny rock fragments. Impelled by the force of the explosion, blinded by the energy backlash, Harry felt his craft veering too far to starboard. He corrected with the thrusters, hoping it would be enough.

It *had* to be. Or else it would end here—*they* would end here—and that was an injustice too grievous for him even to contemplate.

For what seemed like a long time, he stared through the observation port, unsure of the outcome. He couldn't tell if they had cleared the asteroid or if they just hadn't hit it yet. Holding onto his armrests with all the white-knuckled strength he had left, he peered into the face of death.

Finally, he realized there wasn't going to be an impact. Their vessel wasn't going to hit a rock and explode, sending bits of flesh and bone streaming into the void.

They were going to make it.

As the glare of their energy strike dissipated, Harry could make out the void of space in front of him. No asteroids—not a single one. Just the distant sun and the even more distant stars.

The ensign had never seen such a beautiful thing in

his entire life. Nor did he ever expect to, even if he lived to be two hundred.

Switching to rearview again, he tried to locate the transports behind him. It wasn't an easy task, with all the debris from the damaged asteroid cluttering his perspective. Then something happened that made his pursuers even harder to see.

Something collided with one of the asteroids and went to pieces in a ball of crimson fire. Then came a second explosion. And a third.

The other transports, the ensign thought. They didn't make it. Or anyway, the first one didn't, and that doomed the other two as well.

He felt B'Elanna grasp his shoulder. She lowered her face to his and grinned. "You did it, Starfleet."

Harry nodded, drained by his ordeal. "Yeah," he said. "I guess I did. Tom would have been proud of me."

Of course, there was still one pursuer left—the one that had gone after Tolga's vessel. But knowing the Nograkh, he'd probably blasted that one to pieces already. Still, Harry figured he'd better find out.

He switched to forward view again and maneuvered his way around the outskirts of the asteroid belt, looking for a sign of Tolga's transport. At first, there wasn't any.

Then he caught a glimpse of something moving among the asteroids, like a dark, mysterious fish swimming through the shallows of a lake. And it seemed to be moving alone, neither pursued nor pursuing.

But which transport was it—the one Tolga had

commandeered or the one sent to catch him? B'Elanna must have been wondering the same thing, because she hit the communications stud on the control panel.

"Tolga!" she said. "Is that you?"

No answer. Harry swore under his breath.

"Target weapons," he called back to Ram's Horns.

Glancing back over his shoulder, he could see Ram's Horns making the necessary adjustments on his instrument board. Then the ensign turned back to his own controls, to plan an attack.

"Tolga!" cried B'Elanna. "If that's you, I need an answer!"

Abruptly, they heard a familiar voice. "It's me," their ally assured them. "Still in one piece, although—B'Elanna, watch out behind you!"

Harry reacted instantly. Switching to rearview again, he saw what Tolga was shouting about. He swallowed in his dry, feverish throat.

A huge, gray vessel filled the dimensions of the viewscreen. A battle cruiser, unless he missed his guess. Even bigger and more powerful than the ship that had destroyed the Kazon vessel and brought them to the station in the first place.

And it was headed right for them.

CHAPTER 20

B'ELANNA TOOK IN THE SIGHT OF THE VESSEL BEHIND them, with its bristling weapons clusters and its powerful-looking engine nacelles. It made the Kazon ships she'd seen look like excursion craft.

And it was bearing down on them with all the single-minded ferocity of a Klingon targ.

"They're powering up their weapons," Ram's Horns warned her.

But then, the lieutenant could've guessed that. The cruiser had no doubt gotten word of the prisonbreak. And it had probably scanned them with its sensors as well, just to make sure.

She turned to Kim. "Evasive maneuvers, Starfleet."

"I'll do my best," he responded.

Peeling off to port, he avoided a blast of directed

energy. Of course, it might just have been a warning shot, to let them know what they were in for.

"I've got an idea," said the ensign.

"We can use one," B'Elanna replied.

Gunning the thrusters, Kim wove a circle around the top of the cruiser, where it didn't seem to have any armaments. He must have guessed right about their being safe there, because the enemy didn't attempt to fire at them.

But it did try to grab them in its version of a tractor beam.

"We've got to move," B'Elanna said.

"I'm moving," Kim assured her.

But his escape route put them back in the line of fire. And the cruiser seemed eager to take advantage of it.

Weapon-cluster after weapon-cluster lashed out at them, filling the vacuum with blue-white energy beams. Thanks to Kim, none of them found their mark—but they were getting closer with each barrage.

Tolga's vessel wasn't doing much better. It was eluding the cruiser's bursts by only the barest of margins. Then it encountered one it couldn't elude and took a hit to its starboard side.

There was no hull damage—at least none that B'Elanna could see. But Tolga's shields had to have taken a beating.

"We can't dance this dance much longer," Kim told her.

"I know," she said.

The lieutenant racked her brains for a maneuver that would put the transports in the clear. Something . . . anything.

An option came to mind. It wasn't a good one. In fact, it couldn't have been much worse. But it was also the only chance they had.

Clearly, a couple of transports couldn't go head to head with a battle cruiser. They didn't have the speed, the durability, or the arsenal. But if one of them smashed headlong into the enemy, sacrificing his or her vessel and crew in a suicide run . . .

The other transport might get away.

"Tolga," she said out loud. "This is B'Elanna."

"What is it?" he rasped in return.

The lieutenant told him what she had in mind. Her decision drew stares from Kim and the others, but no one objected. *No* one.

"It's a good idea," the Nograkh replied. "Unfortunately, I had it *first.*"

"What?" she cried.

"Go," Tolga advised her. "Get out of here as fast as you can."

Then B'Elanna saw his ship begin to loop around—to double back in the direction of the cruiser. Ice water began to trickle down her back.

"No," she said. Then a little louder: "No!"

But if Tolga still had his communications link open, he wasn't paying any attention to it. He was too busy accelerating on what seemed like a devastating collision course.

The cruiser's commander must have seen it, too, but he was nowhere near as maneuverable as the transport. After all, his ship was a lot bigger. And he didn't have to wind his way through an asteroid belt every day.

So, as Tolga's vessel sped toward him, the cruiser commander couldn't get out of the way. He could only fire at the smaller ship and hope to destroy it before it got too close.

"Tolga," the lieutenant breathed.

Then the transport plowed into the much larger vessel with an impact she could almost feel. Tolga's plasma tanks ruptured, sending out streamers of wild, undulating light. And, a heartbeat later, the view-screen blanched as the transport exploded into flames.

They didn't last long, of course. This was airless space. But they endured long enough to show B'Elanna what was left of Tolga's vessel, which wasn't much at all.

Everything from the middle back had been destroyed in the blast. From the middle forward, it looked like the entryway into hell, an open maw full of fiery plasma that continued to eat at the cruiser's hull.

And there was no life on it at all. *None.* Because nothing living could have survived that kind of fury.

B'Elanna felt a moan deep in her throat. She stifled it. It couldn't be, she told herself. It couldn't *be.*

But another part of her, a colder and harder part, disagreed. It *could* be. It *was.* The warrior called Tolga was gone, destroyed, and the prisoners in his vessel along with him.

Not for nothing, though. All over the Nograkh

cruiser, lights were going out. The nacelles were going dark as well, their propulsion coils cooling. Clearly, Tolga had known where to hit the thing.

But then, he had served on one of these monsters, hadn't he? He had told her so, back in the rest chamber.

The rest chamber . . . where he had saved Kim's life. Where the lieutenant had come to respect the warrior, even develop a certain amount of affection for him. Perhaps if she had known him better, longer, something more might have grown between them.

But not now. Tolga, she thought numbly, was dead.

Before B'Elanna could come to grips with this newfound reality, before the pain of her loss could quite sink in, she heard a beeping sound. Kim turned to her, his features confused—caught in the grip of conflicting emotions just as she must have been.

"Someone's trying to hail us," he told her.

The lieutenant glanced at the screen again and swallowed. The cruiser was almost entirely devoid of illumination now. And it was beginning to drift, the remains of Tolga's ship still protruding from its side.

"What do you think they want?" asked Ram's Horns.

The lines in Kim's forehead deepened as he worked his controls. "Hang on," he said. "I don't think it's them."

B'Elanna regarded him grimly. "It's not another

cruiser, is it?" Not after Tolga had sacrificed himself for them . . .

The ensign shook his head. "No. I . . ." Suddenly, he looked up at her and smiled—with a sense of relief that seemed drastically out of place. "I think it's *Voyager.*"

The lieutenant leaned over him and checked his monitor. As Kim had indicated, the frequency was one commonly used by *Voyager.* The message itself was garbled, perhaps due to the proximity of the raging plasma furnace that had once been Tolga's vessel.

But the frequency . . .

"Let's hear it," said B'Elanna.

Kim did as he was told. A moment later, they could make out the tenuous, static-ridden voice of Captain Janeway as it filled their bridge.

". . . *Voyager.* If that's you in that . . . respond, Mister Kim. Repeat, if that's you in . . ."

The lieutenant put her hand on her comrade's shoulder and squeezed. "You're right," she said, unable to keep the excitement out of her voice. "It's *Voyager.* Can you get a visual?"

"I'm trying," he told her.

What's more, he succeeded. Like the audio portion, the video was wracked with interference. But there was no mistaking the familiar countenance of their commanding officer.

Janeway's voice continued to fill the compartment with its crackle. ". . . you, isn't . . . come in, Ensign. I need . . ."

"Captain Janeway," said B'Elanna. "This is Lieutenant Torres. Ensign Kim and I used this ship to escape the place where we were being held. We're in no danger right now, though that may change."

Janeway's brow creased as she tried to make out what B'Elanna was telling her. Obviously, the interference was affecting *Voyager*'s comm equipment as much as the transport ship's.

After a second or two, the captain turned to Tuvok, who was standing in the background, and said something B'Elanna couldn't make out. The Vulcan checked his instruments, then replied. Finally, Janeway faced forward again.

". . . effect a transport . . ." she said. ". . . raise our shields . . . quickly so we don't leave ourselves vulnerable."

Kim glanced over his shoulder at the lieutenant. "They're going to try to beam us aboard, Maquis."

B'Elanna nodded. "I heard."

It made sense to her. Their vessel was too big to make use of *Voyager*'s shuttlebays and too small to take care of itself. The only way the captain could be sure they were safe was to bring them home.

Of course, it would take a while before *Voyager* could transport them safely. If the plasma display from Tolga's ship was wreaking havoc with communications, it would break up an annular confinement beam as well.

"*Beam* us?" echoed Ram's Horns, obviously unfamiliar with transporter technology.

That came as no surprise. *No* one in the Delta

Quadrant was familiar with transporter technology—which was what had made the Kazon-Ogla so eager to get their hands on it.

"You'll see," the lieutenant told Ram's Horns.

He did, too. And in less time than she would have expected.

One moment they were on the bridge of the mining ship, looking at one another expectantly. The next, they and three of the Nograkh in the hold were standing on a transporter pad aboard *Voyager*.

Janeway had positioned herself beside the transporter operator. There was an expression on her face the lieutenant couldn't quite identify. A mixture, it seemed to her, of happiness and . . . something else.

Relief? she wondered.

"Are you all right?" the captain asked, advancing to the pad.

B'Elanna started to say she was fine, then felt a weakness in her knees. When she staggered, Janeway was there to catch her.

"Radiation," said the captain, figuring out what was wrong with her officer at a glance. She looked to Kim and her eyes narrowed. "You, too."

The lieutenant got her legs back under control. "We're not as bad as we look," she said.

Janeway frowned. "The hell you're not." She looked up at the intercom system. "Sick bay, this is the captain. Prepare some beds, Doctor. I've got some radiation cases for you."

"Bring them on," said the holophysician. "I haven't

treated a case of radiation poisoning in a couple of days now. I can use the practice."

B'Elanna smiled at the ironic tone in his voice. It was good to be home, she reflected. And also to know that she and Kim had rescued half the prisoners on the mining station.

But it would have been better if they had saved the other half as well. She thought again of her friend, Tolga—of his strength and his boundless courage. And it hurt.

"What is it?" asked Janeway, tilting her head to look into the lieutenant's eyes. "Is the pain getting worse?"

B'Elanna shook her head. "It's not that, Captain."

"Then what?" Janeway prodded.

Off to the side of them, the doors to the transporter room were sliding open. No doubt to admit the security people who would escort the lieutenant and her companions to sick bay.

B'Elanna could feel a lump forming in her throat. She shrugged in response to the captain's question. "It's just that . . . a few moments ago, I saw someone die to keep me alive."

"And who was that?" asked a familiar voice.

Scarcely able to believe her ears, B'Elanna turned toward the entrance—and saw Tolga enter the room, accompanied by Tuvok and a few of the other prisoners. The lieutenant shook her head, speechless.

"What . . .?" she finally croaked out.

Tolga's eyes narrowed. Crossing the room, he embraced her as one warrior would embrace another.

Alive, she thought, feeling the reassuring hardness of his arms around her. He was *alive.*

"How is this possible?" asked the Nograkh, releasing B'Elanna. He jerked his heavy-browed head in the Vulcan's direction. "Apparently, your people plucked us out of our vessel before we could hit the cruiser—though I am still not sure *how.*"

Tuvok looked a little discomfited as he turned to Captain Janeway. "I had intended to bring these people directly to sick bay. However, when Tolga learned he might be able to see Lieutenant Torres even sooner . . ."

Janeway nodded. "I understand. And don't worry, Mr. Tuvok—you did the right thing."

The Vulcan quirked an eyebrow. "I *never* worry, Captain. It would be illogical to do so."

B'Elanna was still at a loss. She regarded Captain Janeway. "But how did you figure out Tolga's crew was on our side?"

Now it was Janeway's turn to shrug. "Originally, we were headed for the mining station. Then we saw all those ships take off from it in a hurry—and one of them performed a maneuver Mister Paris found vaguely familiar." She glanced at Kim. "Nice flying, Ensign."

Kim managed a grin. "Thank you, Captain."

"After that," Janeway continued, "it was a little confusing as to whom your allies might be—if you even had any. But when the cruiser showed up and went after the two of you, we had a pretty good idea of what was going on."

"So you established transporter locks," B'Elanna guessed.

"Yes," said the captain. "As soon as we could." She glanced at Tolga. "It was a good thing, too. They came in handy when one of the ships surprised us with a suicide maneuver."

"Which I am told did considerable damage," Tolga commented. He was looking at B'Elanna as he spoke.

The lieutenant was still stunned—but pleasantly so. "That's true," she confirmed. "The cruiser was disabled."

"Good," said the Nograkh, his silver eyes hard and vengeful.

Clearly, he felt as if he'd accomplished something. The fact that he'd lived to tell of it seemed almost secondary.

A voice came to them over the intercom. "Captain Janeway?"

The captain responded. "Yes, Commander Chakotay?"

"We've got them all now. But they're not in the best shape."

Janeway's nostrils flared. "The Doctor's already been alerted. Get them to sick bay, Commander."

"Aye, Captain," came the response. Then he added, "How's Lieutenant Torres? And Ensign Kim?"

Janeway smiled. "Not bad," she said, "all things considered."

B'Elanna put her hand on Tolga's arm and looked up into his eyes. She could see herself in their silver gray sheen.

"I didn't think I'd ever see you again," she admitted.

His brow-ridge lowered. "That makes two of us."

Then a handful of security officers showed up and took them all to sick bay.

CHAPTER 21

Pacria knew something was going on. She could tell by the volume of traffic in the corridors. She could see the crewpeople in their variously colored uniforms rushing in and out of the turbolifts.

Using the communicator badge they had given her, she contacted Captain Janeway. "What's happening?" she asked.

The captain couldn't tell her—not right away, at least. She was too preoccupied with something. Something urgent, judging by the sounds Pacria heard in the background of their brief conversation.

So she went to Neelix's mess hall, hoping to glean some information there. But to the Emmonac's surprise, Neelix wasn't around. In fact, there was no one there at all.

That meant there was only one other place she

could go. One other venue on the ship where she would be known and welcomed.

Sick bay.

As she entered, she saw Kes standing in the Doctor's office. The Doctor was there, too. So was Neelix.

They turned as she entered. The Talaxian raised his arms in greeting. "We found them!" he cried. "We found Torres and Kim!"

Pacria smiled. "Really?" she asked.

"Yes," said Kes. She beckoned. "Come see."

As the Emmonac approached, the others backed off a bit so she could see the Doctor's desktop monitor. It showed her some kind of vessel, gray and spartan in design.

"That's where they are?" she asked.

"Apparently," the Doctor answered. "We have no idea as yet how they got there, but they've answered the captain's hail. It's only a matter of time now before we recover them."

Pacria spent that time standing with the others in the Doctor's office. She was there when Captain Janeway called sick bay to report the imminent arrival of Torres and Kim and their newfound allies. And she was there to see them all enter sick bay, in need of beds and treatment.

The Emmonac could have let the others attend to the flood of patients on their own. But she didn't. She helped out. After all, she was there already, wasn't she? And she sympathized with the patients, having been a victim of radiation exposure herself.

She even got a chance to meet Lieutenant Torres and Ensign Kim. They were different from the way she'd pictured them, Torres being prettier than she'd expected and Kim being quieter.

And after Neelix explained her role in their rescue, they thanked her for all she'd done. So did the Nograkh. After all, if *Voyager* hadn't found its missing officers, it wouldn't have found the other prisoners either. And in time, another cruiser would have shown up to destroy them for their audacity.

It made Pacria feel good. It made her feel as if she'd accomplished something. That was more important to her than ever before, considering how little time she had left.

Then the captain called her back. With all that was going on, Janeway almost seemed to have forgotten she had meant to speak with Pacria. In any case, the captain said, the Emmonac's efforts hadn't been in vain. Torres and Kim had been rescued.

Pacria smiled. "Yes," she said. "I know that. I'm standing here in sick bay with them." Under the circumstances, it wasn't hard to forgive the human her oversight.

As Janeway signed off, Pacria took another look at sick bay. As crowded as it was, everything seemed under control. Seeing she was no longer needed, she started for the exit.

Someone called her name. "Pacria?"

It was Kes. The Ocampa crossed sick bay to catch up with her. "Can I ask you a favor?" she inquired.

"Of course," said the Emmonac.

"Meet me on the holodeck," Kes told her. "Say, in half an hour. I ought to be done here by then."

It was an unusual request. Having learned a bit

about the ship's holodeck, Pacria guessed that Kes had set up a program for her as a gift. Perhaps it was her way of saying thanks for all the Emmonac's help. Or an attempt to distract Pacria from her imminent demise.

No matter the reason, it wasn't necessary. The Emmonac said so.

"To me, it is," Kes replied.

Pacria sighed. But in the end, she agreed to meet the Ocampa in the appointed place at the appointed hour.

Kes activated her program and opened the doors to the holodeck. It was dark inside, just as she'd planned it.

Pacria looked hesitant about going inside. "I warn you, I'm not partial to surprises," she told the Ocampa.

Kes didn't say she would be partial to this one either. She just asked that the Emmonac enter—which she eventually did, despite her misgivings. When they were both inside, the Ocampa asked for illumination.

The lights went on instantly. Pacria blinked as her eyes made the adjustment. Then she looked around the holodeck—or rather, the illusion contained in it.

The room was stark, colorless—filled with metal beds, all of them empty. The Emmonac looked agitated, confused.

"What is this?" she asked.

"I think you know," Kes said gently. "It's the clinic at a Zendak'aan redistribution camp. I was able to reconstruct it using the information from your ship's logs."

Pacria looked at her, still uncomprehending. "But why? Why would you make such a terrible thing?"

The Ocampa bit her lip. She could see the pain in Pacria's face. But now that she'd begun, she couldn't turn back—not after she had promised herself she would see this through.

"Because I want you to see what you're doing," she explained.

"See?" the Emmonac echoed. "What I see is one of the places where the Zendak'aa tortured us. Where they broke and mutilated our bodies, all in the name of science."

Kes sighed heavily. That was all true, she conceded. But it wasn't the *whole* truth.

Pacria took a few tentative steps. The chamber echoed with her footfalls—like a tomb. Her eyes narrowed with dread and loathing.

She turned to the Ocampa again, a haunted look on her face. "Is this supposed to make me change my mind, Kes? Or make me more certain than ever that what I'm doing is right?"

Kes didn't answer her—not directly. Instead, she looked up at the ceiling and said: "Computer, add Doctor Arnic Varrus to the program."

A moment later, a white-robed Zendak'aan materialized in the room. He was taller than Pacria and much more slender. Where her skin was purplish and scaly, his was smooth and a very pale shade of yellow, with long slashes of black on his forehead and the backs of his hands.

But his eyes were his most noticeable characteristic. They were large and black and shiny—the eyes of someone utterly confident in his abilities, utterly secure in his preeminence.

Nonetheless, Varrus just stood there, saying nothing. That was as it should be, thought Kes. He wasn't programmed to do anything besides respond—though in a way, his air of self-assurance was a statement in itself.

The Emmonac regarded the Zendak'aan. After a while, silent tears began to trace their way down her cheeks.

"You must hate me a great deal," she whispered without looking at Kes, "to show me something so utterly disgusting."

The Ocampa swallowed. Part of her wanted to spare Pacria this misery. But it was necessary, she reminded herself. It was absolutely essential if she was going to accomplish anything in time.

"I'm sorry," she told her companion. "I don't wish to cause you any distress. Please—just bear with me."

The Emmonac took a shaky breath and let it out. "What is it you want me to do?" she asked.

Kes tilted her head to indicate the Zendak'aan. "Just talk to him. Ask him questions about his work."

Pacria grunted. "Why? So he can tell me how dedicated he was to the healing of his fellow Zendak'aa? So I can learn to forgive him for his crimes—and benefit from their results?"

Kes steeled herself. "Ask him," she said softly.

With obvious reluctance, the Emmonac eyed Doctor Varrus again. "Tell me about your research," she demanded.

"My research," Varrus replied, warming to the subject immediately, "concerned itself with certain debilitating diseases, aaniatethis in particular. Since there was an analogous virus among the Emmonac, I used a great many of them as test subjects."

"How many?" asked Pacria, her voice devoid of emotion.

Varrus shrugged. "I don't know. A thousand. More, perhaps. I would have to consult my records to give you an exact figure."

Pacria flinched. "Of course. There was no reason to keep count. They were only Emmonacs."

"Precisely," said the Zendak'aan.

"And what did you do to these . . . test subjects?" she asked.

Varrus smiled. "I exposed them to their disease. The strain that worked the quickest and did the most damage."

Pacria turned to Kes. "How much longer must I continue with this hideous charade?"

"Just a *little* longer," the Ocampa assured her.

The Emmonac swallowed and turned to Varrus again. "What happened when you exposed your test subjects to the virus?"

The Zendak'aan didn't answer right away. He seemed to be thinking. Remembering, with something akin to nostalgia.

It turned Kes's stomach to watch. She could only imagine what it was doing to Pacria.

"There were several groups, of course," he said at

last. "In each one, the disease was allowed to take a firm hold before I introduced an antigen. In most cases, the subjects died right away, the antigen having no effect. In other cases, I observed a significant response—but only enough to allow the subjects to linger for a while."

"To linger," Pacria repeated, containing her shame and her anger as best she could.

Varrus didn't seem to notice the Emmonac's discomfort. "Yes," he confirmed. "To linger—and in great pain, since I wished to observe everything I could about the disease, and that would not have been possible with the administration of painkillers."

Pacria swallowed. Tears streamed down her cheeks. "I see."

"But not everyone died," Varrus was quick to add. "There were those who managed to survive, despite the suffering and the crippling effects on bone and muscle tissue. And it was this group of subjects that ultimately produced an antigen."

The Emmonac's lower lip began to tremble, but she regained control of herself. She turned to Kes. "This is pointless."

"No," said the Ocampa. "Though I understand it must seem that way."

Pacria lifted her hands up helplessly. "But what more could I possibly ask this monster?"

Varrus looked at her. "Monster?" he echoed ironically. "I think not. After all, I found a cure for aaniatethis. I saved the lives of thousands of noble Zendak'aa and spared millions more its depradations. In the eyes of my people, I am a hero."

The Emmonac cast a withering glance at the Zendak'aan. "You are a demon. An incarnation of evil. And I would not partake of your cure if my soul itself depended on it."

Clearly, she had endured all she could. Wiping a tear from her cheek, she headed for the exit.

Varrus chuckled as he watched her go. "Good," he responded.

Pacria stopped. And turned to look back over her shoulder. "What did you say?" she asked him, her face flushed with fury.

"I said it was *good,"* Varrus told her, undaunted in the face of her indignation. "Only the Zendak'aa were meant to have benefited from my research. It was for them I worked from early in the morning until late at night, studying blood samples until my eyes wouldn't focus anymore. For *them."*

He dismissed Pacria with a flick of his wrist. "The Emmonacs I dealt with were laboratory animals, nothing more and nothing less. The idea of an inferior reaping the harvest of my labors . . ." He chuckled again. "I can think of few things more loathesome."

Pacria looked at the Zendak'aan as if for the first time. "That would displease you?" she asked.

Varrus' lip curled. "It would be a knife twisting in my belly. Knowing I had helped an Emmonac to survive . . . to spawn other Emmonac . . ." He shuddered. "Fortunately, that will never come to pass—not as long as the Zendak'aan Empire endures."

Pacria smiled. "The Zendak'aan Empire has been destroyed," she said.

Varrus's eyes narrowed. "Never," he insisted.

"It has been destroyed," she repeated. "What's left of your people has been scattered across the stars. And the so-called work you did? The scientific accomplishments of the haughty Zendak'aa? They fuel the ships and ease the lives of the lowly Emmonac."

Varrus' eyes grew big and round. His face turned dark with anger as he jerked his head from side to side. "No! It cannot be!"

"It *can* be," Pacria maintained. "And it is."

"You lie!" the Zendak'aan spat through clenched teeth. "My people were the height of evolution. The Emmonac were nothing. They were *animals!"*

"They were survivors," Pacria replied. "They endured. And when the Zendak'aa grew fat and careless and lowered their guard, the Emmonac and others repaid them for the miseries they'd inflicted."

"No!" shrieked Varrus. He pointed a long, slender finger at Pacria. "You're just trying to confuse me. You want my research, don't you? But you can't have it. It wasn't meant for you. It was meant for *us,* you hear me? For *us!"*

The Emmonac laughed. It was a sound more of triumph than amusement. "I guess," she said with only a hint of sarcasm, "even the noblest of intentions can go awry."

Kes smiled. "Freeze program."

For a moment, there was silence in the holodeck. Pacria continued to consider the Zendak'aan in the white robes, his eyes wide with fury—unable to accept that his worst nightmare had overtaken him.

"I suppose you thought you were being clever," she told Kes.

"Not clever," the Ocampa corrected her. "To be honest, I was clutching at straws." She paused. "Did I clutch at the right one?"

Pacria took a long time in answering. "Yes," she said finally. "It appears you did."

Kes nodded, relieved. "In that case, I don't think we need this place anymore." Looking up, she instructed the computer to terminate the program. Instantly, Varrus and his clinic disappeared, to be replaced by a black-and-yellow grid.

The Emmonac looked around. She shook her head. "It seemed so real. *He* seemed so real."

"In a way," said Kes, "he was. He acted exactly as the real Varrus would have acted—if he were still alive."

Pacria thought about her experience a moment longer. Then she turned to the Ocampa and managed a smile.

"Come on," she said. "I have an appointment in sick bay." And she led the way out of the holodeck.

CHAPTER 22

Captain's log, stardate 49588.4. On Lieutenant Torres' recommendation, I have taken her friend Tolga and his fellow Nograkh to a world of their choosing. Apparently, it's one that already serves as headquarters and staging ground for the rebellion to which they've lent their support.

The non-Nograkh we rescued have chosen to make this world their destination as well. It seems a bond of mutual respect was forged in the mining station that they have no desire to break.

The location of the place would normally be a secret, *of course. Based on his knowledge of Lieutenant Torres and Ensign Kim, Tolga trusted us enough to share it. Naturally I'll erase the coordinates from our files as soon as we break orbit, so we won't give anything away if* Voyager*'s ever captured by Tolga's enemies.*

Not that I anticipate that, of course. But this is the Delta Quadrant. One never knows what or whom one will encounter.

As for Pacria Ertinia, the Emmonac we took on board, things are looking up. Though I still don't know how, Kes talked her into taking the antigen for the virus she contracted. We've agreed to drop her off in Emmonac space, which—fortunately—isn't very far off our intended course.

All in all, I'd say, the last few days could have turned out a lot worse. End of log entry.

Her log entry complete, Janeway sat back in her center seat and watched the forward viewscreen. Pictured on it, Tolga's Class M hiding place spun quietly in space, unaware of the fate the rebels had picked out for it.

Unlike the planet where Torres and Kim had been captured by the Kazon, this world didn't remind the captain at all of her native Earth. Its continents were too orange, its cloud cover too dense, and there wasn't nearly enough water. But when it came to the kinds of nutrients they needed, the place was chock-full of them.

"Captain Janeway?" came a voice over her comm badge.

"Lieutenant Tuvok," she said, identifying the caller. "What kind of progress are we making?"

"Considerable," the Vulcan reported. "We are beaming up the last assortment of roots and tubers now. Mr. Neelix is quite . . ." He paused, seeking the precise word. "Excited."

"I'd be surprised if he weren't," Janeway responded. "He'll have a whole new world of tastes and textures to explore."

And to inflict on the crew, she thought, though she would never say such a thing out loud.

"I should mention," said Tuvok, "that Tolga's people were quite helpful in pointing out the most promising sites. Though they seem to have a penchant for intraspecific aggression, they can also be rather generous."

The captain smiled. "Then our little detour wasn't totally unproductive. We've not only restocked our larder, we've made some friends."

Back at his usual post with all his injuries healed, Ensign Kim nodded in agreement. "I don't think you'll get any argument from Lieutenant Torres on that count. Or," he added hastily, "from me either."

Janeway glanced at Kim, then at Lieutenant Paris, who was manning the helm. Whatever had been straining their relationship, it seemed to be gone now. But then, people tended to appreciate their friends more when they thought they had seen the last of them.

Harry Kim suppressed a yawn.

Despite the level of comfort he felt being here on the bridge, he found himself counting the minutes until his shift was over. Though he'd pretty much recovered from the beating he'd taken on the Nograkh mining station, he was still a little tired. A little out of kilter. And he would continue to feel that way for a while, according to the holodoctor.

To pass the time, he ran some diagnostic checks. On the structural integrity field and the weapons systems. On the propulsion system. On the various sensor arrays.

He would have run a test on the transporters as well, except they were still very much in use. Tolga's hideout was turning out to be a bonanza for *Voyager*. They'd be knee-deep in food for the next couple of weeks.

Finally, it was time for him to get up and let someone else man his station. In this case, it was DuChamps, who had apparently performed the function much of the time Harry was away.

The two men nodded to each other. "I went through some diagnostics," the ensign noted. "You'll see them on the screen."

"Got it," said DuChamps. "And Kim . . . welcome back."

"Thanks," Harry replied, clapping the man on the shoulder. "It's good to be back, believe me."

Glancing at Paris, he saw that his friend was yielding his post as well. Harry waited for him at the door to the turbolift. They entered together, turned and watched the doors slide closed in their wake.

Suddenly, they opened again—to admit Chakotay. "Room for one more?" he asked.

Paris smiled. "I don't see why not."

"Holodeck," said the first officer, giving the turbolift its orders. The doors closed and, almost imperceptibly, the compartment began to move.

"You know," Harry said, "that's not a bad idea, Commander. I think I'll book a little holodeck time myself—in Chez Sandrine." Chez Sandrine was Paris's holodeck recreation of a bistro he'd frequented during his days at the Academy. "Sip a little wine at the bar. Play a relaxing game of pool." He winked at Paris. "Or, the way I feel, maybe kick back and watch *Tom* play a game of pool."

"Fine with me," his friend assured him.

"No way," Chakotay remarked.

Harry looked at him. "Excuse me?"

The doors opened on the appropriate deck. The holodeck was a few meters away, just down the corridor.

The first officer gestured. "After you, Mr. Kim."

The ensign shook his head as he exited the lift. "I don't get it," he confessed.

Chakotay didn't tender an explanation—at least, not yet. Instead, he turned to Paris.

"Have a pleasant shift, Lieutenant."

Paris's expression was a puzzled one as the doors closed between him and Harry. Putting his hand on the ensign's shoulder, Chakotay guided him along the corridor.

When they reached the holodeck, the commander punched in a program. A moment later, the interlocking doors parted for them. Harry could see the inside of a Starfleet shuttle.

He stared at Chakotay, dumbfounded. "What . . . ?"

"You didn't do a *bad* job in that asteroid belt," the commander conceded. "But you could've done *better.* And we're going to keep practicing till you get it right."

Harry's jaw dropped. Then he laughed and said, "You're on."

* * *

As B'Elanna entered the turbolift, she saw Paris standing inside it. He had a bewildered expression on his face.

"Something wrong?" she asked him, as the doors closed behind her.

He thought for a moment. "I'm not sure." Then he seemed to snap out of his fog. "Hey," he noticed her, "you're back."

"So I am," B'Elanna replied.

Paris smiled. "Said your good-byes?"

"I wished them luck—Tolga and all the others. I know what it's like to take on someone big in the name of freedom."

The helmsman grunted, "Sounds exciting. You'll have to tell me about it sometime."

Now it was B'Elanna's turn to smile. And to blush a little. "Sorry. I forgot I was talking to a former Maquis."

"That's all right," he told her. "I was really in it for the challenge. The freedom part was secondary."

She looked at him. "Uh-huh. Whatever you say."

"So," said Paris, changing the subject, "it seems we're done beaming up supplies. As soon as the captain says *her* good-byes, we'll be getting underway." He regarded her for a moment. "Say, you want to do something later? When you go off duty, I mean?"

"Actually," said B'Elanna, "I'm off duty already. I requested some time off."

He seemed surprised—but only for a moment. "After what you've been through the last few days, I guess you deserve time off. Lots of it, in fact."

"Chakotay gave me all he could spare," she elaborated. "In other words, about six hours. From what he tells me, engineering can use my . . ." She cleared her throat. ". . . critical eye. That's a quote."

Paris nodded. "I believe it. Things weren't quite the same while you were gone."

B'Elanna accepted the compliment. "Anyway, I'll take whatever time I can get. And six hours will be plenty for what I have in mind."

Her colleague's eyes narrowed. "Now you've piqued my curiosity. If you don't mind my asking, just what *do* you have in mind?"

She chuckled. "I'm going to celebrate a holiday I should have celebrated days ago."

Paris's brow furrowed. "Not the Day of Honor?"

"That's the one," she confirmed.

"But I thought you *hated* the Day of Honor."

"I did," she confessed. "But I don't anymore."

"Why the change of heart?" he asked.

B'Elanna had to think for a moment before she responded. "What I hated about the Day of Honor was really what I hated about myself. The fact that I was different. I just didn't want to think of myself that way, and everyone kept insisting on it anyway."

"And that's changed?"

"Everyone is still insisting," she conceded. "That part's the same. But I think I've learned to look at it differently. I've come to see that what makes me different isn't bad. It isn't something to be ashamed of. In certain cases, certain places, it's a *good* thing."

B'Elanna sighed. "To be perfectly honest, I'm still

not thrilled about my Klingon half. I don't like having to keep a leash on my emotions. I don't like the fact that my first impulse is always to lash out, to inflict damage on whoever's standing in my way.

"But I see how Klingons aren't the only ones who act that way. Tolga's people are violent, even brutal at times. And yet, there's another side to them. A noble side, you might say. There's courage and passion and a willingness to sacrifice oneself for someone else."

Paris understood. She could tell from the look on his face.

"They were willing to give their lives to save a stranger," he said. "Just as James Kirk was willing to give *his* life more than a century ago."

She folded her arms across her chest. "It's funny, isn't it? We don't expect people we've never met before to be brave or dedicated or self-sacrificing. But if Tolga hadn't shown us he was all those things—and Pacria as well—Kim and I would have been space debris by now."

"And *we* may have surprised *them,*" Paris pointed out. "It works both ways, you know." He stroked his chin. "So you want to celebrate this holiday after all."

B'Elanna pictured Tolga and the way he'd tried to bury his ship in the Nograkh battle cruiser. She pictured Kim weaving his way through that asteroid belt. And she shrugged.

"You know," she said, "I've always had bad luck on the Day of Honor. But maybe my luck has changed."

The helmsman's smile was a sincere one. "I certainly hope so."

Just then, the lift stopped and the doors opened—

on the corridor where Paris had his quarters. He stepped outside.

"See you around," he told her. "And, uh . . . " He shrugged. "Happy Day of Honor."

For the first time in her life, B'elanna was pleased to hear the greeting. "Thank you," she replied. "And a brave Day of Honor to you too, Tom."

Kerdoch stood on the edge of the disrupter cannon platform taking a break while his two neighbors continued to work behind him. The smell of smoke was thick in his nostrils. The colony would stink of it for days. He thought of it as an incentive to work harder and faster.

He and two others had almost gotten one disrupter cannon on the outskirts of the colony ready. Another group worked on a second cannon on the west side of the colony. The other two cannons had been destroyed in the overnight attacks. If the cowards returned for another run in their thin ships, they would find a fight on their hands.

Kerdoch took a long, deep drink of water from a jug. The day had turned out very hot under the two suns, and Kerdoch felt the sweat caked to his back and arms. In midmorning his eldest boy had brought food and water for him and his neighbors working on the gun.

His son reported that the fires were out and that his mother had completed building a shelter inside their dome. He then asked why he couldn't stay and fight with his father on the cannon. Kerdoch ordered him to the side of his mother, where he was needed to defend her. After the boy left, Kerdoch felt pride. He had taught his children well. He hoped they all would live long enough to continue the lesson.

He took another drink from the jug and was about to

return to work, when he felt the odd sensation of a transporter beam. It had been years since he felt one, but it was a feeling not easily forgotten by anyone.

"Kerdoch!" his neighbor shouted, jumping toward Kerdoch as if he might hold him and pull him from the beam. A fruitless but generous gesture.

"Be prepared," he managed to say to his friends before he was gone.

Kerdoch's only thought as the transporter took him was that he wished he had a weapon in his hand. At least that way he'd die fighting.

But as the transporter released him he found himself on a Klingon battle cruiser. He'd been on two before and instantly recognized it. But how? And why? He fought to calm his questions and stay prepared for what would come.

He stepped down slowly from the pad to be greeted by a nod from the Klingon warrior running the transporter. Then through a door strode another warrior, clearly the commander of this battle cruiser.

"I am Kor," the warrior said.

"Kerdoch." Kerdoch hoped his shock didn't show, Kor was a famous commander known for his fighting skills.

"Good," Kor said, nodding his respect to the farmer. "In a moment we will talk."

"I understand, Commander," Kerdoch said.

Behind Kerdoch the sound of the transporter filled the room. He turned as a human form reassembled itself on the transporter pad. Could the humans be behind this cowardly attack? That was not a possibility Kerdoch had considered. The humans in the Federation colony had been more than friendly for the years they shared on Kerdoch's planet.

Besides, what was a human doing on a Klingon battle cruiser?

This was very confusing. Kerdoch shook his head. After this day, and last night, nothing would seem impossible ever again.

This human was puny, but then, all humans seemed puny to Kerdoch. This human also had strength; it was evident in the way he moved, the confidence with which he held himself. He was a warrior, just as the Klingons were.

The human stepped down from the transporter pad and nodded to Kor. "Commander."

Kor nodded back. "Captain."

A Federation captain! With Kor. It was obvious to Kerdoch that these two knew each other, and didn't much like each other. That he might expect, but what was the human captain doing here? And why had they picked him off the surface? Questions. Too many questions.

"This way," Kor snapped, turning and moving out the door without waiting for a response.

The human captain stepped in behind him and Kerdoch followed the human. Fourteen hours before, he had been walking the dirt path in his field, when he was attacked. Now he walked the corridors of a Klingon battle cruiser with a Federation captain and one of the Empire's most famous warriors.

Captain Kirk could not identify the type of room he found himself in. Federation starships had exact configurations. Captains' quarters had a different look from ensigns'. Each room had a designation, and was designed for that designation.

This room could have been an officer's mess or it could have been an emptied crewman's quarters. It certainly didn't seem like a meeting room. The lights were dim—as they were all over the Klingon ship. Klingons seemed to prefer dark colors as well, which gave the whole place the feeling of something underground, something slightly unsavory.

Something dangerous.

The small room was also hot. And stuffy. Kor had placed a pitcher of fluid in the center of the table, but no cups. No one had asked for any either, and Kirk wasn't about to be the first. He wasn't even certain he should taste anything on this ship. No matter how hot and thirsty he got.

The chair, however, was surprisingly comfortable. It had arms that encircled whoever sat in the chair, and the cushion, while not soft, wasn't hard either, although it was a bit larger than he was used to, and he had always thought his command chair was large.

He had been sitting in that chair for some time, as colonist Kerdoch told his story. It sounded like the Klingon farmer and the other colonists had had a very long night. They were more than lucky to be alive.

The farmer spoke in precise detail. His memory was astounding. His ability to recall the trivial, trying. But, like a good soldier, he assumed all details might be important. Kirk had to force himself to listen more than once.

Fortunately, the farmer was finishing his story of the night of flames, as he called it.

"Thank you, Kerdoch," Kor said, nodding in respect as the farmer stopped.

The farmer nodded back and wiped the sweat from his face with his sleeve.

Kirk had been surprised during the last ten minutes at the respect Kor had shown the colonist. It seemed that even in a warrior race like the Klingons, those who supplied the food and built the ships and weapons were highly regarded and respected. It had been an eye-opening detail of the Klingon Empire that a Federation officer would normally never get a chance to see.

There were many other things Kirk had seen since he'd been on the ship, things he doubted any other Federation officer had seen. Kor had tried to keep Kirk away from the main areas of the battle cruiser, but Kirk had snuck a look into various sections. He'd also made mental note of things like layout and size.

Kor turned to Kirk, showing no respect at all now for a Federation Captain.

"Well, Kirk," Kor said, his voice low and mean, "was this attack from one of the Federation's mongrel races? Do you deny it?"

"Of course I do," Kirk said, forcing himself to keep his voice level and not play Kor's game. "If we wanted to destroy the colony, we wouldn't need small ships to do it. And if it were a rogue member of the Federation, we would have had warning. I would also recognize the type of craft used. I don't. When I return to the *Enterprise,* I'll search her database for crafts like that. But I can tell you now, I've never seen or heard of diamond-shaped ships of that size and configuration."

"You would lie to protect your own," Kor said.

"No, I wouldn't," Kirk said. "If members of the Federation made this sort of cowardly attack, I'd want to catch them and punish them as much as you do."

Kirk kept his gaze focused into Kor's eyes.

The silence stretched until finally Kor laughed. "So you defend a Klingon planet to keep Federation races under control?"

Kirk held his temper. "Of course not, Commander," he said, keeping his voice level and cold and staring at Kor as hard as he could. "I defend this planet because it sent out a distress call. Commander, the Organian Treaty would mean nothing if I refused to defend it."

"You are a strange human," Kor said, shaking his head in disgust. "I will play your game for the moment. But do not cross me, Captain."

Both men stared at each other until finally Kerdoch said, "Commander, I would like to return to defend my family in case of another attack."

Kor slammed his fist on the table and stood. "Of course, Kerdoch. I will send men with you to help."

"So will I," Kirk said. He flipped open his communicator before Kor could say a word. "*Enterprise,* have Doctor McCoy, Doctor Rathbone, Lieutenant Sulu, and a security detail meet me in the transporter room. Stand by to beam me back aboard."

"Aye, Captain." Spock's voice came back clear enough for all in the small room to hear.

Kirk turned to the farmer. "Kerdoch, if the cowards who did this return, I will be at your side to defend you and your family."

"As will I," Kor said.

Kerdoch looked first at Kirk, then at Kor. There was a puzzled, intent look in his eyes. But after a moment he nodded his agreement.

"Good," Kor said, slapping the farmer on the back.

Kirk flipped open his communicator. "*Enterprise,* one to beam aboard."

Then he turned to Kor and Kerdoch. "I will meet you at the colony."

Kor laughed, again shaking his head in mock amazement as Kirk beamed out.

But for Kirk, there was nothing to laugh about. At least not until they discovered who had attacked this colony.

Look for STAR TREK Fiction from Pocket Books

Star Trek®: The Original Series

Star Trek: The Motion Picture • Gene Roddenberry
Star Trek II: The Wrath of Khan • Vonda N. McIntyre
Star Trek III: The Search for Spock • Vonda N. McIntyre
Star Trek IV: The Voyage Home • Vonda N. McIntyre
Star Trek V: The Final Frontier • J. M. Dillard
Star Trek VI: The Undiscovered Country • J. M. Dillard
Star Trek VII: Generations • J. M. Dillard
Enterprise: The First Adventure • Vonda N. McIntyre
Final Frontier • Diane Carey
Strangers from the Sky • Margaret Wander Bonanno
Spock's World • Diane Duane
The Lost Years • J. M. Dillard
Probe • Margaret Wander Bonanno
Prime Directive • Judith and Garfield Reeves-Stevens
Best Destiny • Diane Carey
Shadows on the Sun • Michael Jan Friedman
Sarek • A. C. Crispin
Federation • Judith and Garfield Reeves-Stevens
The Ashes of Eden • William Shatner & Judith and Garfield Reeves-Stevens
The Return • William Shatner & Judith and Garfield Reeves-Stevens
Star Trek: Starfleet Academy • Diane Carey

#1 *Star Trek: The Motion Picture* • Gene Roddenberry
#2 *The Entropy Effect* • Vonda N. McIntyre
#3 *The Klingon Gambit* • Robert E. Vardeman
#4 *The Covenant of the Crown* • Howard Weinstein
#5 *The Prometheus Design* • Sondra Marshak & Myrna Culbreath
#6 *The Abode of Life* • Lee Correy
#7 *Star Trek II: The Wrath of Khan* • Vonda N. McIntyre
#8 *Black Fire* • Sonni Cooper
#9 *Triangle* • Sondra Marshak & Myrna Culbreath
#10 *Web of the Romulans* • M. S. Murdock
#11 *Yesterday's Son* • A. C. Crispin
#12 *Mutiny on the Enterprise* • Robert E. Vardeman
#13 *The Wounded Sky* • Diane Duane

#14 *The Trellisane Confrontation* • David Dvorkin
#15 *Corona* • Greg Bear
#16 *The Final Reflection* • John M. Ford
#17 *Star Trek III: The Search for Spock* • Vonda N. McIntyre
#18 *My Enemy, My Ally* • Diane Duane
#19 *The Tears of the Singers* • Melinda Snodgrass
#20 *The Vulcan Academy Murders* • Jean Lorrah
#21 *Uhura's Song* • Janet Kagan
#22 *Shadow Lord* • Laurence Yep
#23 *Ishmael* • Barbara Hambly
#24 *Killing Time* • Della Van Hise
#25 *Dwellers in the Crucible* • Margaret Wander Bonanno
#26 *Pawns and Symbols* • Majiliss Larson
#27 *Mindshadow* • J. M. Dillard
#28 *Crisis on Centaurus* • Brad Ferguson
#29 *Dreadnought!* • Diane Carey
#30 *Demons* • J. M. Dillard
#31 *Battlestations!* • Diane Carey
#32 *Chain of Attack* • Gene DeWeese
#33 *Deep Domain* • Howard Weinstein
#34 *Dreams of the Raven* • Carmen Carter
#35 *The Romulan Way* • Diane Duane & Peter Morwood
#36 *How Much for Just the Planet?* • John M. Ford
#37 *Bloodthirst* • J. M. Dillard
#38 *The IDIC Epidemic* • Jean Lorrah
#39 *Time for Yesterday* • A. C. Crispin
#40 *Timetrap* • David Dvorkin
#41 *The Three-Minute Universe* • Barbara Paul
#42 *Memory Prime* • Judith and Garfield Reeves-Stevens
#43 *The Final Nexus* • Gene DeWeese
#44 *Vulcan's Glory* • D. C. Fontana
#45 *Double, Double* • Michael Jan Friedman
#46 *The Cry of the Onlies* • Judy Klass
#47 *The Kobayashi Maru* • Julia Ecklar
#48 *Rules of Engagement* • Peter Morwood
#49 *The Pandora Principle* • Carolyn Clowes
#50 *Doctor's Orders* • Diane Duane
#51 *Enemy Unseen* • V. E. Mitchell
#52 *Home Is the Hunter* • Dana Kramer Rolls
#53 *Ghost-Walker* • Barbara Hambly
#54 *A Flag Full of Stars* • Brad Ferguson
#55 *Renegade* • Gene DeWeese
#56 *Legacy* • Michael Jan Friedman

#57 *The Rift* • Peter David
#58 *Face of Fire* • Michael Jan Friedman
#59 *The Disinherited* • Peter David
#60 *Ice Trap* • L. A. Graf
#61 *Sanctuary* • John Vornholt
#62 *Death Count* • L. A. Graf
#63 *Shell Game* • Melissa Crandall
#64 *The Starship Trap* • Mel Gilden
#65 *Windows on a Lost World* • V. E. Mitchell
#66 *From the Depths* • Victor Milan
#67 *The Great Starship Race* • Diane Carey
#68 *Firestorm* • L. A. Graf
#69 *The Patrian Transgression* • Simon Hawke
#70 *Traitor Winds* • L. A. Graf
#71 *Crossroad* • Barbara Hambly
#72 *The Better Man* • Howard Weinstein
#73 *Recovery* • J. M. Dillard
#74 *The Fearful Summons* • Denny Martin Flynn
#75 *First Frontier* • Diane Carey & Dr. James I. Kirkland
#76 *The Captain's Daughter* • Peter David
#77 *Twilight's End* • Jerry Oltion
#78 *The Rings of Tautee* • Dean W. Smith & Kristine K. Rusch
#79 *Invasion #1: First Strike* • Diane Carey
#80 *The Joy Machine* • James Gunn
#81 *Mudd in Your Eye* • Jerry Oltion
#82 *Mind Meld* • John Vornholt

Star Trek: The Next Generation®

Encounter at Farpoint • David Gerrold
Unification • Jeri Taylor
Relics • Michael Jan Friedman
Descent • Diane Carey
All Good Things • Michael Jan Friedman
Star Trek: Klingon • Dean W. Smith & Kristine K. Rusch
Star Trek VII: Generations • J. M. Dillard
Metamorphosis • Jean Lorrah
Vendetta • Peter David
Reunion • Michael Jan Friedman
Imzadi • Peter David
The Devil's Heart • Carmen Carter
Dark Mirror • Diane Duane
Q-Squared • Peter David
Crossover • Michael Jan Friedman
Kahless • Michael Jan Friedman
Star Trek: First Contact • J. M. Dillard

#1 *Ghost Ship* • Diane Carey
#2 *The Peacekeepers* • Gene DeWeese
#3 *The Children of Hamlin* • Carnen Carter
#4 *Survivors* • Jean Lorrah
#5 *Strike Zone* • Peter David
#6 *Power Hungry* • Howard Weinstein
#7 *Masks* • John Vornholt
#8 *The Captains' Honor* • David and Daniel Dvorkin
#9 *A Call to Darkness* • Michael Jan Friedman
#10 *A Rock and a Hard Place* • Peter David
#11 *Gulliver's Fugitives* • Keith Sharee
#12 *Doomsday World* • David, Carter, Friedman & Greenberg
#13 *The Eyes of the Beholders* • A. C. Crispin
#14 *Exiles* • Howard Weinstein
#15 *Fortune's Light* • Michael Jan Friedman
#16 *Contamination* • John Vornholt
#17 *Boogeymen* • Mel Gilden
#18 *Q-in-Law* • Peter David
#19 *Perchance to Dream* • Howard Weinstein
#20 *Spartacus* • T. L. Mancour
#21 *Chains of Command* • W. A. McCay & E. L. Flood
#22 *Imbalance* • V. E. Mitchell
#23 *War Drums* • John Vornholt

#24 *Nightshade* • Laurell K. Hamilton
#25 *Grounded* • David Bischoff
#26 *The Romulan Prize* • Simon Hawke
#27 *Guises of the Mind* • Rebecca Neason
#28 *Here There Be Dragons* • John Peel
#29 *Sins of Commission* • Susan Wright
#30 *Debtors' Planet* • W. R. Thompson
#31 *Foreign Foes* • David Galanter & Greg Brodeur
#32 *Requiem* • Michael Jan Friedman & Kevin Ryan
#33 *Balance of Power* • Dafydd ab Hugh
#34 *Blaze of Glory* • Simon Hawke
#35 *The Romulan Stratagem* • Robert Greenberger
#36 *Into the Nebula* • Gene DeWeese
#37 *The Last Stand* • Brad Ferguson
#38 *Dragon's Honor* • Kij Johnson & Greg Cox
#39 *Rogue Saucer* • John Vornholt
#40 *Possession* • J. M. Dillard & Kathleen O'Malley
#41 *Invasion #2: The Soldiers of Fear* • Dean W. Smith & Kristine K. Rusch
#42 *Infiltrator* • W. R. Thompson
#43 *A Fury Scorned* • Pam Sargent & George Zebrowski
#44 *The Death of Princes* • John Peel
#45 *Intellivore* • Diane Duane

Star Trek: Deep Space Nine®

The Search • Diane Carey
Warped • K. W. Jeter
The Way of the Warrior • Diane Carey
Star Trek: Klingon • Dean W. Smith & Kristine K. Rusch
Trials and Tribble-ations • Diane Carey

#1 *Emissary* • J. M. Dillard
#2 *The Siege* • Peter David
#3 *Bloodletter* • K. W. Jeter
#4 *The Big Game* • Sandy Schofield
#5 *Fallen Heroes* • Dafydd ab Hugh
#6 *Betrayal* • Lois Tilton
#7 *Warchild* • Esther Friesner
#8 *Antimatter* • John Vornholt
#9 *Proud Helios* • Melissa Scott
#10 *Valhalla* • Nathan Archer
#11 *Devil in the Sky* • Greg Cox & John Greggory Betancourt
#12 *The Laertian Gamble* • Robert Sheckley
#13 *Station Rage* • Diane Carey
#14 *The Long Night* • Dean W. Smith & Kristine K. Rusch
#15 *Objective: Bajor* • John Peel
#16 *Invasion #3: Time's Enemy* • L. A. Graf
#17 *The Heart of the Warrior* • John Greggory Betancourt
#18 *Saratoga* • Michael Jan Friedman
#19 *The Tempest* • Susan Wright
#20 *Wrath of the Prophets* • P. David, M. J. Friedman, R. Greenberger

Star Trek®: Voyager™

Flashback • Diane Carey
The Black Shore • Greg Cox
Mosaic • Jeri Taylor

#1 *Caretaker* • L. A. Graf
#2 *The Escape* • Dean W. Smith & Kristine K. Rusch
#3 *Ragnarok* • Nathan Archer
#4 *Violations* • Susan Wright
#5 *Incident at Arbuk* • John Greggory Betancourt
#6 *The Murdered Sun* • Christie Golden
#7 *Ghost of a Chance* • Mark A. Garland & Charles G. McGraw
#8 *Cybersong* • S. N. Lewitt
#9 *Invasion #4: The Final Fury* • Dafydd ab Hugh
#10 *Bless the Beasts* • Karen Haber
#11 *The Garden* • Melissa Scott
#12 *Chrysalis* • David Niall Wilson

Star Trek®: New Frontier

#1 *House of Cards* • Peter David
#2 *Into the Void* • Peter David
#3 *The Two-Front War* • Peter David
#4 *End Game* • Peter David

Star Trek®: Day of Honor

Book 1 *Ancient Blood* • Diane Carey
Book 2 *Armageddon Sky* • L. A. Graf
Book 3 *Her Klingon Soul* • Michael Jan Friedman
Book 4 *Treaty's Law* • Dean W. Smith & Kristine K. Rusch